KARMA'S EMBRACE

KARMA'S EMBRACE

Prem Sharma

BOOKWRIGHTS PRESS
Charlottesville, Virginia

This is a work of fiction. The names, events, and characters are fictitious,
and any resemblnce to actual persons living or dead, events, or locales is
coincidental.

Cover photo by Mayapriya Long

Cover and interior design by Mayapriya Long

Set in Adobe Garamond

Printed in the United States of America

Library of Congress Cataloging-in-Publication Data
on file with the publisher

ISBN 1-880404-21-4

Bookwrights Press
2255 Westover Drive
Charlottesville, VA 22901
publisher@bookwrights.com

10   9   8   7   6   5   4   3   2   1

Acknowledgements

To the many from whom I have gained so much: my parents and teachers, family and friends of this particular journey brothers and sisters one and all, my profound gratitude to them and to Carol Wherley and Mayapriya Long for their assistance and as always, my love to Anita, Leena, Madhu, Sol, Raj, Ben and Becca.

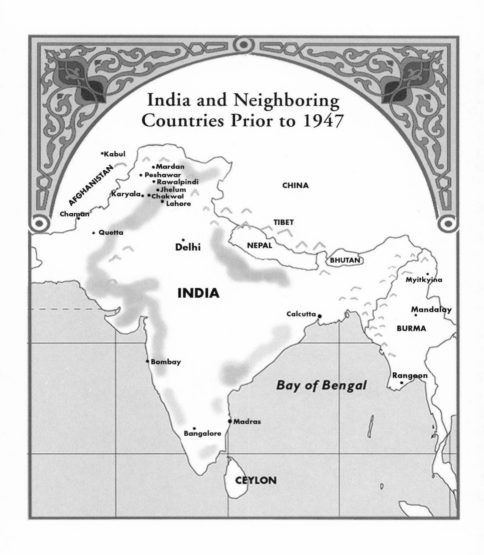

India and Neighboring
Countries Prior to 1947

Kabul

AFGHANISTAN

Mardan
Peshawar
Rawalpindi
Jhelum
Karyala Chakwal
Lahore

Chaman

Quetta

Delhi

INDIA

Bombay

Bangalore

Madras

CEYLON

CHINA

TIBET

NEPAL

BHUTAN

Myitkyina

Mandalay

Calcutta

BURMA

Rangoon

Bay of Bengal

1862
The Beginning

A young man came running down the narrow winding lane along the lower slopes of the hill where the Muslims of the village resided. He was short in stature, stockily built, and with a rugged swarthy face. Reaching the bottom of the hill, he raced through a small barren field toward a cluster of ram-shackle huts. This is where the untouchables lived as outcasts, not allowed up in the village except during daylight hours and then only to clean latrines and sweep the streets.

The man turned towards a solitary hut that stood slightly aloof from the rest and began pounding on its fragile door. His piercing dark brown eyes kept darting back towards the village.

"Stop, you imbecile, whoever you are," a woman's voice screeched from within. "Stop before you break down my door!"

"Come on, hurry up you old hag," he yelled back, taking large gulps of the frigid air, "there's not a moment to waste." His *kurta**
and *salwar* were the typical long shirt and baggy pants worn by men in Northern India. His turban was of fine cotton and a light blanket was carelessly draped around his shoulders. He was clean-shaven except for a thick mustache which covered his upper lip.

**English translations for text in italics are provided in a glossary beginning on page 239.*

"Oh, it's you, Hari Ram. *Jai Ram Jee Kee,*" the old woman cooed, opening the door, her dark prune-like face split by a toothless grin. Her clothes were soiled, gray hair unkempt, and her body reeked of stale mustard oil applied copiously over her cracked leathery skin. "Is it time?" she asked, squinting her tired watery eyes.

"Yes, hurry up," he answered, grabbing her shriveled hand and starting to drag her through the field towards the village.

"Wait, let me close my door, Hari Ram," the woman yelled, stumbling on clods of dried mud, curling her toes so as not to lose her worn slippers.

"It's the middle of the afternoon woman; besides, what's there in your hovel for anyone to steal?" he answered impatiently.

Dense dark churning clouds blanketed the skies and a howling wind was blowing, bringing bone-chilling cold from the snow covered mountains of Afghanistan to the north. Although the village of Shahpur in Northwest India was in the middle of the central arid region of the province of Baluchistan, this winter of 1862 was particularly harsh.

"For God's sake, slow down," the woman pleaded, panting. "Yours is not the first child to be born on this earth. It won't help if I'm half dead by the time we reach your house."

The man slowed down a little.

"Shouldn't we be going up to your house from the north, Hari Ram," the midwife asked. "You're headed towards the street of the Muslims."

"No, we don't have time to go around the hill," he answered angrily. "Come on, keep moving."

"By the way, Hari Ram," the old woman continued, lowering her voice, drawing her coarse blanket tightly around her hunched shoulders, "do you want me to take care of matters, should your first-born be a girl? I will — but you must understand, you'll have to pay me double," she said, looking up at him, grinning, her small beady eyes gleaming.

What was she babbling about, he wondered? What was she going to take care of? Then it occurred to him; she was talking about killing the baby if it were a girl.

How could this creature even contemplate such a vile deed when his wife had been trying to conceive for over five years. His face turning red, he stopped and let go of the old woman's hand, grabbing her scrawny neck instead. "If you so much as harm a single hair of my child, no matter if it's a boy or a girl," he said, glaring at her, "I swear to God, I'll strangle you with my own hands! Do you understand?"

"Yes, all right" she squeaked, gasping, clawing at his hands, "I'll do what you want. Let go of my neck. But remember — if it's a daughter you have, pray that she's fair-skinned and pretty, and even so, start saving for a dowry right away or else you'll never find her a husband."

God, which lowly caste does this ogress come from, he wondered? Could the touch of her wretched hands taint his off-spring? Freeing her, he began wiping his hands on his shirt.

"I try to do him a favour, and instead of showing gratitude, he tries to kill me. What is this world coming to, will some one tell me?" the midwife muttered, rubbing her neck, as she walked up the hill ahead of him.

She was suddenly startled by the call of the *mullah* from up in the minaret of the mosque. "*Allah O Akbar,*" the voice intoned, echoing through the lanes, drawn out and lingering, urging the faithful to prayer. Men entering the mosque paused momentarily to glare at the Hindu with an old woman in tow, rushing along their lane. Hari Ram sensed the quickening of his heart-beat under their gaze and started walking even faster.

They reached the house in the middle of the Hindu and Sikh neighbourhood of the village near the top of the hill and entered a spacious walled courtyard through a heavy, weather-beaten wooden door. The smell of animals and hay in the courtyard was over-powering. A horse in a stable along the side wall, sensed the presence of its master and began neighing softly. Hari Ram led the midwife to the far end of the courtyard and ushered her into a large room along the back wall.

The room was cold and dimly lit by the light coming through the partially open door by which they had entered. A small window in the side wall was shut tight. A young woman lay quietly in a low wide bed in one corner, a thick woolen blanket drawn up to her chin. She was pretty, with delicate features and a smooth fair complexion, but right then her face appeared tense, covered with glistening beads of perspiration. Her fists were held tightly clenched on each side over her chest outside the blanket, and her body suddenly stiffened.

"Is she all right?" Hari Ram asked.

The midwife started hustling him out of the room. "Stay out of my way, Hari Ram. I'll take over now. I don't need you in here," she scolded, closing the door.

Hari Ram walked to a *charpai* in the courtyard and sat down on its wooden frame. He removed his turban and wiped his face with it. "*Hey Prabhu*," he prayed softly, "Take care of Tara and the child."

Time passed, yet there wasn't a sound from the room. Hari Ram stood up and began pacing back and forth. He heard a shrill voice yelling on the street outside and saw the front door pushed open. A young boy, wielding a long stick, herded two cows and a buffalo into the courtyard, coaxing them towards the shed next to the stable. "This cow didn't graze much today," the boy called out, pointing his stick at one of the beasts. Getting no response, he shut the gate to the shed and ran out of the courtyard.

When Hari Ram realized it was getting dark, he lit an oil lamp and knocked on the bedroom door. "How's she doing?" he whispered, handing the lamp to the midwife.

"Leave her to me, Hari Ram," the old woman mumbled. "I know what I'm doing."

"Remember what I told you," he said, tersely.

"Yes, yes, I know," she answered, slamming the door in his face.

It was getting bitterly cold, and he hadn't eaten since the noon meal, yet he was oblivious to any discomfort. Each day he had prayed for his wife and for their child she was carrying, but now he had to wait, unable to help her in any way.

He heard faint voices from behind the closed door. "*Hey Bhagwan,*" he sighed, "be merciful." Then he was startled by the loud cries of a baby. He slid to the edge of the *charpai* and sat staring at the closed door. The crying stopped abruptly and he could hear his own heart pounding. "Now what, God," he moaned, standing up. After what felt like an eternity, the door opened.

"Look, Hari Ram, you have a little daughter," the midwife gushed, stepping out of the room. "Thank God she's not dark- skinned like you. She's fair and pretty like your wife."

The old woman had cut the umbilical cord with a kitchen knife she had found on a table in a corner of the room. She cleansed the infant and had wrapped it in a small, soft, white woolen blanket.

Hari Ram hesitated a moment and then cautiously reached out to take the baby from the outstretched arms of the midwife. In the faint glow of the stars, he saw a beautiful little round face looking up at him, but then the face became a blur as his eyes filled with tears — tears of joy and gratitude. Holding his daughter close in his arms, he bowed his head and prayed to his Creator to give his first-born a long, healthy and happy life.

"Is Tara all right?" he asked.

"Of course she is," the old woman beamed, wiping her hands on her soiled *kurta*. "Go in, see for yourself."

Hari Ram entered the room, cradling his daughter close to him. "How are you, Tara?" he asked gently.

"I'm all right," she answered softly, though in the dim glow of the lantern her face appeared pale.

"Why aren't you smiling?" he asked, cautiously sitting down on the edge of the bed.

She hesitated, and then, turning her face away, answered, "I so much wanted to give you a son, my husband,"

"Well, a girl-child is fine; she's like the goddess *Lakshmi* who brings wealth into a home," he said, looking at his daughter. "There'll be sons born later," he added.

Tara wiped a teardrop that spilled down her face.

"What shall we call her?" he asked. "Have you thought of a name?"

"She is beautiful, isn't she?" Tara said, relieved that her husband had not found fault with her for bearing a girl child. "I'm sure she'll grow to be most graceful and adorable. The word in Sanskrit that describes those three attributes is *Kanti*, my husband."

"Then Kanti it shall be," Hari Ram said, laughing. "We shall call our daughter Kanti."

"Yes, Kanti has such a good ring to it," Tara whispered, a faint smile appearing on her face and her eyelids slowly drooping shut.

"I promise you, Tara, our daughter will have the best of everything that money can buy. I'll work hard, you'll see. Kanti will be the luckiest girl in the entire village. We'll raise her in the finest traditions of our caste," he continued, gently kissing his daughter on her forehead. After all, isn't she the descendent of the proud martial race of *Mohyal* Brahmins, the highest among all of the Hindu castes, and whose Aryan ancestors came all the way from Central Asia three thousand years ago. He would imbue his child with the saga of their ancestors; like King Porus who had challenged Alexander the Great in heroic and epic defiance. She would learn about the great deeds of other Mohyals whose courage, valor and martyrdom, for refusing to give up their Hindu faith, were legendary.

"I'll get an addition built to our house, Tara," he said. "Our Kanti's room won't be of clay and straw but of real bricks. You'll see." He inhaled deeply the early morning dew-like fragrance of his newborn's skin and, turning, gently placed her next to his wife.

"Have you had anything to eat, my husband?" Tara asked sleepily. "There's some food in the kitchen that I cooked earlier."

"Don't worry about me, my dear," he answered, standing up. "You haven't eaten anything either. I'll heat up some milk for you." He left the room and went into the kitchen. It was warmer in here, the air laden with the odor of smoke and stale food. He threw some wood shavings on the embers in the fireplace and placed the milk pan over it.

The flames from the fire faintly lit up the kitchen and he slowly glanced around the room. His eyes came to rest upon the small shrine in a corner where Tara said her prayers twice each day. In the flickering light of the fire, the white marble statue of Lord Krishna appeared ethereal. Hari Ram turned towards it and, with head bowed, brought the palms of his hands together in front of his lips. When the milk was heated, he poured some into a brass bowl and added a lump of jaggery to it. But when he returned to the bedroom, he saw that his wife was already asleep.

The baby had cried once during the middle of the night and Tara had quickly picked her up to feed her. She gazed down at the little soul in her arms and tears threatened to fill her eyes. "You are mine, my precious Kanti, and I'm going to take care of you," she whispered. "I'll pray for you each day and teach you all I know."

The lamp was still burning, filling the room with a soft glow and a faint sooty smell. Tara slowly looked around and saw her husband asleep on the narrow cot along the far wall. He had been so worried about her and their child and she hoped that he hadn't gone to sleep without eating. Then she remembered that he was to leave later that day with the traders' caravan and would be gone for an entire month. She would miss him terribly and pray each day for his safe return. I must cook a hot meal for him before he leaves, was the thought that occurred to her.

The baby had stopped suckling and Tara placed her in the wooden crib next to her bed, which her husband had bought from the village carpenter weeks earlier. She then curled up under her blanket and fell asleep again.

She woke up before dawn and, raising herself on one elbow, peered into the crib. The baby had her eyes closed and lay very still. Tara quickly sat up and, reaching out, touched the infant's forehead with her fingertips. The baby cooed softly and moved its tightly clenched fist towards its mouth. Tara sighed and a smile slowly lit up her face. She lifted her baby into her arms and fed her again. She then returned her to the crib and got out of bed. Wrapping the blanket around her shoulders, she walked quietly out of the room and towards the kitchen. The chill of the early morning air outside stung her face and she covered her mouth with the blanket. She felt faint and had to quickly grab the kitchen door. Moving slowly, she re-kindled the fire and placed the water pan upon it. After she had washed, she sat down in front of the shrine in the corner of the kitchen and closed her eyes. The palms of her hands came together in front of her face, and she began to pray.

Om Bhur Bhu vah Svah
Tat Savitur Varenyam
Bhargo Devasya Dhimahi
Dhiyo yo na Prachodayath

O Supreme Being, the source of existence, intelligence and bliss, Creator of the Universe, may we prove worthy of Thee. May we meet Thy glorious grace. Mayest Thou be the unerring guide of our minds and may we follow Thy lead unto righteousness.

She beseeched Lord Krishna to give her husband and Kanti long healthy lives. She prayed for her parents, brothers and sisters in far away Kashmir, and for the souls of her husband's parents, killed four years earlier when an earthquake had devastated their village of Sibi.

The first hint of dawn had barely begun lightening the sky when Tara went into the shed at the far end of the courtyard to milk one of the cows and the buffalo. She returned to the kitchen in a short while with a bucketful of foaming milk just as Hari Ram came out of the bedroom, stretching his arms over his head.

"Oh, I've slept late today," he said, stifling a yawn. "You shouldn't have milked the cows, Tara. I would have done it."

"No, I'm all right," she answered, pouring the milk into a large pan. "You have to prepare for your journey."

Hari Ram looked away. "I'll try and cut the trip short," he spoke quickly. "You'll be all right, won't you?"

"Yes, I'll be fine," she answered and started to knead the flour which she would bake into *naans* in the *tandoor* later.

Tara wished her husband didn't have to travel to these distant places to trade. Only last month, she had learned at the village well about a caravan of traders from an adjacent village that had been waylaid by armed bandits. Two of the traders had been killed and the entire caravan robbed of its merchandise. She had spoken to her husband the moment she had returned from the well. "Perhaps you could open a shop here in the village, my husband," she had suggested. "Then you wouldn't have to face such dangers yourself."

"Oh no, Tara," Hari Ram had answered, raising his hands. "I'd be bored to death sitting cross-legged all day in a stuffy shop. I couldn't do that even for a day." Then with a smile he had pointed at his wife's belly and added, "Besides, now I'll need to earn more money to help raise our child."

Hari Ram was a shrewd merchant and enjoyed his work, trading in silks, rugs, blankets, kitchen utensils, spices and fruit. He traveled with his caravan of twenty camels, buying and selling merchandise all over Baluchistan and into the neighboring province of Punjab. He went to Quetta and Chaman in the northwest and to Loralai and Zhob towards the northeast.

Travel through these areas was always fraught with danger as Baluchistan was controlled by fierce tribal Muslim chiefs constantly feuding with each other. Merchants and traders, who were mostly Hindus and Sikhs, when passing through the tribal territory were required to pay tariff to the local chief to obtain safe passage. Thieves and bandits added to the dangers, so the traders usually traveled together in caravans often consisting of over a hundred camels, and accompanied by several well-armed guards on horseback.

Hari Ram led the caravan riding his horse, and his camels were tended by three Muslim tribal herdsmen. They traveled the northwestern trade route in the summer, moving away from the boiling desert, climbing through the steep Bolan Pass to the high plateau and then down into the scenic, lush Quetta valley.

After trading in Quetta, and carrying fresh wares, the caravans traveled farther north. They climbed out of the valley and traversed the rugged Khojak Pass to the town of Chaman in the mountains on the border with Afghanistan, where they did much of their trading. Hari Ram sold the pots and pans and rugs made in Shahpur, Loralai and Zhob. Traders from Kandahar in Afghanistan would bring dried fruits, carpets and precious stones. Exquisite silks all the way from China were acquired and later sold to the rich in Quetta and Lahore. Conversations in Chaman would take place in half a dozen tongues, including Punjabi, Afghani, Baluchi, Pushtu, and even, on occasion, Russian.

The trading season in the northwest ended when the first snowfall blanketed the Quetta Valley. The caravans would then ply the northeastern trading route, traveling east to Loralai where they met traders from Dera Ghazi Khan in the Punjab. From there they'd go north to Zhob to meet up with caravans coming from the Northwest Frontier.

The traders felt much safer traveling east through Punjab as the trading routes here were well patrolled by British soldiers. By 1858, Britain had captured most of India and Queen Victoria had proclaimed the country to be a colony of the crown. But the British had been unable to subdue the fierce tribes of Baluchistan and the Northwest Frontier. Well-armed bands of tribal men in these areas often attacked British troops, especially in the mountain passes leading into and beyond the Quetta valley. Yet Hari Ram eagerly awaited the arrival of spring and with it the opening of the northwest trading route.

"Are you sure you'll manage while I'm gone?" he asked again. "I'll have the midwife come and see you each day."

"No, don't do that. I don't need her anymore," Tara answered, then added softly, "I'll miss you, but I don't want you to worry about me. There's a lot to do around the house and now I have Kanti to take care of."

"Well, all right, I won't ask the midwife, but I'll tell my cousin Jeetu to keep an eye on you."

"No, no, husband," Tara blurted out much too hurriedly, "please don't do that." Hari Ram looked at his wife, but she had turned away. How could she tell him that she was terrified of his cousin and detested the way he always stared at her with eyes that made her skin crawl.

Jeetu was a tall man, slim and fair of skin. He wore his turban rakishly tipped to one side, and a childhood injury had left him slightly cross-eyed. Hari Ram had grown up with his cousin in Sibi and was quite fond of him. When Tara had met him for the first time the day they moved to Shahpur, she had quickly covered her face with her *duppata*, for it was most immodest for a married woman to let an older male see her face. But Jeetu had laughed. "Times are changing, Sister-in-law," he had said. "You don't have to hide your face from me. Besides, I'm about the same age as Hari Ram."

At her husband's urging, Tara had stopped shielding her face whenever she met Jeetu. But in her heart she despised the man, especially after the day he had tried to put his arms around her waist when she had run into him on the street. Her shock turned to shame and then to anger as she forced herself free and ran back into her house. She hadn't told anyone about it, not even her husband, and after some time wondered if it had really happened.

Then one day Jeetu's wife Pushpa appeared at the well with an ugly bruise on the side of her face. She was crying but would not tell Tara and the other women what happened. "I'll run away to my parents' home," she sobbed.

"You can't do that," an older woman advised her. "Your parents won't accept you back. They'll force you to return to your husband."

"Then I'll kill myself," Pushpa wailed, covering her face with her hands. Soon after that she had disappeared, never to be seen again in the village.

"Well, someone has to be available, Tara, should you and Kanti need help," Hari Ram persisted.

"All right my husband," Tara conceded, "let the midwife come every other day for a week and after that, should I need her, I'll fetch her myself. Besides, I can always call one of our neighbours for help." She then picked up two large brass pots and started walking out of the kitchen.

"No, Tara, you mustn't go to the well today. It's too cold and you must be exhausted," Hari Ram pleaded, following her out. "Ali, the water-man, can also bring our drinking water for the next few days."

"We can't drink the water he brings, my husband, you know that," Tara answered, placing one of the pots on top of her head and the other next to her hip. "He's a Muslim and eats the flesh of cows. It's bad enough we use the water he fetches for bathing and washing clothes. You watch Kanti. I won't be long," she called out over her shoulder, stepping out of the courtyard. She felt relieved at being able to convince her husband not to ask his cousin to look after her. The scoundrel; she wouldn't want his help even if her life depended on it. What a vile man. It was even rumoured that he was hiding from the British authorities for a crime he had committed in the big city of Quetta.

The well at the edge of the village to the north also served as a social gathering place for the women of the village. They sat on its wide circular platform and chatted, sharing news about their families and neighbours. They sang songs of springtime and a good harvest while drawing water from the well. There was usually a great deal of giggling and laughter, but the women also shared their pain and tears.

This was a new well, dug just a year ago and only a short distance from the old one which had to be abandoned even though it had not run dry. The women arriving at the old well one day were alarmed by what looked like streaks of dried blood going up the steps. One of them had looked into the well and had fallen back, screaming. "There is a severed head of a cow in the water!"

"It's the vile deed of Shahpur's Muslims," the men of the Hindu and Sikh neighbourhood yelled. "Let's get our swords and spears. We'll shed their blood."

They had beaten up Ali the water-man and set a Muslim farmer's house on fire, but then the village elders had quickly intervened. Shahpur's Muslims denied the act. "Tribal Muslims from another village must have been responsible," they stated.

An uneasy truce had since prevailed between the religious groups, but the Hindus and Sikhs had abandoned the old well and dug a new one closer to their neighbourhood.

The well was the domain of women and men usually stayed away from it. If a village elder happened to come by, the women stopped talking and quickly drew their colourful *duppatas* over their heads to shield their faces. But if a young man walked by, the girls taunted and teased the unfortunate youth mercilessly. For many of the women, the well was also a refuge where they could spend a few moments away from the tiresome daily routine of their household chores. For others, it was a respite from the taunts of nagging in-laws and the demands of uncaring husbands.

"Tara, you've had your baby," one of the women drawing water called out. "Is it a boy?"

Tara sat down on the steps of the well without answering: the walk down the winding path had tired her and she was feeling faint. She should have listened to her husband and not insisted on fetching their drinking water herself.

"Oh, you poor thing," a young woman said, interrupting her singing. "It was a girl, wasn't it? Your husband must have been terribly cross."

"No he wasn't," Tara answered softly. "He said that a girl-child was like the goddess *Lakshmi* and would bring great riches to our home."

"You're lucky," another woman drawing water called out. "My husband didn't speak to me for months after my daughter was born. This one I'm carrying now better be a boy."

When her turn came, Tara started lowering the water bucket into the well. "Here, let me help you," one of the women said, taking the rope out of Tara's hands.

When the two pots were full, Tara balanced one on top of her head and, placing the other on her hip, started walking back towards home.

"Be careful now," a woman called out.

Tara felt tired, yet she kept labouring up the path, afraid that if she stopped to rest, she may not be able to continue. Her hands were frozen and her body ached. "Wait, let me help you," a women called from the well and came running. Tara gratefully handed her one of the pots. Reaching home, she placed the pots in the kitchen and crawled back into bed.

During the middle of the day Hari Ram saddled his horse and, bidding farewell to his young wife and infant daughter, rode off to lead his twenty camels, laden with merchandise, to go join the caravan of traders headed northeast.

1876
Fourteen years later

"*I*s father coming home today, Mother?" Kanti's voice lilted down from the highest branch of the tall tamarind tree in the corner of the courtyard. It was springtime and the swirling warm winds from the south had banished winter's chills. Tara was seated on a small wooden stool in front of a clay churning pot outside the kitchen. Her hands alternately pulled a thin rope wrapped around a wooden rod, making its blades flip back and forth through the thick buffalo milk in the pot.

"Yes, his caravan is due back some time today," she answered, and then looked up quickly. "Be careful, Kanti," she cried, getting up and hurrying towards the middle of the courtyard. "You don't have to retrieve your brothers' kite. Let it be. I'll buy them another one."

Kanti's laughter wafted down. "Oh you worry too much, Mother," she complained, stretching and reaching out to pluck the kite from the very tip of the swaying branch to which she was clinging, her legs wrapped tightly around it. "Here you are," she called to her brothers below and released the bright red paper kite which sailed lazily down, twisting and turning in a dizzying zig-zag, towards the two boys jumping joyously, vying to snatch the kite.

Kanti started coming down the tree hugging its trunk, moving her feet from one branch to another. Her mother stood below, arms raised, anxiously watching. "Oh God, be careful, child, slow down," she admonished. The young girl made it to the lowest branch and swung back and forth from it a few times before letting go to drop lightly to the ground. She then sprang to her feet and, laughing, ran off to join her brothers.

Tara's eyes followed her daughter. My baby has grown up so fast, she thought, her heart melting as it did even now after all these years, whenever she heard Kanti's laughter. It was so innocent, full of bliss, and melodious, like the shimmering little rills that trickled down the mountains of the north each spring. Tara never tired of looking at her daughter's face, so fair and her skin smoother than those of the *mem sahibs* the foreign ladies she had seen in Quetta. Soon they would have to start looking for a suitable match for her, she worried. But what a beautiful bride she's going to make, Tara mused.

Yes, time had passed too quickly and so much had happened. She had given birth to her second child two years after Kanti was born and, much to her relief, it was a boy. She and Hari Ram named their son Shiv, after Lord Shiva of the Hindu Trinity. A year later, she gave birth to another son and they called him Shanker, for one of the appellations of God. Tara was ecstatic; Hari Ram, pleased. Yet Kanti remained his favorite and he spent every free moment playing with her. He had bought her a wooden rocking horse and while Kanti would scream gleefully riding it, he would call out, "*Challo ghora, tez jao!*"—"move horse, go faster!"

"You wait and see," he would tell Tara, "our Kanti will be able to out-ride the best of Baluchistan's horsemen. She'll leave them behind to choke in the dust from her horse's hooves."

"Yes, but she'll also have to learn to cook and sew," Tara chuckled. "Our daughter won't be able to raise a family from the back of a horse!"

Yes, so much had happened during the past 14 years. With renewed hostilities between Hindus and Muslims, Hari Ram had seen his trading business come almost to an end. Caravans of Hindu and Sikh traders were being attacked and looted by tribal Muslims and several traders had been killed. But then the call to battle their common enemy, the British rulers, brought the two factions to declare a truce. Hari Ram was relieved: there shouldn't be any animosity between people whose only difference was the religion they professed. He didn't want his children to grow up amidst such hatred nor ever be in harms way.

Each morning Tara read the Hindu holy books of *Ramayan* and *Bhagavad Gita* to her children and taught Kanti how to read and write the Hindi alphabets. Before the children went out to play, their mother painted a small dot with black *kajal* on their foreheads. "There now," she would tell them, "this blemish will ward off the evil eye of those jealous of my handsome children."

At six, Kanti started attending a school for girls in a one-room school house near the center of the village. Vivacious and intelligent, she soon learned to read and write in Hindi, Urdu and Punjabi. The girls wore white cotton *salwar* and *kurta,* and the *duppata* around their shoulders was of a deep blue colour. The morning began with a prayer, followed by a patriotic song in which the children vowed to fight for the freedom of their sacred motherland. They learned about the golden age of Hindustan — the land of the Hindus, their monarchs and sages. They read about the ancient civilization of India, many thousands of years old, when their country was the seat of culture, learning and trade — a time when scholars from the four corners of the earth came to its shores in search of knowledge. The children studied the recent history of the country; about the repeated raids and conquests by marauding Turkish, Afghan and Mogul armies which forcibly converted thousands upon thousands of Hindus to Islam. They learned about the founding of the Sikh religion as a means of protecting Hindus from these Muslim invaders. They read about the British East India Company, which in the early 1600's established trading posts in western India; but gradually began conquering parts of the country, and ended by imposing British rule over the entire nation by 1858.

Each evening before their bedtime, Tara made her children sit with her on the floor in the kitchen, in front of the statue of Lord Krishna.

She helped them pray for their hearts and minds to remain free of hatred, greed and anger. "Our evening prayers must be a time to reflect on our deeds of that day," she told them. "We must assess our actions as well as our behaviour. Did we do or even think of anything that was sinful or hurtful to others? If we did, we must ask for God's forgiveness and promise not to repeat them."

"But what if someone harms us, Mother?" Kanti asked. "Shouldn't we hate them?"

"Our scriptures tell as that when we hate others it is we who suffer by clogging our minds with anger," her mother explained. "When some harm occurs to us, it is the result of our *karmas*, the fruits of our deeds. We are rewarded by good *karmas* when we have been good in a previous existence or in this life. Similarly we are cursed with bad *karmas* for our ill deeds of previous births or of this life. If we consider the person harming us to be simply an instrument of God, delivering to us what we deserve, then we should not hate that person. It isn't easy, I know, but we must try very hard to think that way."

"I want to be a brave general when I grow up," Kanti would say. "I will ride a horse and lead my army to victory over our enemies. You wait and see, Mother."

Tara would smile, "You're a girl, my child, and girls do not ride horses and lead armies. But it's all right to dream."

Hari Ram joined the children during their evening prayers whenever he could and went to the temple to pray before leaving and upon returning from each of his business trips. By tradition the eldest son in most Hindu families became a Sikh, and Hari Ram's older brother had done so. Hari Ram himself on occasions attended the Sunday service in Shahpur's Sikh temple and wore on his wrist a steel bracelet, one of the five requirements of the Sikh religion.

Kanti, with unbounded energy, enjoyed climbing trees and wrestling with her brothers more than playing with the toys her father bought her or the dolls her mother made for her. Her angelic face and large luminous eyes, brimming with child-like innocence, masked the impish side of her. Hari Ram started teaching his daughter to ride a horse and she soon became adept at it.

"You shouldn't encourage her to ride, my husband," Tara complained. "It's not dignified for girls to be seen galloping around on horseback."

"Well, times are changing, Tara," Hari Ram answered. "There's no reason why a girl shouldn't have the same freedom as boys."

Shiv was a gentle shy child, but his younger brother, Shanker, was mischievous and followed his sister wherever she went.

"We'll have to watch this one carefully, Tara," Hari Ram cautioned his wife. "I saw him today trying to pick a fight on the street outside with a boy almost twice his age."

Kanti attended school up to the sixth class, when a girl's formal education was considered complete. Now that she was twelve, her parents kept her home and she spent the entire day with her mother, learning to cook, sew, and manage a household. She was shown how to milk cows and buffalos, deliver a calf, churn milk to make butter, and put a child to sleep by softly singing lullabies. She had turned into a strikingly pretty girl, slim and, like her mother, very fair-skinned. She braided her long black hair into a plait and often tied a red ribbon to its end. Her brothers had taken after their father and were dark complexioned, which to their parents was fine, as it was more important for girls to be fair skinned and pretty in order for them to be married off to a good husband.

Tara had some time ago forbidden her daughter from ever leaving the house alone, following the incident with Jeetu. Hari Ram was away with the traders' caravan and the children had asked their mother if they could go to the village market to buy some sweetmeats. Tara had allowed them to do so, and a little while later the boys returned home.

"Where's your sister?" Tara inquired.

"She went with Jeetu Uncle to get the glass bangles he promised to give her," answered Shiv.

"You two stay inside the house," Tara cried, and grabbing an axe lying near the cow shed, ran out onto the street. She burst into Jeetu's small courtyard and found him with his arm around Kanti's waist, leading her towards the house.

"Kanti, get out of here," Tara screamed, pulling her daughter by the hand.

Jeetu freed the young girl and turned to face Tara. "I was only going to give her some bangles," he said, trying to smile.

Tara raised the axe over her head and leapt at him. Jeetu ran into his house and quickly bolted the door behind him. "If you ever even come close to my daughter again, I swear by *Krishan Jee*, I'll kill you," Tara screamed, pounding the wooden door repeatedly with the axe.

"All right, I'll never offer any gifts to your children, Tara. Calm down," he pleaded.

Tara struck the door several more blows with her axe, making splinters fly, before taking Kanti by her hand and walking out onto the street. "Don't you ever leave the house alone," she scolded, her voice trembling and her heart pounding uncontrollably. When her husband returned a week later she didn't tell him about the incident, as she knew that if she did, he would go berserk and kill Jeetu. And what would that accomplish? She would just have to make sure that this evil beast was never allowed anywhere near her children.

Kanti had felt confused about what had happened. She started spending much of her time alone in her room, and to her mother, it seemed as if her daughter had lost some of her childhood innocence. Tara tried to cheer her daughter up by taking her to the village goldsmith to have her left nostril pierced and buying her a shiny gold nose ring.

When Kanti turned fourteen, Hari Ram and Tara started seriously worrying about getting their daughter married. The boy would have to be from a Mohyal Brahmin family, but not from the Vaid subcaste as marriage between children belonging to the same subcaste was against their religious beliefs and therefore unthinkable.

"We must find a family that will look after our Kanti well," Hari

Ram confided to his wife. "God, I hate the thought of giving our child away to others."

"I know what you mean, my husband," Tara answered. "But such is the *rivaz* of our culture and that's what we have to do."

Now winter had come to an end, the air was warm and the sun dazzling. It was springtime and Tara knew that the priest of the Mohyals would soon come to their village, bringing news of the community and often serving as a matchmaker. She reminded her husband about it and when the priest arrived in Shahpur, Hari Ram invited him to their home.

The priest was tall and lanky and walked slightly stooped over, supporting himself with a long wooden staff. He was of indefinable age and his weather-beaten face was lined and creased. His beak-like nose projected over a mustache and a long gray beard. He wore a *kurta, salwar* and turban made of coarse cotton fabric. Hanging from his right shoulder was a large cloth bag containing all of his worldly possessions.

He lowered himself onto the *charpai* in the courtyard. "Oh, I'm getting too old to be traveling like this all over the country," he moaned.

"Well, you are needed by our community, *Pundit Jee.* Your work is much too important," Hari Ram said, sitting down next to the old man. "In fact, we can use your help right now," he continued, turning towards the priest. "Tell me, do you know of any good family that is looking for a bride? Our Kanti is getting to be of marriageable age and we have to start looking for a suitable boy."

"Well, I guess you're right, my work is important and I must continue," the priest sighed, massaging his knees with his gnarled fingers. "What did you ask? Oh yes, a good family. Yes, Hari Ram, there is indeed one such family looking for a suitable match for their 16-year-old son. They are from the village of Karyala in Punjab and own vast farmlands, large herds of buffalos and cows and many horses."

"Do you think this family will consider our daughter, *Pundit Jee?* I'm only a trader with nothing but this house to my name."

"Well, to tell you the truth, many have approached the boy's father with offers of big dowries, but all have been turned down. The boy's parents are wealthy and interested only in getting a most beautiful bride for their handsome son. I don't know, Hari Ram," the priest continued, shaking his head. "The girl will have to be very fair skinned and slim as well as extremely beautiful. That, I believe, is the only consideration of the parents, provided, of course, the girl has been brought up in a good home and their horoscopes match."

Tara was standing in the doorway of the kitchen trying to catch the conversation between the old priest and her husband. Hari Ram turned towards his wife. "Bring a tall glass of warm milk for *Pundit Jee*, and tell Kanti to come here," he called out.

Kanti came and stood demurely in front of the priest, her eyes cast down. She had on a pale pink silk *salwar* and *kamiz* which her mother had insisted she wear that morning. After a few moments, Hari Ram spoke gently. "All right child, you can go back in now."

Tara handed her husband the glass of milk, who then offered it to the priest.

"What do you think, *Pundit Jee*?" Hari Ram asked, his rugged face masking the annoyance that was building within his heart.

"You have a good reputation in the community, Hari Ram, and I've seen that Kanti is indeed a very beautiful child," the priest said, accepting the milk. "I'll do everything possible to bring about this match."

"What's the family's background, Pundit Jee?" Tara inquired softly, keeping her face shielded with her *dupatta*.

The priest drained the glass and placed it on the ground. "Well, the boy's father, Ashok Raj Chibber, is the chief of Karyala, a settlement of Chibbers in Northern Punjab," he answered, wiping his lips with the back of his hand. "He is highly respected by his people and their family history is also very illustrious. They are the direct descendants of the revered martyr, Mati Das."

"Wasn't he the one who, along with the 9th Guru of the Sikhs, was slain by the Muslim King Aurangzeb?" Hari Ram asked.

The priest placed his hands on his chest and belched loudly. "Yes indeed, he was the one," he answered with a deep sigh. "It happened in the year 1675 when the Muslim King Aurangzeb gave the two men the choice of converting to Islam or being beheaded. Mati Das, a devout Hindu, and Guru Teg Bahadur, the leader of the Sikhs, refused to give up their faiths and were tortured and executed in front of a large crowd in Delhi. Mati Das was made to kneel while two soldiers began sawing him vertically from the top of his head. He suffered agonizingly but kept reciting prayers before dying.

"Guru Teg Bahadur, touched by his friends' courage, instructed all Sikhs to henceforth treat the descendants of Mati Das as brothers and forever protect them from their enemies, even at the cost of their own lives. Two days later Guru Teg Bahaddur was himself beheaded by the soldiers of King Aurangzeb."

"We will consider ourselves most fortunate if our daughter is accepted into such a noble family, *Pundit Jee*," Tara spoke quickly.

"All right," the priest said, slowly pushing himself up, and turning to Hari Ram. "I'll be leaving Shahpur in a couple of days. Give me Kanti's horoscope along with one English sovereign gold coin. I shall describe Kanti to the parents and if the girl's and the boy's horoscopes are compatible, I shall present the gold coin to his parents as an offer of engagement."

Hari Ram gave the priest a fee of two *rupees* with a promise of another five if the match was finalized.

"I don't know if we're doing the right thing, Tara," Hari Ram confided to his wife later. "Trying to get Kanti married into such a wealthy family may not be the right thing for her."

"Of course it will be the right thing for Kanti," Tara answered. "We should consider ourselves blessed if they accept our daughter into their family."

It was autumn by the time the priest returned to Shahpur. *"Jai Ram Jee Kee*, Hari Ram, I have good news for you," he said, limping into the courtyard. "The horoscopes matched and the boy's parents accepted the English sovereign gold coin." The old man began digging into the large bag hanging from his shoulder. "Now where is it?" he mumbled and then brought out a package wrapped in a piece of crumpled red cloth.

"Here you are, Hari Ram," he said, a broad grin appearing on his face. "Here is the *shagan*, a token of commitment from the boy's parents to consummate the engagement."

Tara snatched the package from her husband's hands and eagerly started opening it. "Oh look," she beamed, forgetting to shield her face from the priest. "A beautiful red silk *dupatta*, a coconut and some dried fruit. And see, a thick gold chain with a heavy exquisite locket."

Tears welled in her eyes. "This is the happiest day of my life," she said softly. "By the grace of Krishan Bhagwan, our daughter is engaged. Wait, *Pundit Jee*," she said, hurrying towards the kitchen. "Let me fetch you a big glass of fresh warm milk."

Thus, Kanti at age 15 was betrothed to Hem Raj Chibber of Karyala, who was two years older. The wedding would take place in Shahpur the following spring, during the auspicious month of *Chaitra* of the Hindu calendar. The date and the precise time when the ceremony must be held would be carefully calculated by the Brahmin priest of the village to ensure the success of the marriage of this young boy and girl, who as yet weren't even aware of each other's existence.

The Wedding

*T*ara started planning Kanti's wedding from the moment the priest left. At her bidding, Hari Ram had gone to give the village elders the good news and to buy sweetmeats to distribute among their neighbours. "There is so much to be done, and hardly enough time," Tara complained to her husband. "I'm truly worried," she moaned. They were in their bedroom after the evening meal and Hari Ram was exhausted from all the running around his wife had made him do.

"I suppose you're right," he responded, removing his turban and tossing it towards a small wooden table next to the wall. "Where do we begin?" he asked.

"Well, Kanti is of course very beautiful and also well versed in managing a household," Tara answered, her face softening for a moment. "Yet, a decent dowry will be expected by her inlaws. We must start by deciding what all we need to assemble for her dowry."

Hari Ram slowly lowered himself into a cane chair next to the bed. "That really makes me sick," he said, his face showing the annoyance that had started welling in his mind. "It's bad enough our precious daughter has to be given away to others, but then, we also have to provide gifts for their entire clan."

"Well, it's not all that bad, my dear," Tara consoled, sitting down on the bed. "It's just that we mustn't let Kanti down. She has to be accompanied by a dowry befitting the status of the boy's family."

"You know, this custom of requiring a girl's parents to provide a dowry is a terrible curse of our culture," Hari Ram continued stubbornly. "It's a shameful tradition which should be stopped altogether."

Tara stood up and put her arms around her husband's shoulders. "My friend, Rani, was telling me the other day at the well that we are lucky; we only have Kanti to worry about. She and her husband have four daughters and will have to sell their farm and cattle if they are to get all of them married. She also said that since we have two sons, we'll get back twice as much as we give to Kanti's inlaws."

"Absolutely not," Hari Ram blurted out. "We won't accept a single *paisa*. I'm going to put a stop to this nonsense."

"I don't know about that," Tara mumbled, walking away from her husband. "We'll see when the time comes."

"What all do we need to get, anyway?" Hari Ram asked, sighing.

"Well, there'll have to be jewelry and clothing for Kanti, of course" Tara answered, returning to her husband's side. "Then we must give clothing and some jewelry for her mother-in-law and sisters-in-law. We'll need to provide clothing for the boy, his brother and father, and, of course, there'll also have to be some cash and perhaps a horse and a few cows. Will we have enough money? We'll also need to feed the wedding party during their stay in Shahpur and our friends and neighbours will have to be invited to the wedding feast."

Hari Ram remained slumped in the chair. The last two trading trips hadn't been profitable and he had barely broken even. The Muslim tribal chiefs whose territory the traders' caravans traveled through were now asking exorbitant protection monies and the demands for the merchandise he was carrying were also diminishing. If this kept up, he may have to end up opening a shop here in the village. The very thought sent a shudder through his body, and he slowly pushed himself up.

"Well, let's see what we've got," he answered, bolting the door to the room. Then, placing his shoulder against the heavy bed, he shoved it away from the wall. He went down on his knees and sweeping the mud aside from the floor in the corner of the room, he lifted four bricks and removed a tin box lying underneath them. He placed the box on the bed and opened it.

Tara peered over his shoulder. "*Hey Bhagwan*, how much money do we have here?" she whispered.

Hari Ram counted the pieces of soiled paper. "Well, we have 685 *rupees* and these four English gold sovereigns," he answered, placing the shiny coins in his wife's hands.

"*Lakshmi Mata Kee Jai*," Tara sang in amazement, "when did you collect so much money and this gold?" she asked.

"Well, for the past four or five years, I've been putting away a little after each trip, and the coins I bought in Quetta."

"That's great," Tara gushed, looking at the glittering gold in the palm of her hand. "We'll start tomorrow. You must take me to Quetta. We'll buy Kanti's wedding clothes and jewelry. We'll buy gifts for the boy and his entire family. Oh husband, we'll have a grand wedding for our daughter."

"Yes, I know you will. I guess we must secure our daughter's future happiness," Hari Ram spoke softly. "We must provide Kanti with a suitable dowry even if we have to use up every last damn *paisa* from our savings."

Time was passing quickly and one day Tara beckoned Kanti. "Come sit here next to me, daughter," she called out. "Let's you and I chat." Tara was seated on the *charpai* in the courtyard and Kanti had just finished washing the utensils after the morning meal.

"What should we chat about, Mother?" she answered, laughing, sitting down next to her mother.

Tara placed an arm around her daughter's shoulders. "Do you remember the old priest who came to our house two months ago?" she asked.

"Yes I do," Kanti answered, giggling. "He's the one with the parrot nose."

"Yes, child, he's the one," Tara answered, smiling. "Anyway, he brought us some wonderful news. The wealthy parents of a very handsome young boy have agreed to our proposal of an engagement between you and their son."

"Oh," Kanti said softly, the smile fading from her face. "Is that so?" she added.

"Yes," Tara pressed on, "and now we've set your wedding date for next spring. Isn't that exciting?"

Kanti remained silent for a few moments. "Why do I have to get married now?" she asked. "I'm only fifteen. Why can't I wait till I am twenty, or even older?"

"No my dear, that would be much too late," Tara replied, shaking her head. "In many of our communities, children are married off when a boy is five or six years old and the girl three or four."

"That sounds terrible," Kanti moaned.

"Oh, it's not so bad. The girl stays in her parents' home until the age of sixteen and only then is she sent to live with her husband and his family."

"Well, I'm glad I wasn't married off when I was three," Kanti said, sighing. "But I don't want to get married even now, Mother. Do I have to?"

"Yes, my child. You will be sixteen next spring, and besides, the boy's family is very well off. You'll be most comfortable living with them."

"But Mother, I don't want to live anywhere else," Kanti answered, turning towards Tara, her voice trembling. "I want to stay here in my own home with you, father and my brothers."

"No, Kanti, you mustn't say that," Tara answered patiently. "We can't go against our customs and traditions. As a Hindu woman, your place is with your husband in the home of his parents."

"You and father are just trying to get rid of me, aren't you?" Kanti cried, tears filling her eyes. "You'll get me married off to some stranger and send me away from home, won't you?" she said, standing up and running towards her room.

Tara's heart ached and she wanted to hold her child in her arms. But she left her alone for awhile. Later she went and spoke to her, patiently explaining the responsibilities parents have towards their children. "Someday when you have a daughter of your own," she added, smiling, "you'll also want her to be happily married."

They did not speak about it again for the next few days. Kanti remained pensive and, although she continued to help her mother with all of the household chores, her eyes had lost some of their sparkle.

Recently she had started noticing that some of the older boys would stare at her whenever she went out to the market with her mother. Then when she looked at them, they would smile at her in a silly way. In the beginning their odd behaviour annoyed her and she wished they'd stop gawking at her. Then one day when one of the boys waved his hand at her, she had been suddenly overcome with a strange warm feeling. Even later, in her room, thinking about it had given her a peculiar sensation which she found not altogether unpleasant.

One day Tara invited her daughter into her bedroom. "Come, Kanti, come let me show you the beautiful clothes your father and I have bought for your wedding," she said, opening the shiny tin trunk in the corner. "Here, look at this beautiful *salwar, kameez* and *dupatta* set," Tara beamed, spreading the bright red silk garments on top of the bed. "Look at this exquisite embroidery with pure gold and silver thread. We bought these for you in a fancy store in Quetta, but they were made by master weavers in far-away Varanasi. Here, child, look at your jewelry," Tara continued, placing the gleaming gold ornaments on the fine silk *dupatta*. "Isn't this a beautiful necklace, and here, the matching earrings, bangles, rings for your fingers, toes and a nose ring. Look at the size of this *tikka* for your forehead. These are all made of twenty-two carat gold, the jeweler has assured us. Aren't they all beautiful? Don't you like them?"

"Yes, they're beautiful, Mother," Kanti answered softly, touching the jewelry with her finger tips.

"You're going to make a beautiful bride, my dear child," Tara said, putting the jewelry and clothing away in the trunk. "Your husband and his parents will be most impressed. They'll all fall in love with you the moment they set their eyes on you."

"Will I be going away with them right after the wedding?" Kanti asked, looking at her mother's face.

"Oh yes, my dear," Tara answered, cheerfully. "After your wedding, you'll belong to your husband's family. His parents will be your new parents."

"How can they be my parents?" Kanti blurted out. "I already have you and father."

"We are your parents, my dearest, and will always be so," Tara explained patiently, trying not to let her voice falter. "But after your marriage you'll belong to your husband and be a part of his family. You must look after and heed your husband's parents. Each morning, you are to greet your mother-in-law with folded hands. Bow your head and touch her feet. You must also cover your head and shield your face with your *dupatta* whenever your husband's father or any of the village elders are present."

Kanti remained silent. Tara cleared her throat and pressed on. "You'll be very happy and comfortable — but remember not to forget your place. Never call your husband by name in the presence of others, and serve him his meals first, before you eat. It's also not proper for a woman to boast or brag, but instead maintain your dignity even in the face of adversity. You must do all of the housework your mother-in-law asks you to and no matter what happens, never complain. And remember to say your prayers daily and to read from the Scriptures."

Winter came and passed and, as the wedding was now only two weeks away, Hari Ram went about frantically making final arrangements. "I will get Jeetu to help me," he told Tara.

"No, no, my husband," Tara spoke hastily. "Don't do that. We don't need his help."

"What do you have against my cousin, Tara?" Hari Ram asked. "You've avoided him as if he's the devil himself."

How could she tell him that he was indeed the devil. She knew that her husband would go insane with rage if she told him the truth about what had happened. Yet she couldn't bear to have Jeetu involved in any of the arrangements for Kanti's wedding.

"I just feel terribly uncomfortable in his presence," she said. "You know that he used to beat his wife and would probably have killed her had she not run away to her parents' village. God only knows where she is and what's happened to her."

"Oh you're exaggerating a lot, Tara. Jeetu has been known to have a temper but he wouldn't harm anyone."

"No, my husband," Tara spoke stubbornly. "On this I insist. If you care for me and our daughter you will consent to my wish. You can ask the rest of the village for help, but your cousin must not be invited to participate."

"Why, what has he done?" Hari Ram asked, frowning.

"Don't ask me, please," Tara persisted. "I just have a terrible feeling about what he did to his wife. Call it a premonition but I don't want his presence to soil such an auspicious occasion as the marriage of our daughter."

"All right, Tara, you'll have your way," Hari Ram said, raising his hands. "No matter how unreasonable it appears to me, I'll do what you ask. Jeetu will not be invited to the wedding."

The *baraat*, the groom's wedding party, was to arrive the day before the wedding and proper accommodations had to be readied in the community guest house on the temple grounds. Food would have to be prepared not only for the members of the *baraat* but also for relatives and neighbours who were expected to attend the wedding.

The *baraat*, numbering twenty, consisted of Hem Raj, his parents, brother, sisters, uncles and cousins. From Karyala, they rode in five horse-drawn *tongas* to Chakwal and west from there to Jhelum, where they boarded a train the next morning. Arriving in the town of Multan the following day, they rode *tongas* to Dera Ghazi Khan, where they joined a camel caravan traveling west. Four armed guards on horseback, provided by Hari Ram, accompanied them. After spending two nights on the way in the villages of local chiefs, the *baraat* arrived in Shahpur, exhausted from the arduous journey.

Hari Ram, accompanied by several village elders and neighbours, all dressed in freshly starched turbans and their best clothes, waited at the entrance to the temple grounds and received the guests with their hands held together in front of their faces.

"Welcome brother," Hari Ram spoke politely, embracing Ashok Raj. "Welcome to Shahpur. I am very deeply honoured by this union between our two families."

Ashok Raj turned to a tall, handsome young man standing behind him. "Come, Son, pay your respects to your father-in-law," he said. Hem Raj hesitated a moment and then, bending down, touched Hari Ram's feet.

So this is the boy who, in less than two days, will become my beloved Kanti's husband, was the thought that raced through Hari Ram's mind as he placed his hand on the boy's head. "May God bless you with a long life, my son," he said. "May you always be healthy and happy."

The weary guests were ushered into the community eating hall where hot sweet tea and brass platters with sweetmeats were served to them.

"Please," Hari Ram requested each of his guests, "please have some refreshments."

Kanti had not left home the last three days before her wedding and spent much of the time in her room surrounded by her friends who chatted and giggled incessantly. "Why are you so pensive, Kanti? You should be elated," they chided.

The evening before the wedding, the *mehandi* ceremony was held and all the neighbourhood women invited to attend. Kanti's friends prepared *mehandi* paste from henna leaves and applied it to her hands and feet in delicate floral designs. After an hour they washed the paste away, leaving beautiful reddish-brown imprints that would last several days. "Well, now you've started looking like a bride," they laughed. One of the girls began playing the *dholkee*, beating a fast beat, and the women began singing and dancing around the bride.

Kanti's friends started teasing her again. "We walked by the village temple grounds today," one of them confided. "We saw your future husband."

"What did he look like?" Kanti asked urgently. "Describe him to me," she pleaded.

The girls looked at each other. "Well, we might as well tell you as you'll soon see for yourself," one of them finally answered, a somber look on her face. "He's short and fat and his face is dark-skinned and pock marked."

"Kanti, he has a big fat belly," another girl added, shaking her head. "And his teeth stick out of his mouth like those of a desert rabbit."

Kanti didn't know if she should believe her friends. It was customary for a bride to be teased, she knew. She felt dismayed, but resolved in her mind that no matter what her husband looked like, she'd be a good wife and treat him with respect.

Tara and Hari Ram's house had been thoroughly cleaned in preparation for the wedding. The walls had been whitewashed, the courtyard swept and tidied and the animals temporarily moved to a neighbour's yard. A *mandap*, within which Hindu weddings are performed, was constructed in the middle of the courtyard. On the day of the wedding its red wooden frame would be decorated with fresh green leaves and flowers.

The wedding day dawned and the house buzzed with activity. Large baskets of fresh flowers had arrived from Quetta and the women of the community sat busily preparing garlands of marigolds, which were then placed in a basket and covered with a wet cloth. Long strands of marigold, roses and jasmine were also prepared to decorate the *mandap* and the front door of the house.

Just outside the front door a wooden platform had been erected on the side of the street for musicians who would soon start playing traditional wedding music. They would use a reed instrument called *shehnai* and drums called *tabla* to add to the festive atmosphere. Swastikas, the eight thousand year-old revered Hindu symbol of good wishes and good luck, were painted with white lime paste on the wall on each side of the front door. In a far corner of the courtyard, several men had started preparing the meal that would be served first to the *baraat,* and then to members of the community and the bride's family.

Early in the afternoon, Kanti's friends began getting her dressed for the wedding. Kanti wore her red silk *salwar* and *kameez* and her friends helped her don her jewelry; the beautiful gold necklace, earrings, bangles and the nose ring. They placed the gold *tikka* on her forehead and attached its chain to her hair with a clip. They draped the red silk dupatta over her head and around her shoulders. "Oh, Kanti, you look exquisite," they cooed, slowly turning her around.

The marriage ceremony had to commence precisely at twelve minutes after three in the afternoon, which was the exact time the Brahmin priest of Shahpur had calculated to be the most auspicious. By two o'clock, the *baraat* was ready to leave for the bride's home. A band with twelve musicians dressed in bright red tunics adorned with brass buttons, and wearing green turbans and white *salwars* started playing just outside the door of the temple compound. A large crowd of villagers stood watching and neighbourhood children ran around excitedly. A white mare with silver ornaments attached to its saddle and reins was brought forward for the bridegroom to ride to the bride's home. Strands of bright red and orange flowers were placed over the animal's neck.

Hem Raj wore white silk *salwar* and *kameeze*, and his turban was made of fine pink cotton. A silver wedding ornament called *sehra* was tied around the front of his turban and several strands of jasmine and marigolds hung from the *sehra*, partially covering his face. A richly embroidered silk shawl was draped around his shoulders.

"You look so handsome, my son," Hem Raj's mother, Shanta, exclaimed, her voice tinged with concern. "Wait, come here. Lower your head for me." Observing an age-old practice, she took a fistful of coins and moved her hand several times around her son's head. She then threw the coins onto the street in front of him, to the delight of the children who scampered around scooping up the coins.

"There," she said, relieved, "this will ward off any ill effects of the evil eye of all who may be jealous of my handsome son."

Hem Raj was led to the mare and helped climb it. A six-year-old male cousin of his, selected to serve as the groom's attendant, was hoisted onto the mare to sit behind Hem Raj.

Led by the band, the *baraat* started slowly winding its way along the streets, lined on both sides with curious onlookers. Hem Raj's mother periodically looked up at her son and, praying under her breath, threw more coins onto the street.

As the *baraat* approached the bride's house, the music from the band became deafening. Hari Ram, flanked by his relatives and friends, all holding garlands of marigolds, waited at the entrance to the house. Young girls and women dressed in bright red clothes stood behind the men and chatted merrily. The colour red worn by them was symbolic of joy and celebration. A large red dot, called *bindi*, was painted in the middle of the foreheads of many of the women, which meant that they were married. Widows, who stood back and watched the festivities quietly, wore white clothes, little jewelry and did not have the *bindi* on their foreheads.

A man held a brass bottle above his head and sprinkled rose scented water on the *baraat*. The band stopped playing and moved aside. The men of the *baraat* stood facing Hari Ram and the village elders waiting to receive them. A Brahmin priest came forward to begin the first rite of a Hindu wedding ceremony. The priest wore a *dhoti* draped around his ample waist. He was shirtless and several strands of thin cotton thread were draped across his chest and over one shoulder. His head was clean shaven except for a tuft of hair tied in a knot on the back of his head as a symbol of his religion and priesthood. The middle of his forehead was covered with a large red *tikka* and three chalky white lines radiated horizontally on each side of it.

"*Namaskar*," the priest said loudly. "We shall perform the *Milni* ceremony by which the groom and his family will be greeted and welcomed," he explained, speaking in the Punjabi language. Then, clearing his throat, he continued, speaking in Sanskrit.

"Oh Supreme Lord, free us from all evil and bring into our lives only that which is good," he chanted. "Lead us onto the path of righteousness so that we may perform noble deeds in Your worship.

"As the ancestors of these two families in the past have performed their responsibilities, let them now continue to do so in loving harmony. May the two families eat and drink together in peace and may they worship You together.

"May there be peace, peace on earth, peace on the waters, sky, trees, the air, peace in our minds and peace for all things throughout the universe."

The priest then beckoned to Hari Ram who stepped forward and, with folded hands and bowed head, addressed his guests. "I welcome you with great joy to this very auspicious occasion of the joining of our two families," he said. "I'm deeply grateful to you for having undertaken this long and tiresome journey. My family and I hope that the hospitality of our humble home will meet your expectations."

The musicians on the raised platform, receiving a signal from the priest, began playing loudly. Hari Ram and Ashok Raj placed flower garlands around each other's necks and embraced three times. The exchange of garlands and greetings was repeated until all of the men of the *baraat* had been welcomed. They were then led into the court-yard to be served refreshments.

Next, it was the turn of the women to perform the welcoming ceremony. "Sister, congratulations to you," Tara said with a broad smile, placing a garland of flowers around Hem Raj's mother's neck. "May God Almighty bless the union between your son and my daughter." Flower garlands were then placed around the necks of Hem Raj's two sisters.

Tara, along with the other women of the village, next approached Hem Raj. He and his cousin had been helped off the mare and stood surrounded by a throng of giggling young girls. The women started singing a folk song welcoming the bridegroom. A basket of oats was placed in front of the horse as a gesture of welcome. Kanti's friends pressed closer to Hem Raj and began teasing him.

"Hey, look at the bridegroom," one of them called out, "he's so tall and handsome."

"He seems to be very shy, though," another added. "Do you think he can talk?"

"If he can't, that's good," a third teased. "Kanti will be able to keep him under her thumb." A girl reached up and moved the strands of flowers away from Hem Raj's face. "My, my, he's very fair. But look at him — he's still a boy. He doesn't even have a beard or a mustache."

Tara and the other women pushed the girls aside and approached Hem Raj to perform *aarti,* the traditional rite of offering homage. Tara held a silver platter containing a small pile of rose petals, some red *tikka* powder, a sweetmeat and a little brass cup containing *ghee* and a cotton wick which had been lit. She looked up at Hem Raj's face. The priest of the Mohyals had indeed found a very handsome husband for her daughter. "Welcome to our home, my son," she spoke softly. "May God bless you and Kanti with a very happy, healthy and long married life."

She dipped her right index finger in the red *tikka* powder and applied it to Hem Raj's forehead and then placed the sweetmeat in his mouth. She and the other women took the rose petals and showered them over his head. They then led him into the courtyard and directed him to sit down on a red cushion in the *mandap.*

When the *baraat* arrived, Kanti's friends had run out to witness the welcoming ceremony, leaving her alone in her room. The past several days had been hectic with all of the preparations going on around her and she didn't have time even to think. Now, sitting alone, her thoughts started wandering. She saw her own reflection in a mirror propped against the wall and felt overcome with apprehension. She had known for some time that she would be leaving her family and this house where she was born and had lived all of her life and be taken to the home of her in-laws, many days' journey away. Her eyes slowly moved around the room and started filling with tears. How would they treat her? When would she see her parents and her brothers again? She started sobbing, but just then her friends returned, giggling, and she quickly wiped her tears away.

The musicians were now seated in the corner of the courtyard and began playing softly. Kanti's brothers came to fetch her. They held her hands and, followed by her friends, made their way towards the middle of the courtyard. Those sitting on carpets around the *mandap* turned to look at the bride. Kanti's face was covered with her red silk *dupatta* and she held her head bowed. She clutched the hands of her brothers tightly to stop her own from trembling.

"Come daughter," the priest called out. "Come and sit here to the left of your future husband."

The priest then began the second wedding rite called *homas*, the offering of oblations to the sacred fire. He ignited pieces of dry, fragrant sandalwood and reciting hymns, placed the burning wood in a copper vessel called *havan kund*. He then poured a few spoonfuls of clarified butter on the fire and sprinkled fine shavings of sandalwood *mixed with butter onto the fire*. Tongues of bright flames shot out of the *havan kund* and the air was filled with a rich fragrance.

"O Lord, we purify this place in Your name," the priest chanted, leaning back away from the fire. "We seek Your blessings upon the bride and groom and upon all who have assembled here to witness this auspicious event."

Kanti could feel the heat of the flames through her *dupatta* and her face became flushed. A bead of perspiration slowly trickled down from her temple towards her chin and then ran down her neck. Her mind felt numb and she sat staring at the ground in front of her. She could barely hear the priest's voice above the murmuring from the people around the *mandap* and the shrieks of the children who were now busy playing on the street outside.

"Here, daughter, take this cup," the priest called out. "Welcome your husband-to-be by performing *madhuparka*."

He thrust a small silver cup containing a mixture of honey and yogurt towards her. "Don't be shy," he said softly. "Here, take it and hand it to the groom."

Kanti kept her head bowed and her hands trembled a little as she held the cup towards Hem Raj.

"Now, before you partake of the food your future bride has given you," the priest said, turning towards Hem Raj, "offer it to the six directions; east, west, north, south, up and down. Pray to God that you may imbibe the sweetness and purity of this honey and yogurt." Hem Raj did as instructed.

"Now, offer this drink to your bride," the priest directed.

Hem Raj turned towards Kanti. "Here you are," he whispered. Kanti reached out and took the cup from his hands. Taking the cup under her *dupatta*, she placed her lips to its edge and drank a little of the sweet mixture.

The music of the *shehnai* in the background was soft and slow and the drums became silent. It was time for the poignant ceremony of *Kanya Daan*, when the parents of the bride give their daughter away. Hari Ram and Tara tenderly grasped Kanti's right hand and placed it gently in the groom's right hand. Kanti tried to pull her hand away but Tara held it firmly and folded Hem Raj's fingers over her daughter's hand.

"We give you our daughter to be your partner for life and from this moment on, she is yours forever," Kanti heard her parents repeat after the priest, her father's voice faltering a little. Kanti stole a glance at his face and her heart ached, wanting to reach out to him. She heard the priest say something and slowly turned towards him.

"All right, children, please repeat after me," the priest instructed, wiping the perspiration off his face with a small towel he kept next to him. "Let our union be like that of two streams coming together so that we may live in harmony and peace. May our love for each other remain ever constant and deep." Hem Raj spoke in a firm strong voice, but Kanti could barely be heard.

"Now, son," the priest turned to Hem Raj, "repeat after me the following: Just as the rays of the sun passing through air or water illuminate distant objects, Kanti, you have come into my life. I take your hand in mine so that we may attain happiness together. By the grace of God and the blessings of all assembled, we have become partners for life. You are my lawful wife and I your lawful husband. God has given you to me and I shall provide for you always. May we live together happily for one hundred years."

The bride and groom were then made to recite their marriage vows. Hem Raj invoked the blessings of the Supreme Being and pledged to love, cherish, be faithful to and look after his wife as long as he lived.

His voice sounds gentle, Kanti thought, trying to glimpse his face through her *dupatta*. The priest was asking her to repeat the same promises. "Speak loudly, child," he advised. "All assembled here have to be able to hear you." Kanti raised her voice a little and repeated the vows.

The priest then slowly pushed himself up and stood stiffly, shifting his weight from one foot to the other. "Now the bride and groom will walk around the holy fire four times to symbolize the sacredness of their marriage vows," he said, directing Kanti and then Hem Raj to stand up.

Kanti felt relieved; the wedding must be about over. She yearned to return to her room to stretch her aching limbs. She allowed Hem Raj to take her hand and they slowly walked together around the fire four times. She was about to start towards her room when, to her dismay, she heard the priest instruct her brothers to pick up a small stone lying nearby and place it in front of their sister.

"Set your sister's right foot on top of the stone," he directed, and then turning to Hem Raj, added, "Repeat after me: I promise that our love for each other will be as firm and strong as the rock under my bride's foot."

"Each and every one of us is a pilgrim in this life, on a quest towards a common destination," the priest explained, "a destination where we can achieve inner tranquility and absolute freedom from all limitations. On the way, we are provided a partner via the sacrament of marriage."

The priest then tied the end of Kanti's *dupatta* in a knot to the edge of the silk shawl draped around Hem Raj's shoulders. "Thus united, you will perform the next rite of a Hindu wedding," the priest said. "Together, you will take the first seven steps of your lives. Each step you take symbolizes progress towards a particular goal, a specific end result of life. As you take each step, repeat after me the appropriate accompanying prayer."

"With God as our guide, we take these our first seven steps together.

With this first step we pray for unity and everlasting love between us.

Taking our second step together, we ask God for strength of our relationship   and good health.

With our third step we pray for a joyous and prosperous life together.

The fourth step we take with a prayer for each other's true happiness.

With our fifth step we pray for progeny.

Taking our sixth step together, we pray that the seasons all prove to be favorable for us.

And with this seventh step, we vow to fulfill our duties to our families and pray for true and everlasting companionship between us."

The priest now asked them to face each other and place their right hand over the other's heart. "Don't be shy," he added, smiling. "Repeat after me," he instructed.

"I take your heart as mine. May our hearts beat as one. May God unite us heart and soul."

Kanti by now was exhausted and wondered when the wedding would end.

"Only a few more minutes," the priest said loudly, as if reading her mind.

He was about to begin the next ceremony when a man standing by the courtyard wall started screaming, "Fire, fire." Everyone sitting around the *mandap* quickly stood up. Dense dark smoke was seen billowing over the wall and orange-red flames were now visible rising from the neighbour's yard.

"Get water, put out the fire," several men stared yelling.

"Please take your seats. Do not worry. Every thing will be taken care of," Hari Ram called out to his guests and ran towards the front door. Tara stood up, her hands at her throat, praying that the fire was not an ill omen of some kind.

Hari Ram found the thatch roof of his neighbour's barn to be burning furiously. Two horses in the barn were stomping their hooves and neighing loudly. Hari Ram quickly opened the barn gate and the horses stampeded out, almost knocking him to the ground. Other men came and stood watching the flames quickly consume the entire barn: there wasn't much they could do and it was over in minutes. All that remained were a few burning pieces of timber and the strong acrid smell of smoke.

Hari Ram walked out of his neighbour's courtyard. His first thought had been that the fire was set by Muslim miscreants of the village. But then he had seen a tall man running away in the distance wearing his turban at a rakish angle. It had to be Jeetu, he thought, angrily.

"Everything is fine; please sit down," he said to his guests, gesturing with his hands. "The fire is out. It was only the barn. Pundit Jee, please proceed with the wedding."

The priest appeared uncertain. "Is it all right to do so?" he inquired softly.

"Yes, yes, Pundit Jee, it's all right," Hari Ram answered, sitting down on the ground next to Tara. "Please continue the ceremonies."

The priest hesitated. "*Accha*, if you say so," he said and slowly turned toward the bride and groom. "Come children, look at the sun," he told them, "and recite after me: God, the Supreme Being, who existed before the creation of this Universe and will exist after it, may we pray together to this Supreme Being for a hundred autumns. May we enjoy the blessings of a happy and healthy married life together for a hundred autumns." Kanti and Hem Raj softly murmured the prayer.

"Where are the *jaimalas*?" the priest now asked, turning towards Hari Ram. Tara got up and handed the priest a basket who then gave Kanti and Hem Raj each a thick, brightly coloured garland made of fresh flowers. "As the final ceremonial act, you shall place these garlands around each other's necks," he instructed. Hem Raj had to bow low to allow Kanti to reach over his turban.

"You have today witnessed the sacred rites of a Hindu marriage." The priest addressed the assembled family members and guests, wiping his hands with his towel. "This ceremony has existed in our culture unchanged for thousands of years. The rites performed are extremely important and solemnize this holy union between Kanti and Hem Raj. Had this marriage taken place at night, instead of looking at the sun, they would have been asked to gaze at the polar star and pledge that their devotion and love for each other be as steadfast as this star. They would have looked at the two adjunct stars in the Great Bear constellation, representing the sage *Vasishta* and his wife *Arundhathi*, who personify a perfect marriage. The bride and groom would then have prayed that their marriage be as strong as that symbolized by these two stars in the heavens. From now on, Kanti will, each day, apply a red *bindi* on her forehead to signify her blessed married status."

The priest again wiped his face and smiling, spoke to Hem Raj and Kanti. "The wedding ceremony is over. As husband and wife, you may now go pay respects to your parents."

Hem Raj and Kanti together first touched the feet of Hem Raj's parents and then those of Kanti's parents. The shawl from Hem Raj's shoulders was removed and still tied to Kanti's *dupatta*, placed around her shoulders. The musicians began playing a lively tune and Kanti's friends led her to her room.

"You told me he was short and fat," Kanti whispered to them. "You were wrong. I had to stretch my arms so high to put the *jaimala* around his neck!"

Her friends giggled, "Well, all right, we were wrong," they teased. "He's tall, and you might as well know he's also very fair and handsome." Only her friends standing near her noticed the smile appear on Kanti's face.

Soon Tara and the other women led Hem Raj into the house. "Now that Kanti and you are married," one of the women told him, "you two will play a game to show who is quicker and will therefore dominate the other."

Kanti was seated on the floor in front of a shallow brass bowl half filled with milk. Hem Raj was directed to sit facing her across the bowl. Women and children quickly crowded around them. The air in the room had already become hot and stuffy.

"I will drop three *cowrie* shells into this bowl," a woman seated next to the newlyweds informed them. "You two must quickly grab at least two of the shells to win. The game will be played seven times before a winner will be finally declared."

Kanti's friends took her side. "Grab the shells the instant they're dropped, Kanti," they urged.

Several boys, including Kanti's brothers, went and stood behind Hem Raj and instructed him to grab the shells first. "You must win, brother-in-law," they pleaded.

The woman with the shells stood up and raised her hands. "Hush everybody, be quiet!" she admonished. Then, sitting down on the floor, she spoke to Kanti and Hem Raj. "Place your right hands on the rim of the bowl."

As soon as they did that, the woman dropped the shells and both Kanti and Hem Raj thrust their hands in the milk. Kanti came up with two of the shells, and Hem Raj only found one. The girls shrieked and clapped their hands.

"Well, that was only the first round," the boys boasted. "Kanti will lose the rest."

The second time the shells were dropped, Kanti again grabbed two shells.

"Come on brother-in-law, you must be more aggressive," Shiv and Shanker urged. "Don't let Kanti push your hand out of the way."

Hem Raj did what they suggested and he won the next two rounds, making the boys jump with excitement. When the shells were dropped in the milk for the fifth time, Kanti quickly grabbed two, but Hem Raj pried her grip loose and extracted one of the shells, winning the round. Kanti raised her eyes, and through her *dupatta* looked at her husband accusingly. Hem Raj smiled back at her.

During the sixth round, it was Kanti who wrenched a shell out of her husband's hand to win the round. The game was now tied, and the girls were screaming. "Kanti, you must win this last round." As the shells dropped the seventh and last time, their hands shot into the milk at the same instant but it was Kanti who grasped two of the shells. Her friends jumped and screamed joyously, clapping their hands. "We won, we won!" they yelled. The boys showed their disappointment. "The bride won only because the groom let her win," they complained.

Irrespective of who won, this ancient tradition worked once again, allowing a newlywed couple, who had not even seen each other before, to playfully touch hands.

The sun had now set and Hem Raj was led out into the fresh air of the courtyard, brightly illuminated with lamps and shimmering candles. The *shehnai* and drums played a fast rhythm of celebration and the members of the *baraat* were served the wedding feast. The festivities carried through late into the evening and the guests had a good time. Kanti slept that night in her own room, exhausted from the day's events. She woke the next morning with a sinking feeling, realizing that this might have been her last night in her parents' home.

The *baraat* returned to Hari Ram's house for the *dolee* ceremony, after which they would commence their long journey back to Karyala. Tara had carefully packed Kanti's dowry in four tin trunks which were now placed in the courtyard close to the front door. Hari Ram and Tara were most pleased that the wedding had gone off well, but now that the time to part from their beloved daughter was nearing, they felt heavy-hearted.

The music of the *shehnai* this morning was soft, slow and melancholy, the drums silent. Kanti refused to eat, and Tara had to force her to drink some milk. The *dolee*, a palanquin draped in a shiny red fabric and decorated with flowers, was placed outside the front door by four attendants.

After the *baraat* had eaten a meal served in the courtyard, Hari Ram and Tara came to their daughter's room to bid her farewell. Kanti's friends stood around her quietly and each, with tear-filled eyes, embraced her. Kanti then said farewell to her brothers Shiv and Shanker, who both hugged her, crying.

Kanti wiped their tears. "Hush, my brothers," she said, her voice trembling. "You mustn't cry. Promise me you'll always obey our parents and look after them."

She next went into her mother's arms and clung to her. "Mother, I don't want to go!" she sobbed. "Please don't send me away!"

Tara's heart ached and tears ran down her face. She cradled her daughter in her arms.

"No, my dearest child, you mustn't cry," she said gently. "This has to be the happiest day of your life. You are married into a wonderful family. You'll live happily with your husband and have many children. We will always love you and pray for you. But now your place is with your husband and you must go with him." She led her daughter to the door where Hari Ram waited.

Kanti looked up at her father through tear-filled eyes. Raising her hand, she tenderly touched his face, as she had done so often as a child.

"Don't worry about me, father," she said, controlling her sobs. "I'll be fine. I'll come to see you soon."

Hari Ram, tears streaming down his face, put his arms around his daughter. "May God protect you and bless you, my child," he whispered. "Draw upon the strength of your ancestors. Be brave. You will be in my prayers each day for the rest of my life." He led his daughter out into the courtyard, followed by Tara, Shiv and Shanker, each crying softly.

At the front door of the courtyard, Kanti stopped and lifted her *dupatta* to look at the house and her family. Her lips recited a silent prayer for them before she let the *dupatta* fall and cover her face again. Hari Ram and Tara gently guided her to the *dolee* and, parting its screens, helped her enter it. Tara briefly held her daughter's hands before backing away from the *dolee*.

Hari Ram walked over to Hem Raj's father. He handed Ashok Raj a small package containing the jewelry for Hem Raj's mother and sisters and money for the purchase of four cows. Trembling with emotion, Hari Ram folded his hands and bowed his head.

"This is a small token of our appreciation for your accepting our Kanti into your family. My daughter is now your daughter, and I beg and implore you to look after her."

Ashok Raj embraced Hari Ram. "Be assured, brother," he said, "she will be treated as one of my children."

Hem Raj bowed down and touched Tara's and Hari Ram's feet. The four attendants hoisted the *dolee* on to their shoulders and, accompanied by Hem Raj and the *baraat*, started walking down the street.

Hari Ram stood leaning against the door of his house, tears streaming down his face. "Will these eyes ever see you again, my dearest child?" he whispered, trying to catch a final glimpse of the red *dolee* slowly disappearing in the distance. "Please God, oh dear God, please look after her," he sobbed. "Be merciful. Protect her. Keep her in the shadow of your love," he prayed.

Journey To Karyala

$\mathcal{T}$he *baraat* traveled on foot only a short distance from Shahpur before stopping in the shade of a small grove of *kikar* trees where several Muslim herdsmen were waiting with their camels. Members of the *baraat* were to ride the camels back to the railhead town of Dera Gazi Khan, accompanied by the four mounted armed guards that Hari Ram had once again provided.

The herdsmen yelled at the camels and pulled and tugged their reins, and the large beasts gradually started lowering themselves. Their limbs flailing awkwardly, they slouched down and squatted on the ground.

Hem Raj's sisters, fourteen-year old Murti and Janak who was thirteen, helped Kanti out of the *dolee*. Their mother, Shanta, directed Kanti to get on to one of the camels. Although the saddles on each camel were only for two, both Murti and Janak insisted on riding with their sister-in-law and quickly climbed into the seat behind her. The two girls shrieked with alarm when their camel clumsily lumbered up to a standing position.

"Be careful, girls. Hang on tightly," Hem Raj called out to his sisters as the camels, led by the herdsmen, started shuffling forward.

The sun in the cloudless sky above them was like a red fireball and the air suffocatingly hot, but everyone seemed to be in a jovial mood.

Hem Raj had as yet not spoken to his bride and couldn't even see her face which was covered by her dupatta. She did appear to be riding her camel with ease, swaying gently with the movements of the beast, and he hoped that she was all right.

Except for occasional outcrops of rocks and small hills breaking the monotony of the arid terrain, the desert was flat and barren. The camels were moving steadily towards the east, and had now been traveling for about three hours. The village where they were to stop for the night was still some twenty miles away.

Hem Raj straightened his back and stretched his arms over his head. Peering through the haze, he noticed what appeared to be a small cloud of dust approaching from the south. One of the guards riding with them had also seen it and standing up in his stirrups, shielded his eyes to look intently into the distance.

"Bandits," he suddenly shouted. "Move quickly," he called out to the herdsmen. "Get behind those rocks."

The herdsmen yelled instructions to each other and began sprinting towards the large cluster of rocks some distance away. "Oh God, we're going to be robbed," someone cried. The camels started running, the people riding them clinging desperately to their saddles. Hem Raj looked over his shoulder again. The cloud of dust was getting nearer and through the haze he could discern several horsemen racing towards them. Suddenly one of the girls screamed and Hem Raj quickly turned to see Janak falling, tumbling to the ground. He leapt out of his saddle and landing heavily, raced to his sister. Lifting her in his arms, he ran towards the rocks and lowered her gently onto the ground. Janak was sobbing and her face was bleeding where it had been scraped by the tip of the stirrup during her fall. Hem Raj removed his turban and gently pressed it against the wound on her face.

The four guards had slid off their horses and quickly took positions behind the rocks. The herdsmen coaxed the camels down and the members of the *baraat* huddled together behind a large rock.

The bandits, numbering eight or nine, were now within sight, galloping towards the rocks. The guards fired, and a horse stumbled and fell, throwing the rider from its back. Another bandit was hit and fell off his horse which kept galloping towards the rocks. The rest pulled on their reins and quickly brought their mounts to a stop. They had expected the wedding party to have acquired guards only after joining the caravan at the next village. More gun shots rang out from behind the rocks, and the bandits quickly picked up their two fallen members and sped away.

"Let's go," the guards yelled to the herdsmen. "We must reach the village before they regroup and return."

Everyone rushed to hurriedly climb back onto their camels. The herdsmen started running, tugging the beasts behind them. The men kept looking over their shoulders and no one spoke. It was almost dusk by the time they sighted the village ahead of them. A large caravan of camels was already in the village. The bleeding from the cut on Janak's face had almost stopped. The village *hakeem* was summoned and applied a pungent smelling paste over the wound. The *baraat* spent the night in huts Hari Ram had arranged for them, and early next morning they left, accompanying the caravan.

Kanti's mind was in a blur throughout the journey. She felt heavy-hearted and was also bothered by her sister-in-law's fall. The cut just below Janak's right cheekbone was not deep and would heal, but her face was going to be scarred forever. She wouldn't have fallen if she had not insisted on riding with me, was the thought that kept nagging Kanti. Images of her parents and brothers kept entering her mind and she tried to imagine what they must be doing.

She felt somewhat relieved when they arrived in the home of her in-laws in Karyala. Janak's spirits by now had perked up and she and her sister Murti excitedly showed Kanti around their house. "Can we take her to the river bed to play?" they asked their mother.

"No," Shanta scolded curtly. "She has to be shown to the women of the village in her wedding clothes first. Only after that can she step out of the house." Shanta was a skinny tall woman with a stern narrow pockmarked face, and when she spoke, it was in short sentences that shot out of her mouth in a surprisingly deep voice.

The girls took their sister-in-law up to the roof-top terrace of their house. "There's the river," they pointed out. "It's empty most of the year except when the rains come."

"Is that part of Karyala, across the river on the cliffs?" Kanti asked, pointing at a cluster of small clay structures and huts.

"No, that's Meerpur," Janak answered. "It's a village of Muslims. We don't go there."

Two days after the return of the *baraat*, festivities were held at their home and just about the entire village was invited and served hot tea and sweetmeats. The dowry brought by Kanti was displayed on several *charpais* in the courtyard for the guests to see and admire. Kanti, wearing her wedding clothes and jewelry, was seated on a charpai in one corner of the courtyard with her face partially shielded by her *dupatta*.

"What a grand dowry," a woman said loudly. "Such fine clothing and so much exquisite gold jewelry." Then, turning to her companion, she muttered, "The clothing seems coarse, and look at the jewelry: that's not pure gold."

"I agree," her friend answered, raising her eyebrows. "With such a handsome boy, one would have expected to see a much finer dowry and at least twice this size."

Kanti overheard their conversation and felt stunned. How could they speak such lies? My parents have given me a beautiful dowry, she wanted to scream at them. Shanta stood stone-faced next to her daughter-in-law, chatting briefly with the village women as they came to see the bride and to give her a gift of money.

"Oh, she's so pretty," they cooed. "May she be blessed with many sons," they added, pressing a few coins into Kanti's hands.

"No, no, that's too much, sister," Shanta protested. "Give back half of it, daughter," she instructed Kanti.

"It's really not much," the women would insist, returning all of the coins to Kanti.

The money was passed back and forth three or four times and only then would Shanta say, "All right, Kanti, you can accept the gift."

Shanta noted in her mind the exact amount each woman gave as she would reciprocate accordingly when it was her turn to give a gift to the children of these women.

"I've never been so embarrassed in all of my life," she complained to her husband later that evening.

"Why? What happened?" Ashok Raj asked, wondering what had now upset his wife.

"Well, you're lucky, you didn't have to hear the taunts of the village women about the shabby dowry that we received."

"What shabby dowry?" Ashok Raj spoke calmly. "I've never seen so much fine jewelry anywhere."

"What do you know about jewelry?" Shanta lamented. "Any woman will tell you there's more brass than gold in the few pieces of cheap jewelry our daughter-in-law brought with her."

"Now, now, Shanta, calm down," Ashok Raj admonished. "And don't go saying anything hurtful to Kanti. She's to be treated as our very own daughter."

"You can treat her as a daughter," Shanta answered angrily. "She's caused me such shame already. I don't know how I'll ever show my face in the village."

Kanti felt desperately lonely during the first few days in Karyala in spite of the companionship of Murti and Janak. Her mother-in-law seemed angry all the time and hardly ever spoke to her other than to order her around. Hem Raj tried to make her feel welcomed in their comfortable home, but Kanti's heart yearned to be with her own parents and brothers. Hem Raj caught her crying one evening and gently brushed her tears away.

As the days passed, Kanti gradually became accustomed to her new life and surroundings. Her handsome young husband seemed to be caring and Murti and Janak treated her affectionately and she became particularly close to them. Hem Raj's younger brother, Des Raj, at sixteen, was just her age, but he was shy, and addressed her respectfully as *Bhabi Jee*, the Hindi term for one's brother's wife.

Ashok Raj never spoke to his daughter-in-law directly but often inquired through his wife or daughters how she was doing. "Make sure that she's comfortable and happy in our home," he would tell his wife.

"She's fine, she's a daughter-in-law, not the mistress of the house," Shanta would retort. "I'll take care of her."

Their home was built of red bricks and was the largest house in all of Karyala. It was located next to the temple, at the top of the hill the village occupied. A solid wooden double door opened onto a huge courtyard. Sheds for three buffalos and two cows, as well as stables for three horses were located towards the front of the courtyard, away from the living quarters of the family.

A covered veranda ran the entire length of the house and doors leading to the kitchen and three large rooms opened onto the veranda. One room was occupied by Ashok Raj and Shanta, the second was for the two girls, and the third was used by the family as a gathering place and for their meals, especially during winter. The rest of the year, they ate sitting at a large weather-beaten wooden table on the veranda outside the kitchen. A large bedroom on the upper level of the house was occupied by Hem Raj and Kanti, and a smaller one was used by his brother. Several *charpais* were kept on the open upper level terrace where the family slept during the summer months. A third small room provided storage for the *charpais* during the rains.

A large *banyan* tree and two smaller *kikar* trees in the courtyard produced ample shade. A thick rope was tied to a branch of the *banyan* tree and a wooden swing seat attached to the rope. Murti and Janak, with their friends from the neighbourhood, spent many hours each day taking turns riding the swing. The girls sang songs and screamed merrily as they went higher and higher. Two of them rode the swing together, with one sitting on the seat while the other stood behind her, holding on to the ropes, making the swing move by pushing with her bent knees.

"Come out sister-in-law," Janak called out loudly to Kanti. "Come and see how high I'm going on the swing."

Kanti was in the kitchen and was about to start kneading flour to later bake into *naans* outside in the clay *tandoor*.

"Get the *naan* dough ready and then light the fire in the *tandoor*," Shanta instructed her. "Then you can see what the girls want."

From the day after her arrival in Karyala, Kanti had started cooking all of the meals. After she had served the family, she ate and then washed all the utensils and tidied the kitchen. She didn't mind the work so much since she knew that as a daughter-in-law it was expected of her. What did surprise and hurt her was the way her mother-in-law spoke to her while being ever so sweet to her own daughters.

After school, Murti, Janak and their friends often ran down the narrow, winding, cobblestone lanes to play on the dry, sandy bed of the river. They dug into the sand until water started seeping out, and then splashed each other with the cool liquid. Shanta had started allowing her daughters to take Kanti with them to play, but only after all of the housework had been completed. The first time the girls brought their sister-in-law to the riverbed, Kanti had noticed a girl standing on the cliff of the opposite bank, looking down at them. She was dressed in red and wore heavy silver jewelry. Kanti hesitated and then started walking towards the cliff.

"Don't speak to her," Murti whispered. "We aren't supposed to."

The girl on the cliff slowly turned around and walked away.

Murti and Janak selected a likely spot on the river bed and started scooping out the sand with their hands. They giggled and laughed, racing to make the hole deeper until water started oozing into it.

"See, we told you there's water under the surface!" they yelled, splashing each other and Kanti with the cool liquid.

The girl on the cliff re-appeared and Kanti walked over towards her. "Your jewelry is very pretty," she called out, looking up.

The girl stared down and then spoke softly. "It's only silver. Yours is gold. Are you a bride?"

"Yes," Kanti answered. "I was just married into a family here in Karyala. My name is Kanti. I'm sixteen."

"You're a Hindu? I'm fifteen. My name is Noor. I've been married two months," she said over her shoulder, walking away.

The next time the three of them were on the river bed, Hem Raj came along, riding his horse, and stopped to chat with them. Kanti reached out to pat the horse's head. Hem Raj remembered how deftly his bride had ridden her camel during the journey from Shahpur. "Would you like to ride?" he asked.

Kanti's eyes lit up, but then she shook her head. "No, it wouldn't be proper," she answered. "Besides, what if someone were to see me?"

"Go ahead, sister-in-law, ride," Murti and Janak pushed her toward the horse. "We won't tell our parents, and there's no one else down here at this time."

Kanti hesitated a moment, and then, encouraged by the smile on her husband's face, quickly wrapped her *dupatta* around her slim waist. Hem Raj helped her mount the horse and adjusted the stirrups. The animal spun around, but Kanti brought him under control. Leaning forward, she dug her heels into the horse's sides, and raced down the river bed. Murti and Janak shrieked with delight, clapping their hands, watching Kanti steer the animal around several boulders.

Her hair flying and face flushed, Kanti felt as if she were back in Baluchistan, racing her father's horse on the dry plains around Shahpur. Reluctantly she turned back and galloped to where Hem Raj stood, his face showing his amazement.

Kanti dismounted and came up to her husband, handing him the reins. She glanced at his face, seeking his approval, and their eyes met for an instant before she lowered hers. From that moment, a special bond grew between them and each sensed it as they walked back, side by side, up the hill to the house, oblivious to the loud chatter of Murti and Janak or the clatter of the horse's hooves on the cobblestones. This precious moment in their lives soon blossomed into a deep enduring love and respect for each other.

The next several days that Kanti went down to the river bed she kept looking up at the cliff, but the Muslim girl did not appear. Then one day she was there and Kanti walked over towards her. "I didn't see you for the past few days," she asked.

"I was taken to my parents' village for a visit," Noor answered. "Was that your husband whose horse you rode the other day?" she asked.

"Yes, it was," Kanti answered. "I wish my in-laws would send me to visit my parents."

"How do they treat you?" Noor inquired.

"They're fine, except for my mother-in-law. She's very mean to me."

"Then we have something else in common," Noor said, smiling.

"Won't you come down and play with us?" Kanti asked.

"I'm not supposed to. My mother-in-law would kill me if she found out," Noor answered. But then she looked over her shoulder and added, "Maybe just for a minute." She slid down a narrow rough path and came down to the river bed. The two young girls looked at each other awkwardly for a few moments and then started laughing. They held hands and began running around on the hot sands of the river bed.

"I must leave now," Noor said, looking up at the cliff.

"Shall I see you tomorrow?" Kanti asked.

"*Inshah Allah* (God willing), yes," the Muslim girl answered and scampered up the path.

They met on the riverbed each day and a strong friendship gradually developed between them. They eagerly awaited their brief moments together and chatted, telling each other about their lives.

Noor, though dark in complexion, was a pretty girl and was married to her cousin, Aslam Khan, the eldest of the four sons of a wheat farmer who was also the village chief of Meerpur. She was able to briefly escape each afternoon only after cooking the evening meal and before her mother-in-law awakened from her afternoon sleep.

One day when the two girls were chatting on the river bed, Noor suddenly stiffened. "Oh my God, that's my mother-in-law up on the cliff," she moaned. The girls ran and hid behind a boulder. The woman on the cliff squinted down at them and then slowly walked away.

The next day Noor told Kanti that her mother-in-law had slapped her hard on the face for leaving the house without her permission. "Fortunately for me her eyesight is weak and she wasn't sure it was me playing with you. I told her I was tending to the vegetable garden in the front of our house."

The summer heat had been intolerable but then the monsoon began and it rained for days at a stretch, turning the dry river bed into a raging torrent. The boys ran down to the river and swam in its swift muddy water, while the girls played indoors. Kanti felt restless, cooped up in the house all day, burdened by the oppressive humid air and all the work she had to do.

The first day it stopped raining, she ran down to the river's edge after finishing her chores and was delighted to see Noor waving at her from the cliff across the river. They called out to each other but the roar of the gushing water drowned their words. Noor pointed at her stomach and ran her hands over it. Kanti understood and clapped and waved her hands joyously.

Soon it was autumn and preparations began for *Diwali*, one of the most important religious observances of the Hindus. A festival of lights, *Diwali* celebrates the victory of good over evil by commemorating the triumphant return of Rama, a manifestation of the creator Vishnu, after destroying the evil demon king, Ravana.

Schools close for a week, homes are cleaned and painted and elaborate feasts prepared. *Lakshmi*, the goddess of prosperity, is also worshiped during the festival and merchants and businessmen close their account books for the year and start new ones. Gifts are exchanged and *diyas,* little round clay vessels with oil and cotton wicks, are lit at night, outlining homes and temples. Hundreds of *diyas* are also floated on the surfaces of ponds, streams and rivers.

With the recent marriage of a son, there was special significance to *Diwali* in Ashok Raj's home in Karyala. In Shahpur, with Kanti gone, the celebrations in Hari Ram and Tara's home would be somewhat subdued.

Two days before the festival, Hem Raj took his sisters, brother and Kanti to Chakwal in the family *tonga* to buy gifts, sweetmeats and dried fruit. Later they stopped at a shop on the outskirts of the town where they bought firecrackers to explode on the eve and the night of *Diwali*. To Kanti's surprise, her mother-in-law allowed her to go although the housework was not yet finished. "You can complete it on your return," Shanta had said. The day before the festival, Kanti, at her mother-in-law's behest, prepared a variety of sweetmeats. "Now, follow my instructions carefully," the old woman scolded. "The sugar content in all of the sweetmeats has to be exact."

Hem Raj and Des Raj, helped by their sisters, placed clay *diyas* on window sills, along the ledges of the terrace and around the trees in the courtyard. Ashok Raj and Shanta gave the children gifts of new clothing. Each of the three girls also received a piece of jewelry. As evening approached, the family sat down to say their prayers. When dusk fell, all of the *diyas* were lit and relatives and friends dropped by to wish the family good health, happiness and prosperity. The sound of firecrackers bursting filled the night, together with the joyous shrieks of children who danced around and ate sweets to their hearts' content. Everyone stayed up late. Kanti and Hem Raj would long remember this night of their first *Diwali* together.

Kanti had not gone to the riverbed for a week but the day after the festival she wrapped a few pieces of sweetmeats in a piece of cloth and ran down to see her friend. Noor appeared at the cliff's edge, walking awkwardly, and this time Kanti scampered up the rough path. The girls embraced and sat down holding hands, laughing and eating the sweetmeats Kanti had brought.

Winter brought cold winds from the snow covered mountains of the north and the kitchen was the only room in the entire home that was warm. Kanti kept a fire burning there all day, feeding it with the chopped wood piled high outside the kitchen. Hot sweet tea was kept brewing to warm anyone coming in from the cold. Water for bathing was heated on a separate fire out in the courtyard.

Although Kanti was burdened with all of the chores, Shanta was the one who made decisions in all family matters and in the running of the house. One afternoon Kanti was surprised when her mother-in-law asked her to come and sit near her. "Have I done something wrong, *Mata Jee*?" she asked softly, sitting down on the edge of the charpai.

"No, you haven't. I just want to talk about a family matter," Shanta answered, knitting her brow. "I've been thinking, we have to start looking for a boy for Murti. Your father-in-law talked to the priest about it. Let's hope he finds her a good match. I would like to see my daughters married while I'm still alive."

"They are both so beautiful, and our family name is well known, *Mata Jee*," Kanti said quickly, relieved by the lack of anger in her mother-in-law's voice. "There'll be many offers of marriage for them."

"Let's pray to Krishan Bhagwan that you are right," Shanta answered with a sigh. "If that happens, and you give me a grandson soon, I'll be the happiest woman alive."

Kanti's face turned red and she quickly stood up. "Let me get you your tea, *Mata Jee*," she said, hurrying towards the kitchen. She had also been hoping and praying that she would conceive. It would please her no end to be able to give her husband and his family at least one son and she knew fully well that it was expected of her. "*Hey Parmatma*, help me so I don't let them down," she often prayed.

Noor had given birth and it was a boy. Kanti was happy for her friend, but it made her own inability to bear a child more painful. Springtime came and yet Kanti could not sense any fullness to her flat stomach. "I'm terribly sorry that I'm not with a child as yet," she said hesitantly to her husband one day.

"That's all right, Kanti," he answered gently. "I would like you to have children but there's no hurry."

Kanti worried that she may not be able to bear him any. She went to the temple often and prayed. Soon the women of the village were gossiping behind her back. "She is fair and beautiful, but what good are her looks if she's barren?"

Hem Raj's days were occupied in helping his father manage the family's farms and homes. As the eldest son, he was expected to eventually take over as the head of the family, once his father was ready to relinquish his position. He was being groomed for this responsibility and when that happened, he would inherit the family's farms and homes. He would then be responsible for the care of his parents in their old age, and if his brother and sisters were yet unmarried, he would have to find suitable matches for them. His parents would stay with him but would devote their time to prayers and leisure. Hem Raj would also take his father's place as Chief of the village. He would help arbitrate and settle disputes between the people of Karyala and be their leader.

"You will need great wisdom and must always act justly," Ashok Raj advised his son. Although most of the inhabitants of Karyala were Chibbers and related to them, several other Hindu and Sikh families also lived in the village.

"They will all look up to you," Ashok Raj told his son. "You must treat each impartially and with complete fairness. Not only must you look after your own parents, but as the head of our clan of Chibbers, you must see to the needs of all elders, especially those who do not have a son of their own. This is your sacred duty, my son."

Hem Raj traveled with his father to distant towns where they owned farms and homes which had been rented out. Their tenant farmers knew that soon they would have to deal with this young man and hoped he would be as generous towards them as his father.

Within a year a suitable match had been found for Murti from the village of Dharabi. Her wedding took place and she left with her husband and his family. Janak cried bitterly for days. Soon after that, Des Raj was engaged to a girl from Chakwal, also chosen by his parents.

Kanti's inability to conceive was becoming bothersome for Shanta and she spoke to her husband about it. "Maybe there's something wrong with our daughter-in-law," she complained.

"Why, what do you mean?" Ashok Raj asked.

"She is not with child as yet."

"Give her time," her husband answered patiently. "After all, we had to wait eight years before God blessed you with our first."

"I hope she's not cursed," Shanta persisted. "Look at what happened to Janak. Our poor daughter's face has been scarred for life."

"That was an accident," Ashok Raj answered curtly. "It had nothing to do with Kanti. Besides," he continued with a smile, "Janak looks prettier with that little scar on her face."

"Anyway, I'll speak to the village *hakeem*," Shanta mused. "Perhaps he can give a talisman for your daughter-in-law to wear."

The talisman did not work and neither did a potion given by a wandering *fakir*, which only made Shanta angrier. She started finding fault with whatever Kanti did and scolded her for trivial reasons. "This food is terribly bland," she'd moan. "Didn't your mother teach you how to cook?"

"Why do you serve such weak lukewarm tea?" she'd say gruffly. "Can't you even make a proper cup of tea?"

She made Kanti massage her feet each day, and wash her clothes. She'd then complain that the clothes didn't look clean.

In the beginning Kanti's heart ached and at times she wanted to lash back. But she calmed herself by bringing to mind her own mother's advice and the tenderness of her husband. "Give me the will, oh God," she'd pray, "to do what is right and to be ever respectful towards the parents of my husband."

The date for Des Raj's wedding was set and the family began preparations for it. The *baraat* traveled by *tongas* to Chakwal for the ceremony, and returned to Karyala, bringing Des Raj's young bride, Vimla, with them. Kanti took an instant liking to her and Janak was ecstatic to once again have someone closer to her own age in the house.

It was springtime and Kanti became aware of having missed her monthly curse. Yet she wanted to be absolutely certain before she would tell her husband or anyone, especially her mother-in-law. She ran her hand over her belly often and when two more months went by, she decided to tell her mother-in-law.

"*Mata Jee,*" Kanti spoke softly, "I'd like to speak to you."

"What is it?" Shanta grunted, looking away.

"I believe that I am with child," Kanti answered, lowering her eyes.

Shanta turned and glared at her. "Are you sure?" she asked.

"Yes, *Mata Jee.* Here, feel it," Kanti said with a faint smile.

Shanta placed her hand over her daughter-in-law's stomach. "Go, go to the temple, girl," she instructed. "Go at once and pray that it's a boy."

Pray Kanti did, each day, that the child she was carrying should be a boy. What if it wasn't? Oh dear God, how would she face her mother-in-law.

Vimla, her sister-in-law, was most caring. "You are not to do a single chore in this kitchen," she scolded. "You have to worry about your baby. I'll do all the work for you!" With Vimla's help, Kanti was able to cope with her pregnancy although the morning sickness had been particularly bothersome. As the time approached she wondered if she would be sent to her parents' home to have her baby. That would be so wonderful, she mused. She hadn't seen her parents nor her brothers since her wedding and longed to be back in her home with them. But Shanta had already spoken to the village mid-wife and had worked out the arrangements.

The day her labour pains began, Hem Raj and his father were in Peshawar to collect rent moneys from their tenants. Kanti was in the kitchen and needed Vimla's help to go up to her room and get into bed. The mid-wife was sent for by Shanta and came running. Kanti's labour lasted several agonizing hours. The mid-wife gave her a foul tasting liquid to drink and she drifted in and out of sleep.

After a sudden severe bout of excruciating pain, she began to give birth. She heard the cry of her baby and fell back on her pillow, exhausted. Her mind was in a fog; the potion the mid-wife had forced her to drink made her head spin. She dozed off and then woke with a start. For a few moments she didn't know where she was. She raised herself on her elbows and looked around the room. Just then the mid-wife came in through the door. "Where's my baby?" Kanti asked. "Where's my child?"

"I'm sorry," the woman answered, busying herself, "I'm sorry to tell you that your child was still-born."

"What do you mean, still-born?" Kanti asked, sitting up, her eyes showing the panic that was starting to build in her mind. "I heard my baby's cry."

"No, you must have imagined that," the mid-wife answered, starting to leave the room. "I couldn't do a thing for her."

Kanti got out of her bed. "No, it can't be," she screamed, grabbing the mid-wife's arm. "I want my baby. Where's my child? Tell me now."

Shanta appeared at the door. "Calm down, Kanti," she spoke curtly. "It was still-born. The body has already been sent for disposal. Let the woman go. Why are you making such a fuss? It was, after all, only a girl."

Kanti fell to her knees, sobbing. "Oh my God, no. It can't be," she wailed. Shanta turned and left the room. Vimla and Janak tried to console Kanti but were themselves overcome with grief and cried their hearts out.

Kanti stayed in her room all day, praying and crying. If only she had been sent to her parents' home to have her baby, she knew her mother would have lovingly welcomed a granddaughter. She refused to eat and slept fitfully through the night, her sleep disrupted by strange dreams of dark churning clouds, torrential rains and flooded rivers full of bloated bodies of dead cattle. She woke up early the next morning and lay in bed, trying to clear her mind. Then she remembered. "No dear God, this couldn't have happened," she moaned softly. "This should not have happened." She tried to imagine what her daughter must have looked like and tears flooded her eyes. "What karmas were you born with, my dearest, for your life to have been taken away so cruelly," she moaned and started sobbing.

She got out of bed and changed her soiled clothes. Slowly she went down the steps and into the kitchen. Vimla was already there and had rekindled the fire.

"Oh, you should still be in bed, sister," she said coming over and taking Kanti's hands into hers. "You've gone through such an ordeal, you should stay in bed all day."

"No, I'm all right, Vimla," Kanti answered. "I'll make the tea and take it in for *Mata Jee*." She boiled the water and added the tea leaves to it. She poured some milk into the brew and then sweetened it with sugar. She stood staring at the tea bubbling in the pan, strange thoughts clouding her mind. Is there justice in your Kingdom, oh God, she thought, pouring the tea into a clay cup.

She forced herself to pick up the cup and walk out of the kitchen. By now her mother-in-law would be sitting at the table on the veranda waiting for her tea. But today she wasn't there. This was unusual and since her father-in-law was away, Kanti went and knocked on their door. There was no answer and she knocked again. "I have brought you your tea, *Mata Jee*," she called out, struggling to keep her voice calm. There was still no answer so she slowly pushed the door open. She found her mother-in-law lying on her bed, her eyes wide open. Oh, how much Kanti wanted to throw the hot tea at the old woman's face. But instead she placed the cup on a table next to the bed and brought the palms of her hands together before her face. "*Namaste, Mata Jee,*" she said softly, moving towards the foot of the bed to pay her respects. She sensed Shanta's eyes following her as she bent down to touch her mother-in-law's feet. "Please try the tea, *Mata Jee*," she said, moving to the side of the bed. "If it's not sweet enough, I'll add some more sugar." There was no response from Shanta. Kanti looked at her mother-in-law's face. "Are you all right, *Mata Jee*?" she asked. "Speak to me."

But Shanta lay motionless except for her eyes which darted angrily from her daughter-in-law's face to the door.

Kanti felt faint. There was a stench in the room of which she had just become aware. "Something's wrong with you, *Mata Jee*," she said softly, moving towards the door. "I must get help at once."

Several women from the neighbourhood came running, summoned by Vimla. They crowded into Shanta's room, fussing over her. One of them hastened out to fetch the village *hakeem* and brought him back with her. Des Raj had gone to the farms adjacent to their village, and was sent for. "What's happened? What's the matter with my mother, *Hakeem Jee?*" he asked.

The old man led him out into the courtyard. "I'm sorry, son," he answered, shaking his head. "Your honorable mother has lost her ability to speak or to move any part of her body other than her eyes. This happens to some older people when they become possessed by an evil spirit."

"Can you treat her and make her well?" Des Raj pleaded.

"Unfortunately I do not know of a cure for it but will fetch a talisman which is to be tied to her arm," the old man answered. "I will also go to the tomb of the *fakir* in Chakwal and pray for blessings for her. In the meantime she must be kept alive by forcing food into her."

Kanti felt stunned, her sorrow tempered by the shock of Shanta's sudden illness. "Oh dear God," she prayed that night, "did you have to deliver your justice so swiftly? *Hey Bhagwan*, forgive her sins and let her be in peace." She then began praying for the soul of her baby but her sobs interrupted her words.

The next day Kanti went through her rituals of preparing tea and taking a cup for her mother-in-law. She propped Shanta up with pillows and forced the tea down her throat. With Vimla's help, she changed Shanta's soiled clothes and sheets. She then bathed herself and said her prayers.

Late in the afternoon Hem Raj and his father returned. Kanti stayed in her room and only at night when her husband came to her did she tell him of the still-birth of their child. It was then for the first time ever that she saw tears flood her husband's eyes.

Shanta's condition remained unchanged; the talisman brought by the village *hakeem* didn't help, nor did his prayers at the tomb of the *fakir* of Chakwal. The old woman was unable to move any part of her body, nor speak a single word. Kanti had taken over the care of her mother-in-law and fed her three times a day by forcing food down into her throat. The village mid-wife was engaged to bathe Shanta each day and to wash her clothes out in the courtyard.

Months went by and Kanti sensed that she was once again with child. She prayed each day that it would be a boy. When the time came, Hem Raj stayed beside his wife and rejoiced with her at the birth of a son. Ashok Raj was ecstatic at the birth of his first grand-child. "We shall name him Devi Lal, in memory of your mother's father, Devi Chand who was chief of his village near the Khyber Pass," he told his son. "He was a very brave man and died in his saddle, fighting British soldiers."

The naming ceremony was held at the temple and the newest born of the clan of Chibbers named Devi Lal. Kanti carried her son into Shanta's room and held him so the old woman could see her grandson's face. "Here you are, *Mata Jee*," she said. "Here's the grandson you wanted."

Shanta's eyes remained expressionless, staring blankly straight ahead. Kanti cuddled her child in her arms.

"You, my son, will grow up to greatness and will help and heal others," she said softly, walking out of the room and into the bright sunshine outside. "You'll perform many noble deeds and atone the sins of your ancestors."

Over the years Kanti gave birth to two more sons and they were named Mohan Lal and Sohan Lal. They were followed by two daughters who were given the names of Shanti and Sheila. Her friend Noor had given birth to three sons and a daughter. Des Raj's wife Vimla gave birth to two girls and then to a boy. A match had been found for Janak from a family in the village of Saagri and her marriage held. She had then gone to live with her husband and in-laws in their village.

Then one day when Kanti had taken the morning cup of tea for her mother-in-law she found Shanta lying with her eyes closed and, for the first time, with a peaceful look on her face. "I've brought your tea, *Mata Jee,*"Kanti called out, but Shanta's eyes remained shut. The old woman had died in her sleep during the night.

Her body was taken to the cremation grounds east of the village where a priest performed the last rites, and Hem Raj, as the eldest son, lit the pyre. Two days later they collected her ashes and took them to Haridwar, the sacred city for Hindus. There, Hem Raj and Des Raj gave up their mother's ashes to the holy waters of the river Ganga.

Within days of his wife's death, Ashok Raj handed over all the responsibilities of the family to his eldest son and withdrew into a quiet life of prayer. He asked to be moved to the smaller bedroom on the upper floor, giving up the larger one on the ground floor to Hem Raj and Kanti.

The year was 1889 and Hem Raj, at the age of 29, thus became the head of his family and the chief of the village of Karyala. Kanti, just 27 years of age, was now the matriarch of the household. As pretty as she had been when she was a young girl, she had turned into a stunningly beautiful woman. She was adored by her husband and treated with respect by the other women of the village.

A week after Ashok Raj had named his eldest son chief of the village, a special ceremony was held at the temple. In the presence of the villagers, the priest helped Hem Raj recite prayers, asking God for wisdom and courage in meeting his responsibilities and fulfilling his obligations to his people. At the conclusion of the prayers, the priest applied a red *tikka* on Hem Raj's forehead, and the villagers rejoiced.

Hem Raj felt awed by the sudden change in his life and doubts began flooding his mind. Will he be able to carry out all that was expected of him? He accepted the congratulations of the villagers crowding around him and only Kanti noticed the uncertainties that momentarily clouded his eyes. Her heart reached out to him and she prayed, asking God to help her husband meet his new responsibilities.

Duties and Traditions

*H*em Raj gazed at the faces of the village elders seated with him in a circle on the floor of the temple assembly hall. His mouth felt dry and his shoulders began to sag.

"It's time to start the meeting, Hem Raj," the elder sitting next to him whispered.

"Yes, yes. It is time," Hem Raj answered, clearing his throat.

"The meeting of the village Council will come to order," he finally spoke, barely recognizing his own voice. The elders looked at him attentively. Hem Raj continued speaking, his voice shaking a little as he thanked them for the trust they had placed in him. He pledged that, as their chief, he would act justly; would remain impartial and treat each person with fairness.

There were two disputes between villagers that the Council needed to resolve. The first resulted from a villager picking mangoes from the branches of his neighbour's tree that had grown over onto his yard. The owner of the trees had become irate and threatened his neighbour with violence if he ever caught him picking the mangoes.

"He's welcome to the fruit that falls on his ground, but he's stealing the mangoes still on my tree," the man complained.

Hem Raj pondered for a few moments. "Yes, your neighbour is entitled to the fruit that falls from the tree onto his yard," he said in a firm voice. "As to the branches that have overgrown on to his property, you must either cut them off or agree to share the mangoes from them with your neighbour. That is my judgment."

The village elders looked at each other and, much to Hem Raj's relief, nodded approvingly.

Hem Raj now sat up straight and heard the second dispute, involving grazing rights between two farmers. This time he remembered to consult the elders before dispensing judgment. The meeting over, he returned home with a smile on his face and a distinct jaunt in his stride, neither of which went unnoticed by Kanti.

"How did the Council meeting go, my dear?" she asked.

"It went very well, actually much easier than I had anticipated," he answered, grinning. "Now, in two weeks, I have to represent our village Council at the *Zila Parishad*, the District Council. We will then act on disputes between people from different villages in the entire district."

"My goodness," Kanti exclaimed, "that sounds like an even bigger responsibility."

"Yes it is! But don't worry, Kanti, I'll be a good leader. After all, I am a Mohyal Brahmin and I finished high school," Hem Raj said, placing his arm around his wife's shoulders. "You'll be proud of me."

"I'm already very proud of you, my dearest. You're handsome, brave and an educated man. Everyone in the entire province will one day hear of you and admire you."

Hem Raj began embracing his role as the head of the family and chief of the village with passionate vigor. He engaged a village woman to come and wash clothes and the kitchen utensils in his home each day. He required the village Council to meet twice a week, and assigned specific tasks to each of the members. The irrigation of the farms owned by the villagers was going to be improved. The lanes adjacent to their homes had to be swept clean, and the old roof of the school house had to be replaced.

He returned from his first meeting of the District Council excited and full of ideas. "A bandit by the name of Gulzari is becoming a menace in our area," he had been told at the meeting. "Each village must defend itself and try to apprehend this miscreant."

"We must be vigilant and fight off any attempts to rob us," he told his Council members back in Karyala. "We must bolster the defenses of our village. We'll collect a little money from every household and buy four large bells to hang at each corner of our village. Ringing of a bell will alert the entire village of trouble. We must encourage our people to buy guns and those who don't know how to use them will have to be shown."

"We must protect one another," he told them. Let this Gulzari try and attack our village. We'll have his head," he boasted.

Hem Raj allowed his moustache to grow, and curled its tips upwards. He took to carrying his rifle with him all the time and hung a dagger called a *kirpan* by his waist. He purchased a handsome white stallion from the *Ghora Bazaar* in Jhelum and named the horse *Kamaan*—a warrior's bow.

By tradition, the eldest son in most Hindu families was encouraged to embrace the Sikh religion. Although Hem Raj had remained a Hindu, he had from a very young age started wearing a steel bracelet around his wrist and the *kirpan* by his waist, two of the five symbols of the Sikh religion. Like many other Hindus, he often attended religious services at the Sikh temple in the village.

In their home, the cooking chores were taken over largely by Des Raj's wife, Vimla, and Kanti started spending more time with her children. Eight-year old Devi Lal and his younger brother, Mohan Lal, who was six, attended the village school. The younger children, five-year old Sohan Lal and his sisters, Shanti, three, and Sheila, two, played in the courtyard all day. Devi Lal was a serious young boy and enjoyed reading books more than anything else. His two younger brothers, unlike him, were full of mischief, often quarreling with each other and with the other boys of the neighborhood. Kanti raised her children by the precepts of their Hindu faith and led the family during their evening prayers. She taught them how to recite the *Gayatri Mantra* which she herself had learned as a child.

Oh Supreme Being, the source of existence, intelligence and bliss, Creator of the universe, may we prove worthy of Thee, may we meet Thy glorious grace, mayest Thou be the unerring guide of our minds and may we follow Thy lead unto righteousness.

After their prayers, Kanti read the *Bhagavad Gita* for the family. "The *Gita* states that our minds are often cluttered with conflicting thoughts just like the battlefield where Prince Arjuna faced his dilemma of having to engage in a battle against his cousins. Lord Krishna told Arjuna that he had the ability to discriminate between right and wrong. Sometimes the right choice may be painful but it is what we have to do." The children and Hem Raj listened attentively.

"The *Gita* tells us that we must do away with ignorance and strive to gain knowledge," she explained. "When we perform our duty, we must do so without expectations of reward. The results of our deeds, our Karmas, come to us as a gift from God. We must be content and grateful for what we have, and not be envious of others, or constantly crave for more.

"We must banish evil thoughts from our minds and always speak the truth. Each of us must aspire to the best we can. Nothing is unachievable if we put our heart and soul to it."

Hem Raj would tell his children stories of the brave deeds of their ancestors; their valor and the battles they had won. "Now we have a new enemy, the English" he told the children. "We have to drive these foreigners away and free our motherland. As Mohyals, we have the sacred duty to uphold our faith and to fight to protect our nation. I want you, my sons, to grow up strong and help free our country."

"I will fight, *Pita Jee*," Mohan Lal would answer.

"I will too," his younger brother would add. "I'll beat all the foreigners and chase them away."

For the past several years, Hem Raj had accompanied his father to their farms near the town of Sargodha to collect and sell the grain cultivated by their tenant farmers. They also traveled to Peshawar twice each year to collect rent from tenants occupying their buildings. As the head of the family, he now gave his brother the responsibility of look-ing after their farms adjacent to Karyala, and planned to continue trav-eling to Sargodha and Peshawar to collect the grain and rent.

"I'll ride Kamaan and leave for Sargodha tomorrow," he told Kanti. "I'll be gone two or three days."

"Will you spend a night at brother Saleem's home?" Kanti asked.

"Yes," he answered, "I'll do that both going to Sargodha as well as on my way back."

"That's good, my husband," Kanti said, relieved. "Then you won't have to ride after dark. Perhaps you should take Des Raj with you," she added. "It may not be safe for you to travel alone, especially after you receive the money from the sale of the grain."

"Nonsense," Hem Raj answered, "I can outshoot any bandit who tries to rob me. And now I have the fastest stallion in all of Punjab."

Kanti's eyes glowed with pride as she watched her husband ride away the next morning, sitting tall in his saddle. "Protect him through his journey, *Krishan Bhagwan*," she prayed softly.

Hem Raj's long standing friendship with Saleem Khan, a Muslim, had surprised both of their families. But they had known each other since attending school together in Chakwal almost twenty years ago, and shared the same passion for freedom for their country. Saleem's wife, Naseem, called Hem Raj *Bhaijan*, the Urdu word for brother.

Years ago when Naseem had met Hem Raj for the first time, it was the day of a Hindu observance symbolizing the bond between sisters and brothers. On this day, sisters tie bright colourful threads called *raakhi*, around the wrists of their brothers and pray for their health and happiness. The brothers in turn, give their sisters gifts and pledge to always protect them. Even though she was a Muslim, Naseem had tied a *raakhi* around Hem Raj's wrist, taking him as her brother, and since then, Hem Raj had treated her as his sister.

Saleem received his friend warmly and the two stayed up late chat-ting. Early the next morning Hem Raj rode away towards the south and outside the town, crossed the Jhelum River by boat. Kamaan acted skittish getting into the boat, and once across, barely gave his master time to mount before galloping up the sandy embankment and onto the dirt road to Sargodha. Hem Raj rode into the bazaar of the small town late in the morning and stopped at the grain merchant's shop. He arranged for a camel cart to accompany him to his farm a few miles beyond town.

When they saw Hem Raj approaching, the three tenant farmers came running and bowed their heads low. So he has come alone, one of them thought, wondering whether this young landlord would reduce the amount of grain they would be allowed to keep. To their surprise, the farmers found Hem Raj to be as generous as his father. They thanked him profusely and rushed to help load the bags of wheat onto the camel cart.

Hem Raj sold the wheat to the grain merchant in town, and tucked the money away in a pouch under his *kurta*.

"Be alert on the journey," the grain merchant cautioned. "The bandit Gulzari and his gang have recently been attacking travelers in these parts."

"I'll be all right," Hem Raj answered, waving his hand, and walked his horse away towards a food shop where he planned to have a meal before returning to Khushab. An old blind beggar was sitting by the side of the road and Hem Raj dropped a coin in the man's outstretched palm before entering the shop. The beggar got up and hurried out of town.

Hem Raj was in high spirits. The wheat crop this year had been excellent. Even after giving his tenant farmers more than the usual quantities of grain, he was taking home the largest amount of money ever since he had started accompanying his father to Sargodha. He had eaten well and was looking forward to another pleasant evening at the home of his friend in Khushab.

Kamaan trotted along the dusty road. A warm strong wind was stirring up a cloud of dust and Hem Raj wrapped the tail of his turban around his face, covering his nose and mouth. He had ridden a short distance out of town when, coming around a bend, his horse almost stumbled over a large tree limb lying across the narrow path.

"Halt!" a loud voice came from up ahead. "Get off your horse at once," it ordered.

Several men with swords in their hands rushed onto the path from behind trees. The one leading them carried a rifle. Hem Raj's mind was racing: they'll not only take my money, horse and rifle, but will most likely slit my throat. If I die, I'm going to take some of you dogs with me, he snarled angrily. Swinging his rifle from his back, he bent down low. The bandit with the gun fired a moment before the bullet from Hem Raj's rifle shattered his left shoulder. Hem Raj dug his heels into his horse's sides and Kamaan reacted swiftly, vaulting over the branch and racing towards the startled men. They leapt aside and tried vainly to slash at the stallion racing by them in a blur of powerful limbs and pounding hooves.

Hem Raj did not slow Kamaan until they were close to the river bank. Once on the boat, he felt his legs weaken, and quickly sat down. He took off his turban and wiped the perspiration from his face and the back of his neck. There was a burning sensation on the side of his face. He touched the skin gently and flinched, but there was no blood on his finger tips. He knew how close he had come to taking a bullet in his face. He had seen the bandit who had shot at him spin around and drop. "I hope I killed the swine," he muttered under his breath.

When he returned home, Kanti noticed the angry welt on his face. "Are you hurt, my dear?" she asked quickly. "What happened to you?"

"Oh, it's nothing," he answered. "The branch of a tree must have scratched my face during the journey," he lied.

"How are brother Saleem and sister Naseem?" she inquired.

"They were fine. They asked about you and the children," he replied. "Saleem told me about a national organization he has joined."

"What organization is that?"

"I think he said it's called *Azad Hind.* They lead demonstrations and marches, demanding our freedom."

"That certainly is a worthy cause."

"Yes, except marches and demonstrations won't get us anywhere," he spoke angrily. "The rest of India has to do what the Pathans have done in the Northwest Frontier. The English have built forts in the Frontier, but they haven't been able to subdue the people. The only language these foreigners understand is that of the gun."

"Violence may not be the right answer," Kanti spoke softly. "Look at what happened four years ago. Thousands of brave Indians died at the time of our armed uprising."

"To die a martyr for one's country is a glorious death," Hem Raj answered. "I want our sons to grow up to be brave and not afraid to sacrifice their lives for their country as long as they take some of the enemy with them."

"They are but children as yet," Kanti said, her eyes softening. "This is the time for them to gain knowledge and grow."

Hem Raj was silent for a moment. "I'm concerned about our eldest, Kanti," he said. "I've tried to teach him to ride and to shoot, but he seems not too interested."

"Devi Lal is a very gentle and caring child. He'll be fine," she answered.

"Yes, but I want him to grow up strong and bold," Hem Raj persisted. "After all, as our eldest son, he'll have to one day take my place as the head of the family."

"Devi Lal is a very good boy and he looks up to you," Kanti said, placing her hand on her husband's arm. "He'll listen to you. He will learn whatever you teach him."

"I hope so," Hem Raj said with a sigh. "I certainly hope so."

Devi Lal loved and admired his father greatly and listened attentively whenever Hem Raj told his children about the brave sagas of their ancestors. The young boy was proud of his heritage, but was bewildered by the history of conflicts and killings. Why couldn't people simply stay in their own villages and look after their own families and animals, instead of attacking other villages and occupying other countries?

As time passed, Devi Lal did learn how to ride and to shoot a rifle. Yet he was more interested in his books and in learning all he could. He enjoyed listening to his mother, especially when she read the *Gita* to the children.

One day he startled her by asking, "Mother, what is death? What happens to us after we die?"

"Well, the *Gita* tells us that death is the end of one life but the beginning of another," Kanti explained to him. "Our souls are indestructible. The *Gita* says that when the body dies, the soul continues in another body; just as we take off one set of clothes and don another."

Devi Lal spent hours sitting in the courtyard under the trees or in his room, reading books that he brought from his school. He relished the stories of the legendary Emperor Ashoka and read about the lives of Hindu sages and kings. He was touched by the stories on the life of Gautama Buddha and his teachings of *Ahimsa;* non-violence and respect for all life form. Hem Raj, however, wanted his sons to be brave and adventurous. He embraced life with bold enthusiasm living it with exhilaration, and expected the same of his boys.

"Live life to its fullest my sons," he would advise them. "Who knows what the future has in store for us."

Shortly after returning from Sargodha, Hem Raj traveled to Peshawar to collect money from the agent who looked after the four buildings owned by the family. Hem Raj was born in a village not far from Peshawar where his mother had gone to her parents' home to give birth. Hem Raj related well to the carefree lifestyle of the Pathans of the Northwest Frontier. Much of the land around Peshawar was inhabited by tribes who lived in fortified villages. When not feuding with each other, they were engaged in an ongoing struggle against the British who for years had tried vainly to conquer this rugged land and its fierce people.

Hem Raj traveled by a horse-drawn *tonga* from Karyala to the city of Jhelum, where he boarded the Frontier Mail headed north. The train station in Peshawar was in the middle of the bustling city. Hem Raj walked out of the station and started making his way through the heavy traffic and crowds of people. He would stay the night with Jagat Singh Dhaliwal, a close friend of the family, and someone whom he had known since childhood. He turned off the main road and entered a narrow winding lane, crowded on both sides with small shops.

A heavy-set man sitting in a luggage shop stood up and came out. "Welcome, brother, how are you?" he said, embracing Hem Raj.

"I'm very well, thank you, Jagat Singh. I hope you and your family are well?"

Jagat Singh was a Sikh and as a requirement of his religion, did not cut his hair, but tied it in a knot on top of his head and wrapped a turban around it. His beard was long and thick and, as a further symbol of his religion, he wore a steel bracelet around his wrist and carried a *kirpan* at his waist.

"We're all fine, thank you," he answered. "You must be tired after your journey. It's almost dinner time. Please come, let's go upstairs."

The two men sat down on a mat on the floor of the kitchen. Jagat Singh's wife, her face shielded by a *dupatta*, served their meal in large round brass *thaalis* which she placed before them. She sat on the floor in front of the kitchen fire and made round flat *chapaatis* for them while her two-year old son, Bir Singh, stood clinging to her.

"How's your respected father doing?" Jagat Singh asked.

"He's well," Hem Raj answered. "He spends most of his time at the temple or praying at home."

"You must be very busy as the head of the family and the chief of your village," Jagat Singh added. "It must be tough."

"No, it's quite straight forward. I've really had no problems," Hem Raj answered. "We've started making plans to improve the irrigation of our farms, and to secure the village against robbers. How about you, Jagat Singh, how are things with you?"

"My shop produces adequate income to meet our needs, Hem Raj. I'm also able to send some money to my parents in our village of Rakhra each month," the Sikh answered, and then lowered his voice. "I have become active in a secret organization called *Azad Hind*," he added.

"Oh, yes, I heard about this group from my friend Saleem Kahn in Khushab. He said that a *fakir* from the Khyber Pass is their leader."

"Yes, the *Fakir* of the Afridis, Nazir Mohammed, has formed *Azad Hind* to fight the British. They are now developing a nation-wide underground network."

"What else have they done so far?" Hem Raj asked.

"They are providing training to anyone who wishes to become a freedom fighter," Jagat Singh answered. "They've started manufacturing large quantities of firearms and have carried out several impressive raids on British Government installations. Only last week they attacked and destroyed a small fort north of Bannu. The British suffered heavy losses and retreated, abandoning the fort."

"Jagat Singh, I'd like to buy a good rifle for my son."

"I can take you to Dera Gulab, in the Afridi territory north of here, Hem Raj. That's the village where you were born, isn't it?"

"Yes. My grandfather, Devi Chand was the chief of the village and my mother had gone there to give birth. In fact, my oldest son is named after my grandfather."

"The *Fakir* of the Afridis is now chief of Dera Gulab," Jagat Singh explained. "The village is a distribution center for arms for members of the Azad Hind. After we finish our meal, I'll contact my associates and arrange for us to go to the village tomorrow morning. You'll be able to buy the arms you need."

It was still dark early the next morning when Hem Raj and Jagat Singh left. They walked quickly down the narrow lanes and came onto a wide road. The red stone walls of a fort appeared on the right. A sign in front of it read Bala Hissar Fort. Two Indian soldiers armed with bayonets affixed to their rifles were guarding the entrance to the fort. Another soldier sat next to a machine gun mounted on a tripod within a protective wall of sandbags. Hem Raj glared at the soldiers and spat on the ground as he walked past them.

After walking a short distance beyond the fort, they turned into a deserted narrow dark alley. At the far end of the alley, Jagat Singh knocked softly on a door.

They waited and then Jagat Singh knocked again. The door opened a crack and the tip of a revolver appeared through the narrow opening.

Then the door was opened wide enough to allow the two men to quickly slip through. They stood in the darkness while a man behind them closed and bolted the door. The air around them was warm and stale. Someone lit an oil lamp and Hem Raj saw that they were in a long narrow room. The man with the lamp also held a revolver. He now turned around and, opening a door in the rear of the room, beckoned to Jagat Singh and Hem Raj to follow.

They emerged into a dark alley and walked quickly along it. A *tonga* was waiting on a road where the alley ended. As soon as the three men climbed aboard, the tonga started moving. They rode in silence, with the clip-clop of the horses hooves echoing loudly in the early morning quietness. They were approaching an army post on the outskirts of the city. The Indian soldiers on guard looked disinterestedly at the passing tonga. Once beyond the city limits, the driver whipped the horse into a fast gallop.

Two hours later, just as the sun's rays began penetrating the morning haze, the *tonga* pulled off the road and onto a dirt path. Two armed men on horseback suddenly appeared and rode on each side of the *tonga*. The narrow path climbed up towards the top of a hill, and a high mud and stone wall appeared ahead, surrounding a village. Below a watch tower, a large wooden gate was swung open by guards to allow the tonga to pass through. One of the horsemen dismounted and indicated to Jagat Singh and Hem Raj to follow him.

They walked to the middle of the village and entered a small mud house. In a back room, a thick soiled carpet was pushed aside to reveal a trap door in the floor. They climbed down a narrow flight of steps and stepped into a cavernous room. Rows upon rows of revolvers, rifles and even machine guns, were neatly displayed, lying on the floor. The glow of several oil lamps reflected off the polished metal of the weapons. A giant of a man was seated next to a low table on a rug at the far end of the room.

"I am Nazir Mohammed, chief of the village," he said, touching his forehead with the fingertips of his right hand. "The grandson of our hero Devi Chand is welcome to Dera Gulab."

"I am pleased and honoured to return to the village of my birth," Hem Raj answered, bowing his head and bringing the palms of his hands before his face.

"Look around," the chief smiled and waved his hand towards the display of arms. "Select any weapons you wish."

Hem Raj walked through the room, inspecting a revolver here, and picking up a rifle there. These hand-crafted weapons appeared to be excellent. All were exact replicas of arms made in the factories of the British and were true to the most exacting details. Although not able to read or write English, the Afridis even engraved the serial numbers from the guns they duplicated.

Hem Raj selected a long-muzzled revolver for himself and a rifle for his son and placed them on the low table next to the chief.

Hot sweet tea was served, poured from a silver urn into small cups. Jagat Singh and Hem Raj sat down on the rug and accepted the tea. The chief chatted with them for awhile and then mentioned the price of the rifle selected by Hem Raj. "The revolver is a gift from me," he added.

Hem Raj thanked Nazir Mohammed and put the money for the rifle on the table. He would not refuse the gift of the revolver as doing so would be to slight his host.

The rifle was wrapped in a cloth and placed in the *tonga*. Hem Raj tucked the revolver into his *salwar*, under his *kameez*, and they rode back into the city.

Later that morning, Hem Raj went to Hazari Bagh, a maze of narrow streets, to see the agent who looked after the buildings owned by the family.

"*Namaste*, Hem Raj Jee," the agent beamed, showing a mouthful of betel-nut stained crooked teeth. He was short and plump and came waddling from behind his wooden desk. His small one-room office was cluttered with piles of frayed ledgers and papers. The strong smell of incense burning in front of a framed painting of Lord Shiva filled the room.

"I have all of the receipts ready," the agent said, producing a brown paper folder. "Everything is in order, *Sahib Jee*. All the rent collected is listed plus the few costs for repairs."

Hem Raj took the folder and started looking at the receipts. He was never sure if he could trust the man. "What's this fifty rupee entry for the repair of windows?" he asked, waving a piece of paper. "Who did you have do the repairs, your brother-in-law?"

"Oh no, *Sahib Jee*," the agent whined, rolling his eyes. "I swear to you, on the honour of my dear deceased mother, the repairs were done by a Government certified carpenter."

The agent then quickly opened a safe in the wall behind him and took out a bundle of notes. "Here you are *Sahib Jee* — all of the rent money minus the cost of the minor repairs and a very meager commission for me, your servant."

Hem Raj glared at the agent and put most of the money in an inside pocket of his *kameez*. With the rest, he later bought gifts for Kanti and the children.

When he returned to Karyala, the children were excited to receive the gifts their father brought from Peshawar. Hem Raj, however, was disappointed at his eldest son's lack of enthusiasm upon receiving the rifle.

"I brought him a simple little book and a beautiful rifle," he said to his wife. "My son didn't get anywhere near as excited seeing the rifle as he did about the book. I can't understand it."

"He's only a child," Kanti consoled her husband. "Now he likes reading. When he's older, he'll be different."

The years flew by and the people of Karyala came to look up to their charismatic chief with affection. They liked his flamboyance and admired his courage and boldness. He was firm in imposing their village laws, but also showed great compassion. Improved irrigation had resulted in more bountiful crops, and no one went hungry. The village was secure: only once had a gang of bandits attempted to raid the village but an alarm had been raised and the villagers fought them off. The miscreants had fled, leaving two of their dead behind.

The school building had been repaired and a third teacher hired. A flour mill had opened for business along with several new shops. The community hall on the temple grounds had been enlarged. Tension between the Hindus and Sikhs living in Karyala and the Muslims of Meerpur had been somewhat eased.

"We are the same people," Hem Raj would tell his village Council. "We hurt and bleed the same when injured. Our children cry the same cry when hungry. The only difference between them and us is in the name by which we call our God. To them it's *Allah* and for us it's *Bhagwan.*"

"Yes, but Muslims have for centuries forcibly converted Hindus and Sikhs to Islam," an elder complained.

"Well, if we ask them, they'll complain that we have discriminated against them for centuries," Hem Raj answered. "We need to forget the past and learn to live as one. We must join our efforts to rid the country of these foreigners who have made slaves out of all of us."

Kanti loved her husband dearly and considered herself infinitely blessed to be his wife. He treated her with respect and affection and often sought her counsel. Kanti had traveled to Shahpur once to visit her parents and attend the wedding of the older of her two brothers.

Besides his journey to Sargodah and Peshawar, Hem Raj also eagerly awaited the annual *Ghora Mela* near Jhelum. Traders and expert riders from far and wide attended the week-long fair. Tent pegging competitions were held where riders at full gallop used lances, trying to pierce and carry away wooden pegs driven into the ground. Bareback riders thrilled the crowds with their skills.

The grand finale of the fair was a race around the grounds to crown the fastest horse and the champion rider of the year. A keen competition existed between the Indian *sowars* of the British Cavalry and civilian riders from the various districts of Punjab and the Northwest

Frontier. Ever since acquiring Kamaan, Hem Raj had won the race each year, proudly bringing the trophy back to his village.

"This is life at its best, Kanti," he would tell his wife. "This is how one should live. I told you I would be a good chief, Kanti. See, I didn't let you down!"

"No, you haven't, my husband," Kanti would answer. "I'm so very proud of you."

The children were growing up fast and Devi Lal was soon going to be fourteen. "It's time to think about the high school we should send him to," Kanti told her husband one evening.

"Well, he can attend the one in Chakwal just as I did," Hem Raj answered. "I received a good education, didn't I?"

"Yes you did, but Devi Lal is a very good student." Kanti paused for a moment and then hesitatingly added, "Perhaps we should think about sending him to a school in one of the cities."

"If the high school in Chakwal was good enough for me," Hem Raj answered impatiently, "it should be good enough for my son."

"The school you attended certainly was good, my dear, but times are changing. Our son should receive the best education we can provide for him. Perhaps on your next trip to Jhelum you could find out if there are any good schools there," Kanti suggested.

"All right, Kanti, if you say so. Who knows, maybe going to a larger city will toughen our son and make him more suitable to one day be the head of the family and the chief of our village."

Early that autumn, after attending the monthly District meeting in Chakwal, Hem Raj made the trip to Jhelum. He returned home and excitedly told his wife about a new school he had visited.

"It's run by the disciples of Swami Dayanand," he said. "This school not only gives young boys a good education, but they also have a very disciplined daily regimen. I think it will be good for Devi Lal to attend this school. The boys exercise for an hour each morning and in the evenings they have to play games and participate in wrestling matches. Our son is bound to become more aggressive after two years at this school. Then I will teach him everything that I know."

Winter was upon them and it was once again time for the *Lohri* festival. The villagers went to the temple in the morning for special prayers and then assembled on the dry river bed to celebrate. Children played and the women sang songs to the beat of drums. A group of Muslim boys gathered on the cliffs above and stared at the Hindus and Sikhs on the riverbed. A horse race was to be held for boys, and Hem Raj told Devi Lal to take part in it.

"I don't really want to compete in the race," Devi Lal whispered to his mother.

"Why don't you try it, Son? It'll make your father happy," she answered gently. Devi Lal reluctantly agreed.

"What do you know, our son won the race!" Hem Raj said to his wife. "See, I have taught him well," he beamed.

After sunset, the villagers lit a huge bonfire. Children ate special sweets made from jaggery and sesame seeds and the older boys exploded firecrackers. The drums beat a faster rhythm and the women sang and danced.

Several young Muslim men had joined the boys on the cliffs and some of the boys began mimicking the women dancing on the riverbed. "Stop that," the men on the riverbed yelled, but instead of stopping, the boys continued dancing wildly. The men, by now infuriated, picked up pebbles and started pelting the boys. The Muslim boys and young men picked up stones and clods of mud and started hurtling them down on the people below.

A shot rang out and everyone froze. "Stop this madness," Hem Raj yelled, still holding his rifle pointing towards the sky. "You children up there, go back to your homes," he directed the Muslims on the cliff. He turned to those around him on the river bed. "The celebrations are over; it's late," he said. "Put out the fire and go home."

Springtime came, and then it was summer. Schools reopened and Hem Raj was to take his son to the boarding school in Jhelum. Devi Lal was only fourteen and was leaving home for the first time.

"You're going to a big city, Son," Kanti had said, trying to hold back her tears. "Look after yourself and remember to write at least once a month."

"I'll be all right, Mother. Don't worry about me." Devi Lal had assured her.

"Yes, I know you'll be fine, Son, you're almost a man. May God bless you," she said, embracing him.

The school was located just outside the city and was surrounded by a brick wall. There were playing fields for hockey and football. Classes were held in a squat brick building. The hostel where the boys lived was towards the rear of the grounds and the school temple was to one side.

The first day Devi Lal felt lonely, but then he settled into the daily routine of the school. The boys were awakened at six in the morning and after an hour's exercise drills and breakfast, attended class from eight until noon. They had an hour off for lunch, and classes resumed at 1 o'clock and ended at four. They then practiced wrestling and played football or hockey. The evening meal was served at six, after which they did their homework until nine-thirty. Brief prayers were said each evening and morning. On Sunday the students gathered in the school temple for a prayer service. In the afternoon they went to the Jhelum River and swam in it. The few weeks during winter when it was too cold to swim, the boys were taken for long walks in the countryside.

Devi Lal was relishing his studies and spent every free moment in the school's small library. When he went home for the *Diwali* holidays, Kanti was ecstatic to see him. He has grown so tall and handsome, she thought, just like his father. His brothers and sisters showered him with questions. After dinner Hem Raj wanted to know what his son had learned during the first four months at school.

"I am learning physics, chemistry, physiology and anatomy, as well as history, geography and arithmetic," the boy answered.

"What is it that you are enjoying most, my son?" Kanti inquired.

"I like my science subjects very much, Mother. We have a very good science teacher. It's interesting to learn how the body functions and what we need to do to keep in good health."

Hem Raj looked perplexed. "Aren't they teaching you anything about being a leader? How about sports? I hope you're doing well in wrestling."

"We have to exercise every morning, *Pita Jee*," Devi Lal answered. "Then in the evening we have to play games. I've learned how to wrestle, but I don't really enjoy it that much. May I go and read my books now?"

Later, when they were alone, Hem Raj spoke to his wife. "I'm wondering if we've picked the right school for our son, Kanti. What good will all of this science stuff be for the role he has to play in the future?"

"Our son will do very well. Don't you worry," she said, placing her hand on her husband's arm. "He's very gentle and so intelligent. He's also tall and handsome like you."

As eager as young Devi Lal had been to come home for the holidays, he was now anxious to get back to school. When he returned, he once again immersed himself in his studies. Time flew by and soon the school year was to come to an end when he would have to return home for the summer holidays. He had done very well in all of his examinations, but was worried about the questions his father would ask him. He hated seeing the disappointment on his father's face the last time they had talked about what he was learning. He knew his father wanted him to be bold and aggressive, like him. He also knew what was expected of him when he grew up.

During the holidays, Devi Lal did what his father asked of him. He traveled with him to Peshawar to collect rent from their tenants. He rode with him and journeyed to Sargodha to collect and sell the grain harvested by the tenant farmers. He was appalled by the sight of the poor farmers toiling under the blistering noonday sun. Yet they seemed to be grateful for the grain they were allowed to keep.

Devi Lal's thoughts often went to the life of Gautama Buddha who was born a prince, but seeing all the suffering around him, relinquished his life of luxury and had gone seeking enlightenment. The Buddha's teachings of *Ahimsa*, and of detachment, compassion and charity now appealed to Devi Lal even more than when he had first read about them.

During their stay in Khusahb, Hem Raj learned from Saleem Khan that a protest march was to be held by *Azad Hind* volunteers in Chakwal the following week. "You, my son," he told Devi Lal on their way home, "will join me. We will both attend this rally."

When Kanti heard about it, she tried to dissuade her husband from taking their son to participate. "Won't it be dangerous?" she asked. "There might be trouble and he's not even sixteen as yet. Perhaps you shouldn't go either."

"Nonsense," Hem Raj answered with a wave of his hand. "Even if there's trouble, our son needs to learn how to handle himself. Don't worry. He'll be all right. I'll be with him."

The day of the march, the father and son rode their horses out of their village towards Chakwal. They were dressed alike in white cotton *salwar kameez* and freshly starched turbans. Kanti is right, Hem Raj told himself; their handsome son did, indeed, look like his father.

"It'll be very exciting, you'll see," he kept telling his son. "We'll have a great time."

The town was crowded and the main street packed with a mass of humanity holding flags and banners. Cries of "*Inkalab Zindabad* — Long live freedom," and "*Hindustan hamara hai* — India is ours," rose over the din of the crowd.

Devi Lal felt awed. He had never seen so many people in one place before. He got off his horse and followed his father to join the end of the procession. People were still pouring in from the side streets and soon the father and son were engulfed by children, women and men waving flags and calling out slogans. The procession moved slowly towards the center of town where it was to end in front of the office of the British District Commissioner.

The people seemed to be in a festive mood and only a few raised their fists defiantly at police constables standing on the side of the road. Devi Lal felt a strange feeling of excitement flow through his body. He heard his father's voice angrily calling out the slogan with the other marchers, "*Inkalab Zindabad.*"

The front of the procession neared the District Commissioner's office where a large number of Indian police constables under the command of British officers, were waiting. One of the officers yelled an order. The constables moved quickly and formed a solid column across the road, blocking the path of the procession. The marchers kept advancing, their voices now even louder as they yelled their slogans for freedom and liberty.

The constables readied the thick bamboo sticks in their hands and looked on, stern-faced. The marchers had now reached the police line. The officer barked a second command, and suddenly the constables plowed into the marchers, swinging their sticks. Banners and flags were wrenched from the hands of the marchers. Those who resisted were being beaten. Men with broken arms and bleeding heads fell to the ground. The constables kept advancing, swinging their sticks and striking anyone within reach. Women screamed and children started weeping.

"Move back! Get into side streets!" the organizers of the march yelled at the people.

The police constables who were standing along the side of the road had also started beating those marchers who couldn't escape.

Hem Raj was livid. He wrenched a stick from the upraised arms of a constable and threw it into the gutter by the side of the road. Another constable was about to strike Devi Lal. Hem Raj lunged forward, and grabbing the constable from the back, threw him to the ground.

"Come on, Son, let's get out of here," he yelled, getting onto his horse. They galloped down a side street and turned onto the road towards Karyala. "To hell with these peaceful protests and marches," he muttered angrily. "They aren't going to work." Guns are the only answer, he told himself. I'm going to join *Azad Hind.* I'm going to be a freedom fighter. He was especially angry at the Indian constables who were willing to beat up their own countrymen while addressing the foreigners as *sahib* —master. "The damn traitors," he swore.

Soon the summer vacations were over and Devi Lal returned to Jhelum. He found out that he had stood first in the Ninth grade examinations and was to receive an award.

"If you do equally well in the matric examinations" his science teacher told him, "you'll receive a full scholarship to attend the college of your choice in the city of Lahore."

Devi Lal's face had lit up as, to him, that would be the most wonderful thing that could happen. There was so much more he wanted to study and learn. But then he remembered his father's expectations. Maybe he'll let me attend college in Lahore for a few years before asking me to return to Karyala, he hoped. What if his father didn't let him, he worried.

That evening, after school, he obtained permission from the games teacher to go for a walk instead of attending wrestling class. He walked through the crowded city and headed towards the Jhelum River. He sat down on the stone embankment next to a temple. Bathers were going down the steps to take a dip in the river before returning to the temple for their evening prayers. The laughter of children playing at the water's edge drifted up to him. Across the river, in the distance, he could see the spire of a church and a row of neat bungalows where the British lived. A large flock of parrots came sweeping across the river like a thick cloud and settled in the trees above him. Their loud chirping added to the confusion in his mind as he pondered on what the future held for him. Did he really want to take his father's place? He wasn't sure.

The river's surface was aflame from the rays of the setting sun. He didn't know how long he had been sitting there but suddenly realized it was starting to get dark. He stood up and began walking quickly through the city towards his school. By the time he reached the open fields outside the city, dusk had fallen. He didn't wish to be late for the evening roll call. A narrow path led away from the city and, circling a little village, ran to the school gates. Hurrying to get back quickly, Devi Lal decided to take a shortcut and go through the village instead of following the path.

By now it was almost dark and he started running towards the village. He could see cooking fires burning outside the huts and heard the sound of children at play. His heart was pounding but he kept running. Suddenly he tripped over something lying on the path and went sprawling to the ground. He lay there for a moment, trying to catch his breath.

"Well, well, young *sahib*," a voice spoke from the dark, "you must have been chased by the devil to be running so fast."

Devi Lal was startled and quickly sat up. He peered through the darkness and saw a small, crudely-made wooden cart over which he had tripped. Sitting on the cart was a grotesquely deformed person. A few white teeth glistened through a scraggly beard and dark sunken eyes appeared over two holes where a nose should have been. The man did not have any hands or feet. Devi Lal leapt to his feet and hearing footsteps, quickly turned around. Several children had come running and stood staring at him. He gasped at their appearance; their faces were covered with sores and their ears and noses looked like they were being eaten away. They were dressed in dirty torn rags. A young boy raised a fingerless hand to brush his hair away from his eyes.

Oh my God, these are lepers, Devi Lal suddenly realized. This must be their village he had stumbled into. He felt horrified and wanted to flee, but the children were in his way. He looked at their faces again. They appeared timid. Surely they meant no harm. It was he who had intruded into their village.

His horror was slowly replaced by compassion and guilt. He turned to the man in the cart. "Forgive me, I wasn't looking where I was going," he said gently. He looked at the children and smiled. They parted to let him through. A little girl reached out and brushed her stubby fingers against his arm. Devi Lal almost cringed but then he waved to her and slowly walked out of their village.

"Why, almighty God," he prayed that night, "why does there have to be so much suffering? What have these children done to deserve such a horrible fate? Are they the victims of their karmas from a previous existence? How terrible could their deeds have been for You not to have forgiven them? Why, dear God, why can't someone cure them now?"

October 24, 1895
Voyage to India

The expansive decks of the S.S. Caledonia were abuzz with activity. The crew was scurrying around, preparing the large steamship for arrival at its destination, the port of Bombay. All of the brass railings and fixtures had been polished before dawn and every deck scrubbed clean. The voyage of twenty-one days had at times been very rough, but now, in good weather and calm waters, the Caledonia was sailing majestically in bright sunshine, on a glistening sea.

Elegantly dressed passengers were strolling on the promenade deck high above the turquoise waters of the Arabian Sea. A pleasant breeze was blowing, connivingly masking the stifling humidity and searing heat awaiting them ashore.

"Ah yes, there's India," a man with a clipped English accent haughtily announced, waving a cigar towards the distant horizon where a dark line was barely discernible. He was wearing a morning coat, pinstriped trousers and a stiff black silk top hat.

Sarah Dormsbury Smythe stood on the deck, clutching its smooth teakwood railing, her delicate angelic face flushed with excitement. She raised herself on her toes and craned her neck, trying to get a glimpse of the mysterious land she had yearned to visit since childhood.

Sarah was born and grew up in the village of Willoughby on the Wolds in Leicestershire, surrounded by the affluence of her titled family. As a child, she had been rather plain looking with ash blond hair and a very pale complexion. She was the only girl among the five children of her parents and was born eight years after the youngest of her brothers. With few children of her own age to play with, she spent most of her time in her room, reading. She was quiet and un-selfish, and her childhood had been uneventful.

Sarah had been fascinated by India from the time she first read children's story books about the exotic country and its people. In her day dreams, she often fantasized about traveling through this vast land, experiencing one thrilling romantic adventure after another. Then, later, as she grew older, she read about the thousands of hapless Indians who died each year from floods, famines, the pox and the plague. Her heart ached seeing pictures in the newspapers of beggars and starving children near death, with bloated bellies and sunken, tear-filled eyes. Her romantic fantasies about India gradually turned to thoughts of helping the poor and healing the afflicted.

When she was sixteen, Sarah announced to her parents that she was going to become a medical doctor. Although taken aback, her father humoured her for awhile, believing she would soon get over this passing fancy. His daughter had grown into quite an attractive young girl and he hoped she would one day marry some wealthy, titled young man. Sarah, however, surprised her parents as well as her friends by remaining stubbornly single-minded.

She had found out that the practice of medicine, even in late 19th century, was to a very large extent dominated by men. She spoke to her family's doctor about her interest in a medical career. "You could try nursing," was the advice she received from him, which made her just all the more determined.

She had read that a law enacted in 1889 started requiring medical schools in Britain to admit female students. Yet, if members of the faculty did not wish to have women in their classrooms, they couldn't be made to do so, and the school had to arrange separate instructions for them. Most medical schools, therefore, continued to enroll only male students.

Then Sarah heard about the newly opened London School of Medicine for Women. She applied for admission and much to her delight, was accepted. She studied hard and having passed all of her examinations, received a medical degree in the summer of 1893. With her father's influence, who by now was quite proud of his daughter's achievements, Sarah was able to obtain training positions at the Guys Hospital for Sick Children and at St. Mary's Hospital Medical School. At these two fine establishments she received further instruction in treating the ailments of children as well as the many peculiar diseases prevalent in the colonies.

Sarah had met her future husband at a charity ball in London held to raise money for the Guys Hospital for Sick Children. It was a gala affair and she danced with several young men. One in particular, a young Subaltern by the name of Cedric Henry Smythe, didn't seem to be able to keep his eyes away from her. He was of medium height and slim, and to Sarah, looked quite dashing in his red tunic and navy blue trousers.

For Cedric Smythe it was love at first sight and he danced only with Sarah all evening. Before she left, he asked her if he could call upon her. She agreed and they met the next day and several times after that. Sarah was a year older, but she found the shy young Cavalry officer interesting and felt comfortable being with him.

Cedric would not talk much about himself other than to say that he was born and raised in London and that he was expecting soon to be shipped out to India. Sarah's eyes had lit up and she told him about her yearning to go there herself. Within six months of their first meeting, he had proposed and, in spite of her parents' protestations, she accepted. Five months after their wedding they sailed for India.

Cedric was born near Bow Road in the slums of East London. He was raised by his mother in a one-room flat of a rundown row house on a narrow crowded alley. His mother worked as a charwoman at an East End hospital and his father, a wily Cockney, earned a meager living wheeling and dealing, managing to stay barely a step ahead of the law. He had changed his name from John Smith to Jonathan Smythe as to him it sounded "more highbrow."

The only remembrance Cedric had of his father was from a faded sepia-coloured photograph taken at Brighton-on-sea, which showed him standing nattily dressed, with the tips of his moustache waxed to a fine point, in front of an ocean-front amusement park. Jonathan Symthe had bought two prints and signed his name at the lower right corner of each of them. The photographs came in identical wooden frames with small sea shells glued onto their lower edge. He had given one of the framed photographs to Cedric's mother, which she kept on her bedside table even long after her husband had deserted her. All she knew of his whereabouts was that he had gone overseas to one of the colonies. "I think it's to India," she had told a neighbour.

Cedric had vague, troubling memories of his father coming home drunk and beating up his mother. He also used to have confusing nightmares of his father hitting and abusing him. Growing up, he worked hard, determined to provide a better life for himself and his mother. He finished high school but was able to find only a part-time job as a clerk in a shoe shop.

"You've got to go to the colonies, lad, if you're looking for a job that pays more than a few quids," he was told wherever he went seeking work. For no particular reason, he chose India and started studying for the Indian Civil Service examinations. He took them twice but failed each time. Disheartened, he directed his efforts to joining the Indian Army and traveled to Woolwich to inquire at the Royal Military Academy.

"If you'd like to be an officer in an artillery or engineers regiment, you can apply for admission here," he was informed. "If it's the infantry or cavalry you're after, try out for the Royal Military College at Sandhurst."

He was advised to engage a tutor to help him study for the entrance examinations but that was costly and so Cedric started preparing in earnest on his own. He brushed up on his Latin, English, mathematics and chemistry and to his delight, passed the examinations on his second attempt. He opted for infantry training and arrived at Sandhurst on a fine spring day. The cadets had to learn to fence, shoot and ride. Cedric developed a great fondness for riding and immediately switched to cavalry training.

As much as he had enjoyed his year and a half at the Royal Military College, he was never comfortable amongst his fellow cadets who were mostly from the upper middle class of English society. He was fascinated by the sport of polo, new to the British Isles, having been brought back by officers returning from India. But at Sandhurst, only those cadets who could afford to keep two or three of their own ponies could play the game.

Cedric worked hard and was able to pass in the top half of his class. He immediately requested an assignment to an Indian regiment.

"We'll have your name placed on the Indian Staff Corps," he was told by an officer at Sandhurst. "It might be a year or more before you get picked. In the meantime, you'll serve with the 6th Dragoon at Aldershot."

Over the next year, Subaltern Smythe became quite adept as a Cavalry officer through countless drills, mastering cavalry formations and maneuvers. He engaged a private tutor to learn to speak Hindi. He loved Sarah dearly and the few months he spent courting her were the happiest times of his life. He was conscious of the differences in their backgrounds and socially felt inferior to her. After their marriage, they lived in a small but quaint flat near Aldershot. Cedric was somewhat annoyed by Sarah's insistence on using her maiden name along with his last name, but had not objected. He was anxious to leave for India as, once there, he knew things would be different. There in the colony, as an officer in the

Army of Her Majesty Queen Victoria the Empress of India, he would command respect wherever he went and Sarah would be his wife and a social equal.

Finally one day he was summoned to the Commandant's office and given the news he had long awaited. "You've been picked to serve with the 11th Bengal Lancers, Smythe. Pack your bags; you'll be sailing for India in two weeks." The Lancers, it seemed, had lost several men during a campaign in the Northwest Frontier. Cedric was promoted to the rank of Lieutenant and was to accompany three other officers assigned to join the regiment.

Sarah was ecstatic and started preparing for the journey. "You'll need some things to wear other than your uniform, darling," she told Cedric. "It's going to be beastly hot and you'll also need proper clothing for social events." She bought him a three-buttoned morning coat, two stiff collared shirts, pin-striped trousers, a black silk top hat and two silk cravats. She found a pair of knee-length knickerbockers and stockings to go with them.

At Cedric's insistence, she bought two evening gowns for herself. One, high-waisted with large puffed sleeves and a low back, the other an ankle-length skirt made of layers of sheer pink silk with a red satin blouse and matching elbow length gloves. She also bought four light, summery simple cotton dresses.

"Shouldn't you get a few more evening outfits?" Cedric asked when they were packing.

"Heavens no, darling!" Sarah answered, "I'm going to be working there as a doctor. I've taken all the formal clothes I'll need."

They said goodbye to their families. Cedric went alone to see his mother and left some money with her. He accompanied Sarah to her parent's manor and they stayed there two nights. Sarah's father gave her a hefty sum of money. "Wire if you need more, darling," he said.

For Cedric, the voyage to India turned out to be extremely unpleasant. "The weather at sea gets beastly by October," he had been warned by friends of Sarah, but he was not prepared for this. The constant rolling and pitching of the ship, and the sight of the huge waves made him feel nauseated and he remained violently seasick through much of the journey. Sarah, on the other hand, was unaffected by the heaving oceans. While her husband spent all of his time in their tiny cabin, unable to keep even liquids down, she ate heartily in the dining room and enjoyed the voyage immensely. Sarah had given Cedric some pills to take, and although the medicine stopped him from throwing up, it made him feel very drowsy.

When Cedric had gone to book their passage, he was delighted to learn that they were to sail on the Peninsular and Oriental Steam Navigation Company's newest ship, the Caledonia.

"I saw a picture of the ship: she's a four-masted, sparkling beauty," he had informed Sarah excitedly. "She was launched less than a year ago and has several decks, large cabins and electric lights. Believe it or not, they even have refrigeration machinery to keep all the food fresh."

Cedric had made sure they were given an outside cabin on the port side of the ship. "That'll be the shady side," he had explained to Sarah. "My friends at Sandhurst told me that when sailing to India, one should remember the acronym POSH—portside out starboard home. It cost a little more but I want you to have the best, darling."

"Thank you, Cedric," Sarah had responded, hugging him. "You're such a dear."

The day they sailed down the River Thames, the sun was shining brightly and Cedric stayed on the deck with Sarah, excitedly watching the shores and the other vessels on the river. By the time they entered the English Channel, the skies had become heavily overcast and the wind gale like. Cedric returned to their cabin. Once the ship reached open seas nearing the Bay of Biscay, he wished they had taken an inside cabin. The constant sight of the turbulent ocean visible through their porthole made him nauseous and weak-kneed. It had taken them six days to go around the Iberian Peninsula and to reach Marseilles, and the weather had remained stormy throughout. Then when the ship traversed the Suez Canal, he felt a little better.

"Until fifteen years ago when the canal opened, we had to sail clear around the Cape of Good Hope and the entire continent of Africa," a ship's officer informed them. Cedric shuddered at the very thought of a longer voyage.

Sarah had coaxed him to accompany her to the deck, but the glare of the sun was blinding and its heat unbearable so he soon returned to their cabin. Now, as they stood on the deck with the ship fast approaching land, Sarah's face was flushed with excitement but Cedric looked pale. "Christ, I wish we'd get there," he moaned to her.

Several steamships and scores of smaller sailing vessels lay at anchor at the entrance to Bombay harbour. Finally, with a lot of excited shouting of orders and ringing of bells, the Caledonia docked at a pier. The gangplanks were lowered and hundreds of dark-skinned Indian coolies came aboard. They wore red turbans and shirts and white *dhotis*, a loincloth reaching just below their knees. The heat under the sweltering sun was intense. Cedric was wearing his scarlet cavalry tunic and dark blue trousers, both made of wool, and could feel little rivulets of perspiration run down his chest and back.

Sarah wore a long-sleeved pale pink silk morning dress which showed off her slim waist. Her long delicate neck protruded from the V-shaped opening of her close-fitted bodice. A straw hat with bright silk flowers on one side adorned her head. She held a silk parasol with one hand and, with the other, tried to help her husband walk down the gangplank.

Lieutenant Ronald Hancock, an Aide from the Adjutant General's office of the Indian Army was at the Apollo Bunder pier to receive the four officers assigned to the 11th Bengal Lancers. He ushered them to a corner of the crowded and noisy pier, out of the blistering sun, to await their luggage. So this is India, Sarah thought, looking around and savouring her first glimpse of the people and the country she had for so long yearned to visit. She was surprised to see several Indian men bowing low before the British, addressing them as *sahib*. A group of beggars tried to surround them but a cane-wielding Indian policeman wearing a khaki turban, shirt and shorts chased them away and then smartly saluted Cedric.

Lieutenant Hancock had their luggage loaded onto a horse-drawn cart. Cedric and Sarah rode with him in one carriage, and the other three officers climbed into a second carriage to be taken to the Queen Victoria Railway Terminus. "You have several hours before your train leaves," Lieutenant Hancock informed Sarah and Cedric. "I've told the driver to take us past some of the city's landmarks."

The roads were wide and lined with Victorian Gothic buildings constructed by the British, interspersed between rows of squat brick buildings with covered balconies. Narrow lanes led away from the main roads to mysteriously disappear deep inside the city. Ornate Hindu temples and domed Muslim mosques were crowded with worshipers. An occasional high-steepled church rose majestically towards the clear blue sky. Indian women in their colourful *saris* and dark-skinned men with turbans, long shirts and *dhotis* packed the sides of the roads and the shops.

The carriages rolled past an open field where British men all dressed in white clothes were playing cricket. Lieutenant Hancock showed them the University of Bombay and several other imposing Government buildings. A large ornate fountain stood in the middle of an intersection where five roads met. "This is the Flora Fountain," the Lieutenant pointed out. "The statue on top is that of Flora, the Roman goddess of flowers. It's a pity we don't have more time. I would like to have taken you up Malabar Hill on the west side of the city. The view from the top is rather spectacular and you might also have been interested in seeing the Towers of Silence."

"What are those?" Sarah inquired.

"Oh, they belong to the local Parsi community. Their prophet, Zoroaster, forbid them from defiling the elements of earth, fire and water which he considered sacred. They don't bury or cremate their dead, but instead, the bodies are left on the top of towers for vultures to consume."

"Oh how horrible," Sarah moaned. "I don't think I would have wanted to see that."

"No, we wouldn't have gone inside the grounds," Lieutenant Hancock assured her, laughing. "All one can see from a distance are the tops of the towers and the vultures flying over them."

Queen Victoria Terminus was huge, and the heat under its cavernous ceilings less searing. The train platforms were teeming with a confusing mass of humanity. The nauseating smell of stale perspiration and decay was only partially masked by the annoying odor of some strong disinfectant. Coolies, dressed like those at the pier, scurried along carrying incredible loads of suitcases, boxes and bundles on their heads and under their arms, yelling warnings to others to step aside. Indian families sat on the ground waiting patiently to board their trains. Some had spread sheets and appeared asleep while children played around them. Food vendors were walking about carrying trays and baskets laden with spicy fried snacks and a variety of fruits. Two Indian police constables wielding canes cleared a path for an English couple and their entourage. Their three children, carried by Indian *ayahs*, were followed by four dogs straining at their leashes trying to get away from a harried servant.

The noise on the platform was deafening. Sarah held on to Cedric's arm and watched everything around her. Several beggars followed them. "*Baksheesh*," they pleaded, their palms stretched out imploringly. Sarah didn't have any money on her and turned to her husband.

"Ignore them," Cedric advised her. "If you give to one, dozens will descend upon you like flies."

They reached the sanctity of the first-class compartment reserved for them. It was two o'clock in the afternoon and their train, the Frontier Mail, was not due to leave until four. Cedric hadn't eaten a square meal since leaving England and suddenly felt ravenously hungry. Lieutenant Hancock suggested they have lunch in the station's refreshment room.

Cedric ate heartily, accepting a second helping of the roast chicken and fresh vegetables seasoned with Indian spices. He drank several cups of tea and then lit a cigar. They walked out of the refreshment room arm in arm.

"I'm so glad you've gotten your appetite back, darling," Sarah said, squeezing his hand. "You've had a devilish time."

"I'm sorry, darling," he apologized. "I must've been rotten company on the ship."

"That's all right, dear," Sarah smiled up at him. "We've arrived, and I'm so looking forward to living in India."

The train left promptly at 4 o'clock and slowly steamed out of the city. Their compartment was surprisingly clean and spacious. A comfortable berth covered with soft green leather was on each side next to three windows with curtains and wooden shutters. A narrow door between the berths led into a small bathroom, and affixed to the floor near the opposite wall were a small round table and two leather covered chairs. They opted to have their meals brought to their compartment instead of going to the refreshment car. They were served tea and, later, dinner at stations where the train stopped. Indian waiters carrying trays of food covered with clean white linen napkins brought their meals to the compartment and returned later to remove the dishes.

Sarah had washed and changed into a light cotton frock. She sat looking out of the window, fascinated by the panorama of rural India flashing by as the train sped northward. The hot wind caressed her face and she held her hair back with her hand. The train was racing past an unending array of villages nestled in a sea of small fields. Children seemed to be everywhere, as were cattle that looked much skinnier than those back home. Farmers were toiling late into the evening, urging bullocks to pull wooden ploughs, and Sarah could smell the fresh dry earth dug up by the ploughs.

The train rolled past fields with neat rows of little bushes laden with white fluffy balls that glowed in the last light of dusk. Sarah had read that Indians were not permitted to weave cloth but the cotton grown by them was bought and shipped to England, to keep the mills there busy. Woven fabrics were then brought back ten thousand miles to be sold all over India.

A full moon had risen and the wind blowing into the compartment was warm and pleasant. Their beds had been prepared by an attendant and Cedric began lowering the wooden shutters of the windows and then secured the bolts on the two doors.

"We have to be careful, darling," he said, climbing into his bed. "India is full of thieves and robbers."

"Oh, we should be all right, Cedric," Sarah answered, lying down next to him on his bed. "These people are so courteous. I can't imagine them harming anyone."

Cedric kissed his wife on the tip of her nose. "You're too trusting, darling," he said gently. "Just remember, we aren't in England. This is India."

Sarah snuggled closer to him. There had not been much intimacy between them during the voyage and she had missed her husband's caresses. The warm breeze and the jolting of the train made her want to press her body against his. But Cedric drew his arms away.

"Let's turn in, darling," he said, stifling a yawn. "You must also be tired."

"Yes, of course, darling," Sarah answered, masking her disappointment. She kissed him on the cheek and, getting up, went to her bed and lay down. Soon she heard Cedric start snoring softly. Turning onto her side, she drew her knees up and let the rocking of the train slowly lull her to sleep.

The next morning, Sarah found the terrain outside to have changed from the lush green of the coastal region to a drier flatter land but still with an unending array of villages. Large green trees grew in clusters between wheat and sugar-cane fields. Towns and cities where the train stopped all appeared to be very congested. Then the train traveled through a desert-like area with scant vegetation and camels replacing bullocks as beasts of burden. The women wore bright coloured ankle length skirt-like garments instead of the sari and the men wore long shirts, *dhotis* and large colourful turbans.

The journey to the north lasted three days and the train entered the province of Punjab with its green wheat fields and many rivers. They arrived in Jhelum where Cedric's regiment was stationed. They were met by a Major Alan Duckworth, the Deputy Assistant Quarter

Master General of the regiment and a veteran of the Indian Army.

"Smythe, you've been assigned a bungalow," he informed Cedric after greeting them. Then, turning to the three bachelor officers, he added, "and you gentlemen will share a bungalow. Good housing in the cantonment is scarce. But mind you, it'll be a hell of a lot cheaper to share digs and servants."

"What's a cantonment?" Sarah asked Major Duckworth who rode with them in a horse-drawn carriage.

"That's where we British live, my dear," Duckworth explained, "away from the crowded, noisy Indian towns and cities."

"Aren't Indian people allowed to live in them?"

"Heavens, no!" the Major answered. "We can't have them living among us. We've built cantonments everywhere for that reason. We have our homes, barracks, clubs, hospitals, parade grounds and polo fields there. Oh, mind you, an occasional servant or two may live in the servants quarters of some of the senior officers, but by and large Indians are kept out of cantonments."

"What about Indian troops?" Cedric asked. "Where do they stay?"

"Oh, their barracks are usually between the cities and cantonments. A nice barrier, if you know what I mean," the Major answered, chuckling.

The tree-lined roads were clean, with flowers blooming in circular islands in the middle of intersections. The carriage turned onto a smaller road, entered an open gate and came to a stop before a red brick cottage. "Here you are," Major Duckworth announced. "This is where you'll be staying."

"Oh, it's so quaint," Sarah exclaimed, stepping out of the carriage.

Their servants came scurrying and greeted them by bowing low, bringing the palms of their hands together in front of their foreheads. There was a gardener, a cook, a houseboy and a maid.

"Welcome, *sahib*, welcome *mem sahib*. Welcome to your house."

Cedric and Sarah were surprised to hear the houseboy speak English.

"My name is Nathu Ram" the middle-aged Indian continued in

heavily accented English. "I will take care of all of your needs, *Hazoor*." He wore a *salwar* and a white cotton tunic with brass buttons. A wide green belt was held around his waist by a large brass buckle, and his turban was of the same green colour as the belt.

"How do you do?" Sarah smiled, offering the man her hand. "I'm Mrs. Sarah Smythe. Did you say your name is Nathu Ram? You speak English."

Cedric cringed seeing his wife shake hands with the servant.

"Yes, *mem sahib*," the houseboy answered with a broad grin. "I have worked for English *sahibs* all my life."

"Will you present the rest of the house staff?" Cedric asked stiffly.

"Yes, *sahib,* right away. This is the gardener," the house boy said, pointing at the old Indian standing at some distance. "His name is Murli. This is Ali, the *khansama*. He will be cooking all of your food for you, *sahib*." Then turning to the young Indian girl, he said. "This is your *ayah*, *mem sahib*. Her name is Laxmi. She, Murli and I are Hindus. Ali is a Mohammedan."

Each of the servants again brought their hands together in front of their forehead and bowed.

"How do you do," Sarah greeted them cheerfully before turning to look at her new home.

A covered veranda circled the front and sides of the single-storied bungalow. Sarah entered the drawing room through an ornately carved wide wooden door. The wicker furniture inside, though old, looked comfortable. Two large paintings hung on the white-washed walls, one of a fox hunt and the other, a seascape with a sailboat on a stormy ocean. A long heavy piece of cloth suspended from the high ceiling started slowly swaying back and forth. Sarah glanced over her shoulder and saw the gardener, Murli, standing on the veranda pulling on a rope which ran through a hole in the wall and was attached to the piece of wood from which the long cloth was hanging.

"That's a *punkah*, a native contraption to fan the cooler air down," Cedric explained. "I'll tell the servant to pull faster. The bloody thing's hardly moving."

"You mean to tell me the poor man has to stand out there and slave just to keep us from perspiring?" Sarah exclaimed. "I can't believe it."

"Of course, darling," Cedric answered, his voice showing signs of impatience. "That's what he's being paid to do."

"But its hellish hot out there and he's an old man."

"Oh, he's a bloody native. They're used to the heat," Cedric spoke curtly. "And besides, Sarah, I don't want you going around shaking hands with the servants."

"And why not?" she asked.

"This is India. You mustn't touch these people," he answered angrily.

I'll damn well do what I please, she felt like saying, but instead, moved away. This was their first open disagreement and she didn't want to make it any worse. Yet she realized their relationship was going to be tested. How could he be so callous.

Sarah tried to shrug off her annoyance and walked out of the drawing room to explore the rest of the house. There was a dining room, a pantry, a large and a second smaller bedroom. A covered passage at the back next to the pantry led to the kitchen. *Punkahs* hung from the high ceilings of the dining and bedrooms. The dining table and six chairs were of a dark polished wood and a vase full of white and purple chrysanthemums was placed on the table. Each of the bedrooms contained two narrow beds with posts attached to their corners. Mosquito netting hung from the top of the posts. The larger of the bedrooms had a chest of drawers, two wicker chairs and a small table. A vase with several fresh red roses in it lay next to a pitcher and a glass on top of the table. Laxmi was waiting at the door of the bedroom.

"*Mem sahib*, I help you?" she spoke haltingly in English. She wore a bright orange cotton *salwar* and *kameez*. A red *dupatta* was draped around her shoulders and head and a large red *bindi* was painted on her forehead.

"Oh, you speak English," Sarah said, surprised.

The girl smiled. "Little, little. I work other *mem sahib* three year. She show me."

"That's wonderful, Laxmi. Now you'll have to teach me Hindi," Sarah said, placing her hand on the young girl's arm.

"I happy to do that," Laxmi smiled. She had large brown eyes and a finely chiseled face. Her dazzling white teeth glistened in contrast to her smooth dark skin.

"Come, help me unpack the luggage," Sarah said, entering the bedroom. "And while we do that, you can tell me all about yourself. Where do you live, Laxmi?"

"I live in city, *mem sahib*."

"Are you married?"

"Yes, *mem sahib*, my husband soldier. I have two child."

"Who looks after them while you're here?"

"My husband mother and young sister, they look after childs, *mem sahib*."

Tea was served in the drawing room under the swaying *punkah*. "We'll have dinner at the club tonight, darling," Cedric informed his wife, helping himself to a small cucumber sandwich. "Major Duckworth invited us. Why don't you bathe first and get ready. He's sending a carriage for us at six."

Sarah would have preferred to stay home their first evening in Jhelum, but she did not protest. "I'm going to look at the gardens, Cedric," she said, getting up. "You may bathe first."

An oval lawn to the front of the bungalow was surrounded by neat beds of flowering shrubs. Butterflies flitted among the flowers and the air was filled with the fragrance of the blooms and the freshly watered lawn. On each side of the house were several fruit trees. Sarah walked past the kitchen to the rear of the bungalow and was surprised to see a wide river not too far from the brick wall of their compound.

She opened a wooden gate in the wall and, stepping out of the compound, crossed a wide path, and then climbed up a few steps to a stone embankment. The river appeared to be flowing sluggishly, divided into two streams surrounding a long sand bar. Further down, the spire of a church appeared rising high above the river's edge. On the opposite bank, in the distance, she could see several Indian temples, and the city. A herd of cattle had come down to drink from the river. The voices of children playing in the shallow waters drifted across to her.

Sarah watched, fascinated, her face aglow in the rays of the bright sun still high towards the west. She was startled by a large flock of parrots that flew noisily out of the tree above her and went sweeping like a cloud across the river towards the temples. She stood there for a while, mesmerized by the panorama before her, and knew she was going to love it here. She sighed and slowly walked back to the house to bathe and get ready.

"Good evening, Mrs. Smythe," Major Duckworth beamed, coming toward Sarah and Cedric as they entered the Officers Club. The large front room of the club was dark and smelt of old furniture and stale cigar smoke. "Delighted to see you. Could use a few more beautiful young women like you to liven up this old club," the Major added, chuckling.

"Why, thank you," Sarah smiled, offering him her hand. "Won't you please call me Sarah?"

"Be delighted to, my dear," Duckworth answered.

A middle-aged, skinny, tall woman in a plain white dress had followed the Major. "I'm Mary Adele Duckworth; please call me Adele," she said, smiling down at Sarah and gripping her hands. "I've been so looking forward to meeting you. It's nice to have another woman to talk to in this dreadful club."

The Major had turned to Cedric. "Welcome to the club, Smythe," he said, shaking his hand. "Come on over. Let me get you a whiskey soda and introduce you to some of the others here."

They walked towards three men standing in the middle of the room under a large *punkah* slowly swaying above them. "Gentlemen, allow me to present Mrs. Sarah Smythe and Lieutenant Cedric Smythe," Duckworth said with a flourish of his hand.

A tall chubby man with a red beard and bushy eyebrows took the hand that Sarah offered. "Captain Ian Campbell at your service, madam" he said, clicking his heels together. "It's such a pleasure to meet you,"

"How do you do," Sarah answered with a smile.

"This is Lieutenant Leslie Howard and this is Captain David Habersham," Major Duckworth continued.

"Since I was the first to have met you," Ian Campbell beamed, "would you do me the honor of sitting next to me at dinner?"

"I'll be delighted to, Captain," Sarah answered, laughing.

"Would you like a sherry, my dear?" Duckworth asked Sarah.

"Yes, I'd like one."

The Major waved a hand and an Indian waiter came running. "Bring the *mem sahib* a sherry," he ordered, "and a whiskey soda for the *sahib*. That's all we drink here, Smythe. I hope that's what you like."

"That'll be fine. Thank you very much, Major."

Lieutenant Howard was of medium height and stockily built. His pale skin and blond hair gave him a boyish look. David Habersham was skinny and tall with small dark eyes that stared out of a deeply tanned face.

"You'll enjoy India, my dear, as long as you don't let the heat and the mosquitos get to you," Ian Campbell said, patting Sarah's hand.

The men had been drinking all evening and were conversing in loud voices. "You've got to watch your back at all times, Smythe," Habersham was advising Cedric. "If they're not stealing you blind, the bloody niggers will stab you in the back the moment you let your guard down."

Ian Campbell sensed Sarah stiffen. "Oh, it isn't all that bad, Habersham," he said, more for Sarah's benefit. Then, turning to Cedric, he continued, "Don't you be bothered by all of this, lad. There are a lot of nice people in India. Wait till you meet some of the VCO's and *sowars* of the regiment. You won't find a more loyal lot anywhere else in the world."

"What's a *sowar* and who are VCO's?" Sarah asked.

"*Sowars* are Indian cavalry men and VCO stands for Viceroy's Commissioned Officer, again, Indians," Ian Cambell explained.

"Do they have the same ranks as us?" Cedric inquired.

"The senior VCO in a cavalry regiment has the rank of *Rissaldar* Major," Duckworth explained. "You can tell them by the insignia of a crown they wear on their uniform, the same as I do. But a British Subaltern outranks them. Let me advise you, though, Symthe, treat *Rissaldar* Majors with respect. These are seasoned cavalrymen who you may have to count on in a tight spot. The junior VCO's are called *Rissaldars* and *Jemadars*. They and their *sowars* obey their *Rissaldar* Majors implicitly."

"Do you speak Hindustani?" Ian Campbell asked.

"I had a tutor in Hindi for about a year in London," Cedric replied.

"That's good. It'll at least get you started," Campbell said. "The Mohammadens speak Urdu; the Hindus, Hindi; and the Sikhs, Punjabi. Hindustani is a mixture of all three. It'll help you converse with most Indians."

"These natives are a bloody strange lot," David Habersham complained. "Those who speak English will do so when it suits them. Then at times they'll act dumb to annoy you. You've got to keep them in their place and not take any nonsense from them."

"Don't you believe half the things these gentlemen are saying, my dear," Adele Duckworth interjected, patting Sarah's hand. "They do tend to exaggerate a lot."

"Mrs. Duckworth is perfectly right," Ian Campbell added. "There's no need to bother your pretty little head with any of this."

"Oh, it's not going to bother me," Sarah answered. "I've looked forward far too long to coming to India."

"How soon we forget," David Habersham persisted. "The mutiny of 1857 showed us how bloody treacherous these niggers are."

"I've read that the Indians refer to the '57 uprising as their War of Independence, and I guess in their minds what they did was justifiable," Sarah answered coldly.

Adele Duckworth quickly changed the topic and they started talking about London and the latest fashions.

A gray-haired man walked over from an adjacent table. The men stood up and greeted him courteously. Colonel Harry J. Bidley-Halden, the Commandant of the 11th Bengal Lancers, shook Sarah's and Cedric's hands, welcoming them to Jhelum, and then went back to his table.

By the time Sarah and Cedric returned to their bungalow, it was quite late. Sarah was feeling disturbed over some of the dinner conversation. She detested the things Captain Habersham had said about Indians and particularly abhorred his use of the word nigger. She was surprised and angered that the other men, especially her husband, hadn't objected.

Cedric settled with ease into the daily routine of the life of a British Cavalry officer in India. He had been assigned a horse and a *sowar* to look after it. He rode out to the parade ground at six in the morning and drilled with the other officers, VCO's and *sowars*. He returned home at noon for lunch and to rest during the hottest part of the day. At five o'clock, it was off to the polo ground. Then in the evening they went to a party at the club or the regimental mess or to the home of one of the senior officers.

This was the life Cedric had yearned for and he was relishing every moment of it. It pleased him no end to have scores of Indians scurrying around, eager to fulfil his every wish. If only Sarah's friends could see them now. They wouldn't be able to look down their bloody noses at him. He was an officer in the Cavalry and the master of his house.

Sarah busied herself the first few days getting settled into their new home. All the boxes were unpacked. The clothes had to be aired before being hung in closets and their personal belongings had to be sorted and put away in the right places.

"I'm so glad to have you helping me, Laxmi," she said to her maid. "I know I couldn't have managed without you."

"I happy to help, *mem sahib*," the young girl answered with a shy giggle.

Sarah knew she was going to be working with the poor in India, but hadn't decided how she would go about it. They had been in Jhelum for almost a month, and she was already tiring of the daily parties and long evenings at the club.

"I want to start working, darling," she told Cedric one day while they were having lunch.

"You are working, my dear," he answered, raising an eyebrow. "You're managing the servants and our home very well."

"I didn't mean that, Cedric," Sarah said softly, "I meant professionally, as a physician."

"There's no need for you to work as a doctor, Sarah. The Regimental Dispensary is well staffed. Besides, there aren't that many European women here for you to treat."

"I didn't come to India to treat Europeans, Cedric," Sarah answered, her voice sounding a little more touchy than she would have liked.

"You came to India as my wife, to be with me," Cedric said, a complacent grin on his face.

"Well, yes I did," Sarah answered, looking at him, "but I also came to provide medical help to the poor and ailing."

"How do you plan to do that?" Cedric asked, his voice getting tense with the annoyance he was no longer able to control. "No, let me guess. You plan to set up a bloody clinic for these damn natives all by yourself."

"Well, actually that's exactly what I'd like to do," Sarah answered. "I'd also like to go to the villages nearby and help the people."

"You can't be serious, Sarah!" Cedric said, exasperated. "For Christ's sake, use some sense. This is not Willoughby and England. This is India. These are natives. They won't look at you kindly even if you go around trying to treat their bloody bizarre diseases."

"I know what I want to do, Cedric," Sarah said, getting up from the dining table. "Don't try to stop me. I shan't listen to you."

Cedric left the next morning for the Northwest Frontier. A British garrison east of Peshawar was surrounded by hostile tribes and a battalion of the 11th Bengal Lancers was to go to their aid. Sarah was guilt-ridden for having quarreled with Cedric the day before he left. They had not spoken much during the evening and he had slept that night in the small second bedroom. Early the next morning he gave her a perfunctory peck on the cheek before leaving.

Sarah moped all day, taking turns being angry with herself and then with Cedric. They had done nothing but quarrel with each other since coming to India. "He damned well knew what I wanted to do in this country," she mused. "If he was so dead against it, he shouldn't have asked me to marry him," she muttered under her breath.

"*Mem sahib* not feeling well?" Nathu Ram asked Sarah as she toyed with her food at dinner.

"I'm sorry, Nathu Ram," she answered, looking up, "I wasn't paying attention. Did you say something?"

"*Mem sahib* looks worried," the houseboy said gently.

"No, I'm all right. I've just been thinking," Sarah answered, still deep in thought. Then she looked up at the houseboy. "You probably don't know, Nathu Ram, but I am a medical doctor. I came to your country not only to be with my husband, but also to serve the people who may need my services."

"That is very good, *mem sahib*," Nathu Ram answered. "There is plenty illness here. But, *mem sahib*, you are a lady and also English. Your place is not among poor Indians."

"I want to serve where there is the greatest need."

"There is a charitable dispensary in Jhelum City where the poor can go to receive medicines. There are always a lot of sick people there, especially during the cold winter months," the houseboy offered.

"I would rather serve those unable to receive medical care, Nathu Ram, like the untouchables and lepers," Sarah answered, a determined look on her face.

"Oh my God, *mem sahib*," the houseboy said, shaking his head. "You cannot work among them. That will not be right."

"But that's what I want to do, Nathu Ram. Will you help me? Will you take me where the untouchables and the lepers live?"

"There is a village of lepers outside of the city," the houseboy answered, hesitatingly. "I will do what you order me, *mem sahib*, even though I do not think it is right."

"Thank you, Nathu Ram," Sarah said, starting to eat her dinner. "We'll go there tomorrow."

"But tomorrow is Sunday, *mem sahib*. You go to church. Perhaps you can go to the lepers village some other day," Nathu Ram said, smiling.

"No. It's settled. We'll go in the afternoon, when I return from church. You'll take me there."

The houseboy looked worried. "The Lieutenant *sahib* will be very angry at me, *mem sahib*."

"Well, I'll tell him that I made you take me. Then he won't be able to find fault with you."

"All right, *mem sahib*, if you say so. I will engage a city tonga tomorrow. But we must take Laxmi with us. It will not be proper for English lady to ride tonga without being accompanied by maidservant."

Laxmi was pleased to have been asked by her mistress to go for a ride in the tonga until she found out where they were headed. A look of horror appeared on her face.

"Why? Why *mem sahib* want to go to the lepers' village?" she blurted out to Nathu Ram in Hindustani. Laxmi was sitting in the back of the tonga with Sarah and the houseboy was next to the driver in the front.

"*Mem sahib* is a doctor," Nathu Ram answered. "She plans to provide medical treatment to the lepers."

Laxmi turned to Sarah. "No, *mem sahib*, no go. Not good," she said, shaking her head vigorously.

"Don't worry, Laxmi," Sarah assured the maid, patting her hand. "You won't have to enter the village with me. You can wait in the tonga."

They crossed the Jhelum River by a road bridge and entered the city. The narrow streets were crowded and the people stared at the English woman riding a tonga through their city. Several young boys started running after the tonga yelling, "Foreign *mem sahib*, foreign *mem sahib*." Sarah smiled and waved at them.

The tonga had to slow down going through the main bazaar where the street was lined on both sides with shops. Bright coloured saris were displayed in front of several shops, while others offered pots and pans and piles of yellow and red pungent ground spices.

They arrived at the outskirts of the city and Nathu Ram pointed at some squalid structures in the distance. "There, *mem sahib*, that is the village of the lepers."

"*Mem sahib* not go," Laxmi pleaded again.

"It's all right, Laxmi. You can wait here for me. I shan't be long," Sarah said, getting out of the tonga.

She walked towards the middle of the village, followed by Nathu Ram carrying her medical bag. Several children playing in the dirt suddenly stopped and stood staring at them. A grotesquely deformed leper lying on a wooden cart started yelling.

"Everyone, come out!" he called out in Hindi. "Some strangers are coming to our village."

Their dwellings were nothing but stones and bricks piled four or five feet high, with odd pieces of wood and thatch for roofs, and torn gunny sacks hanging in front serving as doors.

An old man limped out of one of the hovels and several women came out of others. Their faces and limbs were ravaged by the disease, and they were dressed in filthy rags. The children huddled together behind the leper women and stared at the foreign lady in her strange clothes coming toward them.

"Have they come to kick us out of the village?" a leper woman asked nervously.

Sarah came and stood in front of them. She smiled and with the palms of her hands held together before her face, greeted them.

"*Namaste*," she said.

The lepers stared at her. "What has the *mem sahib* come here for?" one of the women whispered to another standing next to her.

Sarah turned to the houseboy. "Nathu Ram, would you please tell them why I am here?"

"This *mem sahib* is a lady doctor. She has come to treat any of you who may be ill," the houseboy said in Hindi.

"No, we mustn't let her touch us," one of the women quickly told her companions. "She has come to poison us. The *sahibs* want to kill all of us."

"That's not true," Nathu Ram spoke again. "This *mem sahib* is a very kind person. She wishes to serve you."

"Why does she want to do that?" the man in the cart asked. "We have no money. She should go and serve the rich Maharajas."

"No, no, she does not seek money," Nathu Ram explained patiently. "She's a very charitable lady. She has a good heart."

"Well, if that's what she wants to do," the old leper who had limped out of his hut said, "let her first treat the sore on the bottom of my foot."

The man slowly lowered himself to the ground and, lifting his right leg, pointed at an ugly open sore on the heel of his foot. Sarah took the medical bag from the houseboy's hands and knelt down in the dirt in front of the leper. The stench from the wound and the man's body was nauseating. She hesitated for a moment, but then reaching out, took the leper's foot in her hands. She gently cleaned the wound with cotton wool and applied a soothing balm to it. Placing more cotton wool over it, she tied a bandage around the leper's foot and ankle.

"There, that should make you feel better," she said, standing up.

"*Hai Bhagwan*," one of the women spoke softly. "The *mem sahib* humbled herself before a leper. She has touched his feet."

The old leper stood up and gingerly tested his bandaged foot.

"Tell the *mem sahib* that she can come back next week," he told Nathu Ram. "If she hasn't poisoned me and I'm still alive, then we'll let her treat us."

Sarah had understood enough to know that at least for now the lepers would not trust her beyond what she had been allowed to do for the old man. "All right, Nathu Ram, we'll leave now," she said. "Please tell them I'll be back next Sunday afternoon." Then, turning to the lepers, she put her hands together in front of her face and, smiling, said, "*Namaste.*"

"Look, there is *Chotta Sahib,*" one little boy yelled out, and the children all turned and ran towards the end of the village.

Sarah saw a young Indian boy walk into the village. The leper children surrounded him and were greeting him cheerfully. Sarah was surprised that the boy didn't seem to mind being among these lepers. She walked over towards him.

He appeared to be in his teens, a handsome young fellow, dressed in a clean white *salwar, kameez* and turban. He was busy giving the children some fruit and sweetmeats he took from a cloth bag he was carrying.

"Well, hello. Who are you?" Sarah asked pleasantly.

The boy looked up, startled. "I am Devi Lal, a student from that school," he blurted out in heavily accented English, pointing behind him.

"Oh, you speak English," Sarah said, reaching out and placing a hand on the boy's shoulder. "You're not afraid to come here. The children trust you."

"I bring them fruit and sweetmeats each Sunday afternoon," he answered and then asked, "Why are you here?"

"I'm a doctor. I would like to help these people."

"But you are British. You are supposed to hate Indians."

"Not all of us are like that," Sarah answered softly.

"Are you actually prepared to treat the lepers?" the boy asked.

"Yes, that's what I want to do, if they'll accept me. I plan to come back next Sunday." Sarah paused for a moment. "Actually, I have a suggestion," she added. "If you also come here Sunday afternoons, maybe you can help me. They trust you and, until I learn enough Hindi, perhaps you can interpret for me."

Devi Lal thought for a moment. "I will be happy to do that," he answered with a smile. "If that is what you want, I will help you."

"Good. I'll see you next Sunday then," Sarah said, turning and walking away.

When she climbed into the tonga, Laxmi slowly slid to her corner of the seat.

"I get bath ready when we return, *mem sahib*. Then you burn clothes."

"Don't be silly," Sarah laughed. "I'm not doing any such thing. Look, their disease is not contagious. You don't catch it unless you live among them for many, many years. So don't worry. I'm not going to get it, and neither will you."

The next day, Sarah made Nathu Ram take her to the charitable dispensary in the city. Dev Suri, the Indian doctor at the one room dispensary, welcomed her graciously. He appeared to be middle-aged and wore a western style shirt and trousers. He was bald except for a narrow strip of graying hair along the sides and back of his head.

"I'd like to work where medical care is scarce," Sarah told him. "Is there a need for a physician in some of the neighbouring villages?"

"Yes, Madam, very much so," Dr. Suri informed her. "In fact, a maternity and children's clinic has been established by a wealthy Indian family in a village called Rajpur, just north of the city. They don't have a doctor available to them, only a midwife. You may wish to go there."

"Are there any other places where I can work?" Sarah inquired.

"Well, there is an orphanage in the city which I visit once a week. The children there can certainly benefit from the services of a second doctor."

"Thank you, Doctor Suri, thank you very much," Sarah said, shaking his hand. "I'll go to Rajpur. I'll also visit the orphanage and offer my services."

On the way back to the cantonment, Sarah asked Nathu Ram to instruct the tonga driver to take them to the city school. There, she spoke to the headmaster who helped her hire one of the teachers to provide daily private tutoring in Hindi at her home.

Christmas was fast approaching: Sarah was reminded of it by the invitation she received to attend a Christmas Eve ball at the Club. You couldn't have guessed by the weather, she thought. Although the humid heat they had faced upon arriving in India in October was gone, it was still quite warm and sunny. Cedric wasn't expected to be back in time for Christmas and she was going to miss him terribly. Her mind drifted back to Christmas last year in London, soon after they were married. What a happy time that had been. She started remembering Christmases at home in Willoughby with her family. "Come on, stop reminiscing and get going, woman," she scolded herself. "You have work to do."

By Christmas Eve, Sarah had worked out arrangements to visit the orphanage once a week and the Rajpur Clinic twice each week. The orphanage, run by a Hindu organization called Arya Samaj and supported by philanthropists in the city, provided shelter to over one hundred and fifty boys and girls ranging in age from infancy to sixteen years.

Rajpur was a tiny village a short distance northeast of the city. Surrounded by wheat fields, it consisted of two hundred or so small houses made of sun-dried mud and straw bricks, nestled between a large grove of mango trees and a long shallow pond with stagnant reddish-brown water. The clinic, the only brick building besides a small temple, consisted of one large room. A table with three chairs around it was in the middle of the room and several wooden benches lined two of its walls. A cloth partition was hung in one corner and shielded an examination table behind it. The door to the clinic was wide, as those patients too ill to walk or unable to be carried were brought in on their *charpais*.

Sarah had turned down invitations to the Christmas Eve ball at the club as well as to dinner parties at the homes of some of the married officers. Instead, she went for long walks along the river each evening, accompanied by Laxmi and Nathu Ram and chatted with them, practicing the Hindi she was learning from her tutor.

"Tell me about Hinduism, Nathu Ram," she asked the houseboy. "I know it's origin dates back several thousands of years before my religion was founded and that Hindus pray to many gods."

"Yes, *mem sahib*, it is very ancient religion and we have infinite number of gods. But there is only one Brahma - one ultimate creator. The rest of our gods are the manifestations of this Supreme Being and sent by Him wherever and whenever there is too much evil."

"That is Shiva temple on other side of river," Laxmi added, pointing to the largest of several temples on the opposite bank.

"Hindu scriptures speak of there being only one all pervading final power in all of the universe," Nathu Ram continued, ignoring Laxmi's interruption. "It does not matter what name we give to this supreme being: we all worship only Him."

"Do Hindu's try and convert others to their religion?" Sarah asked.

"What is there to convert, *mem sahib*, if we are convinced there is only one Lord, one Master for all. Yet if other people wish to embrace Hinduism and perform our rituals, nobody stops them."

Christmas day, Sarah attended church and returned home as soon as the service was over. It was a Sunday and she was anxious to go back to the lepers' village. She ate her lunch hurriedly and then called out to her maid. "Let's go, Laxmi, the *tonga* is here."

Yet, during the ride to the village, she was apprehensive, not knowing if the lepers would accept her. She got off the tonga and took the medical bag from the houseboy's hands.

"You can stay here in the tonga, Nathu Ram," she said. "The young Indian boy I met last week, promised to help me, and he's here."

"*Namaste, mem sahib*," the leper in the cart hailed, flashing a broad smile. "Come out, everybody," he yelled. "The foreign doctor-lady *sahib* is here."

The old leper appeared at the door of his hut and slowly followed the women who were coming out of their huts. Sarah tried to read their faces. The old man came and stood in front of her and mumbled something.

Sarah turned to Devi Lal. "What did he say?"

"He said his foot feels better," the boy answered. "He thinks your medicine is all right."

Sarah's face lit up. "Oh thank you," she said to the old leper, raising her hands, stopping short of embracing him. "Thank you so much."

For the next two hours, Sarah examined several children and women while Devi Lal interpreted for her. More lepers had returned from the city after begging all day. They stood crowding around the strange English *mem sahib* who was willing, not only to be among them, but to wash their wounds and treat their ailments.

The last leper needing medical attention had been seen. The children, no longer curious, were busy playing. "Thank you very much for your help," Sarah smiled at Devi Lal. "I couldn't have managed without you."

"I did not do much," the boy said shyly.

"Tell me about yourself. What are you studying?" she asked.

I'm in the tenth grade in the high school here in Jhelum," he answered. "I'm from the village of Karyala."

They had started walking towards a large tree at the far end of the village, under which a small statue was placed on a low narrow platform made of loose bricks. "Is this where they worship?" Sarah asked.

"Yes, this is a temple of Lord Krishna," Devi Lal answered. "Above it is a *peepul* tree which is considered sacred."

"Does the village have a name?"

"The lepers call it *Hari Niwas*, which in our language means God's Abode."

"What a beautiful name, and so appropriate," Sarah answered.

The lepers now all seemed to be converging toward the *peepul* tree.

"It is time for their Sunday prayers," Devi Lal explained.

"Can we stay?" she asked. "Can I watch?"

"Yes, most certainly. Everyone is welcome to pray at Lord Krishna's temple."

The lepers sat down on the ground before the shrine. The children jostled each other, vying to be in front. A brass *thaali* containing a lit *diya* and a pile of puffed rice was placed before the shrine. The old leper conducted the prayers reciting mantras which Sarah did not understand. Then a woman picked up the *thaali* and performed *aarti* while they all sang what sounded like a hymn. Sarah stood next to Devi Lal and like him, held her hands in front of her face with the palms together.

The prayers over, the leper women with the *thaali* started giving a few grains of the puffed rice to each of the lepers. She approached Devi Lal and Sarah.

"This is *prashad* — an offering from God. We must accept it," Devi Lal whispered, putting his right hand out. The leper woman dropped a few grains of puffed rice into his palm. Devi Lal put his hands together and bowed his head. He then put the *prashad* in his mouth and ate it. The woman hesitated a moment in front of Sarah and then started to walk away.

"I would also like to have some," Sarah spoke softly and put the palms of her hands out. She accepted the grains of puffed rice and placed them in her mouth.

She returned home, overcome with a strange feeling of serenity. This is what she had wanted to do for a long time. This is what Christmas is all about. There <u>was</u> a purpose to her life and she had discovered it in Hari Niwas. She sat down to have dinner alone, her mind at peace. If only she could have shared these feelings with Cedric. The thought of him brought a sense of guilt to her mind. Perhaps she should be missing him more. Before going to bed, she prayed, thanking God for helping her and asking Him to keep her husband safe from harm.

The children at the orphanage as well as the women coming to the Rajpur village clinic had quickly accepted Doctor *mem sahib*, and allowed her to tend to their medical needs. Yet Sarah looked forward more eagerly to her Sunday visits to Hari Nivas and found working with the lepers somehow to be more fulfilling. Returning from the village clinic one day, she told Nathu Ram to have the *tonga* stop in the city bazaar. "Laxmi, help me buy some Indian clothes. I'd like to get a sari."

"Why *mem sahib* want Indian cloths?" the maid asked. "*mem sahib* already have beautiful cloths."

"Well, I'd like to try wearing a sari," Sarah answered. "Come, help me choose what else I need to wear with it." Sarah bought four cotton saris and Laxmi helped her pick the right sized petticoats and blouses to go with them. With her maid's help, Sarah learned how to drape the six-yard long garment around her waist.

"You beautiful, *mem sahib*," Laxmi gushed. "Just like a *rani*."

The following Sunday, after returning from church and having lunch, Sarah changed into her sari and when she came out to leave for Hari Niwas, Nathu Ram and Laxmi nodded their heads with approval.

"For a moment I almost did not recognize you, Madame," Devi Lal said when Sarah walked into Hari Niwas and greeted him.

"Do you approve?" she asked with a smile.

"Yes, most certainly," he answered shyly.

They worked side by side and, within an hour, Sarah had attended to all of the lepers who were waiting to be seen.

"Are you going back to your school now?" she asked Devi Lal.

"I have permission to stay out until the evening roll call. I like to go walk by the river. I think I'll do that."

"Oh, I also enjoy walking along the river," Sarah said eagerly. "Perhaps we could walk together."

"But your's is the other side of the river, Madame," Devi Lal said, looking up at Sarah. "I walk on the city side."

"Yes, of course. You're right," Sarah answered.

"I would like to see this side of the river, though," she continued. "I can see some temples from across. Will you take me to visit one of them?"

"Yes, I shall be happy to show you."

They walked out of Hari Niwas and towards the city. Sarah asked Nathu Ram and Laxmi to wait for her by the *tonga*. The city streets were crowded and they walked without talking.

"This is the main temple," Devi Lal said, stopping at the bottom of marble steps leading up to a large ornate temple. "It is devoted to the God Shiva."

"Can we go in?" Sarah asked.

"Yes, but first we have to take off our shoes, and you'll have to cover your head with your *sari*."

They climbed the steps and at the top, stopped to look at a large black marble statue of a bull seated on the ground, around whose neck devotees had placed garlands of orange and red marigolds. "That is *Nandi*, the mount of Lord Shiva," Devi Lal explained, entering the temple through a huge silver plated door. Sarah followed him, placing the end of her sari over her head. The inside of the temple was dimly lit except for a tall statue at the far end which glowed in the illumination of several *diyas*. Sarah felt strangely drawn towards it. Devi Lal reached up and rang a silver bell hanging just inside the entrance. The sharp peel of the bell reverberated down from the temple's high dome.

They walked towards the shrine, the palms of their hands held together in front of their faces. The black marble floor felt cool under their feet. The exquisitely carved white marble statue of Lord Shiva looked down serenely upon them. In the flickering glow from the *diyas*, the statue appeared ethereal. A thin, curling wisp of smoke rose from the incense burning in front of the altar, and filled the air with its sweet fragrance.

Devi Lal knelt down and, bowing low, touched his forehead to the floor. Sarah felt moved by the passion of the young boy's faith, and she, too, bowed her head in prayer. A priest appeared from one side of the shrine and applied red *tikka* on their foreheads. They accepted the *prashad* he gave them and, bowing their heads, left the temple. Neither spoke until they started walking along the river.

"That is the cantonment there," Devi Lal said pointing to the row of neat bungalows and a church across the river.

"Yes, I see it. I live in one of those homes along the bank," Sarah answered. They went down the steps and onto the sand near the water's edge. "I'm very grateful for your help, Devi Lal. You're so good with the children. Tell me, what do you plan to do after high school?"

"I don't know," the boy answered. "I don't know what I'll do."

"Have you thought about becoming a doctor? I think you would make a very good physician."

Devi Lal looked up at Sarah. "How does one become a doctor?"

She noticed the excitement in his eyes. "Well, I'm sure there are medical schools in some of the major cities of India. Perhaps you should talk to your teachers at school. They should be able to advise you."

"My father wants me to return to Karyala after high school. He wants me to eventually take his place as the head of the family and be the chief of our village," Devi Lal said, looking away.

"But what is it that you want?"

"I don't know. I see people suffering. If I could, I'd like to help them."

"Perhaps if you were to explain to your father what you wish to do, he may agree."

The young boy did not answer.

"Tell me about your family, Devi Lal, won't you?" Sarah asked.

"My mother's name is Kanti. She is most beautiful. She explains the passages from our Holy Books to us after our prayers each evening. I have two brothers and two sisters. My father is very handsome and brave. He wants his sons to grow up to be strong and to help chase the British out of our country. Oh, I'm sorry," he added hurriedly. "I would not want you to leave India, Madame."

Sarah laughed. "That's all right. There's nothing wrong with being patriotic. You should want to chase all Britishers out of your country."

Then she continued. "Won't you call me Sarah? I would like to be your friend."

"Oh, no, I cannot call you by your first name. You are older than I, and that would be most disrespectful. If it's all right, I will call you Madame Sarah."

Sarah laughed again. "Oh, all right. If that's what you want."

As the sun started setting, they climbed up the steps and walked back to Hari Niwas.

"Where the hell have you been?" Cedric asked, coming out of the house just as Sarah got out of the *tonga*. "Oh good Lord! What in blazes are you doing in that bloody outfit?" he continued angrily.

Sarah tried to smile. "Welcome home, darling. I didn't know you were back."

"I've been back for hours," Cedric fumed, following his wife into the house.

"How was your trip?" Sarah asked, turning and facing her husband.

"To hell with my trip," Cedric glared at her. "Tell me where you were."

"I was at a village outside the city, treating some poor people," Sarah answered, desperately trying to keep her voice under control.

"What people? What village?"

"Well, if you must know, it's Hari Niwas, the village of the lepers."

Cedric's mouth fell open. "Have you gone completely bonkers? Do you have no sense left at all?"

"How dare you speak to me like that." Sarah lashed out angrily. "You knew damned well what I planned to do in India."

"Well, I forbid you," Cedric shot back. "You aren't going to waste my money running around looking after bloody natives."

"Let me get you to understand, Cedric," Sarah spoke icily. "As far as my work is concerned, I shan't listen to you. I'll do what I think is right. As for the money, I'll use my own and not a farthing of yours!"

Cedric flinched. Here it was again; her bloody money. She would never let him be her equal.

"I'd like to go to the club now," he said, controlling his voice. "I'd like you to come with me."

That was the last thing Sarah wanted, but she didn't protest. She went to take a bath and change her clothes.

"Well, hello there, stranger," Ian Campbell beamed, standing up and taking Sarah's hands in his. "Where've you been hiding yourself these past few weeks?" The men were seated in the smoking room of the club.

"Oh, I've just been busy doing odd things," Sarah answered.

"Well, don't you know?" David Habersham spoke, his voice tinged with sarcasm. "Our mysterious Sarah Dormsbury Smythe has been sighted riding a *tonga* all over the city. It's been rumoured that she's even switched to wearing native garb and has gone to the village of the lepers."

"Am I being spied upon?" Sarah asked, raising her eyebrows.

"No, just being protected, my dear," Habersham answered with a grin.

"I don't need any protection, Captain," Sarah spoke coldly and turned to Ian Campbell. "I've kept myself busy working at an orphanage and at a couple of villages. There's so much sickness among the poor and they need help."

"You're a doctor?" Ian Campbell asked. "Really? I didn't know that."

"They breed like bloody rabbits," Habersham cut in, angrily. "There're too many of them around anyway. Let more of the bloody niggers die. The world will be better off for it."

Sarah felt a deep hatred towards the man and turned away from him. "Where's Lieutenant Howard?" she asked Major Duckworth.

The men looked at each other uneasily. "He didn't quite make it back," Ian Campbell said gently, patting Sarah's hand.

"What do you mean, he didn't quite make it back?" Sarah asked.

"He was killed, Sarah," Cedric answered.

"Oh my God, the poor boy. He was so young," she moaned.

She somehow endured the rest of the evening and felt relieved when they left the Club.

"Now I'm the damn laughing stock of the regiment," Cedric blurted out angrily as soon as they got home.

"Why's that?" Sarah asked.

"You know damn well why. It's you! Running around dressed like a bloody native, and then going out to that damn lepers village."

"You know, in some ways I envy the lepers," Sarah spoke softly. "They seem to accept their fate and don't complain. They're grateful for what little they have. Perhaps you should come with me to their village. We can all learn lessons from them."

Cedric's face turned red. He tried but failed to speak and turning around, stormed into the second bedroom, slamming the door behind him.

They argued and quarreled throughout the next day. Cedric accused Sarah of marrying him just so she could come to India.

"That's not true," she protested. "I married you because I fell in love with you. It's you who has changed. You knew damn well what I was going to do here. You should respect my wishes."

Laxmi and Nathu Ram were shocked by Cedric's anger and, as much as they could, stayed out of his way.

"How can *sahib* be so mean to *mem sahib*?" the maid whispered to the houseboy. "She's so nice. I'm scared of him. He's evil!" she added, shuddering.

Cedric and Sarah barely spoke to each other for the rest of the week. At the end of it, they came to an understanding. Sarah would continue her work unhindered. She, however, agreed to accompany Cedric to the Club and help him meet his social obligations. Unknown to Cedric, Sarah did wire her father, asking him to send her more money.

The Kumbh Mela

*I*n spite of their disagreements, which Cedric felt were entirely Sarah's fault, he was still deeply in love with her and wanted to make the best of their marriage. He tendered a half-hearted apology and even tried to show interest in what she was doing.

Sarah had immersed herself in her work and was devoting more time to the orphanage and the Rajpur clinic than she had anticipated. Yet the few hours she spent each Sunday at Hari Niwas seemed to bring a deeper sense of satisfaction. She had become particularly fond of young Devi Lal and looked forward to their time together.

"He has so much wisdom for someone so young," she told Cedric one afternoon while they were having tea on the front lawn. "I've learned such a lot from him."

"What has he taught you?" Cedric asked, continuing to scan the newspaper in his hands.

"I've learned about the Hindu way of life which is based upon a deep and unquestioning belief in God, acceptance of *karma*: the fruits of our deeds of this life or an earlier existence which determines our ultimate fate, our destiny. It is not only what we do, but also our thoughts and desires determine our *karma.*"

"Oh that's a lot of rubbish," Cedric muttered.

"No it's not," Sarah persisted. "Even the Bible says that as we sow, so shall we reap. Devi Lal also told me that their religion requires the performance of one's duties with diligence and treatment of all elders with respect. He's always talking about his mother and father. I'd like to meet them someday."

"What's so great about them?" Cedric asked.

"He says that his mother is very beautiful and reads to them from their holy book called *Gita*. From her he has learned the importance of performing one's duty, of compassion and love for all creation and a tolerance of the belief of others. She told him that God is like the top of a mountain and each of us seeks to reach Him, taking a path that is convenient for us and most appealing. As long as our ultimate goal is the same, it doesn't matter what path we take to reach the mountain top, or the name by which we call our God. Isn't that beautiful?"

"It's all right, I guess, if you accept their heathen beliefs," Cedric answered, disinterestedly, putting his newspaper down. "What about his father? What does he do?"

"He's the chief of their village. He wants his sons to grow up brave and help chase all Britishers out of India," Sarah answered with a smile.

"The bloody nerve of the man," Cedric retorted angrily. "He should be shot for such treasonous ideas."

"Oh, I don't find anything wrong with their wanting to rid their country of British domination. To the Indian, he must be a hero and we the villains."

"That's rubbish, Sarah. Don't you see, they're an inferior race," Cedric answered haughtily. "They need us to rule them."

"Cedric, that's a lot of nonsense. I'm surprised you even entertain such thoughts. You've started to sound like David Habersham, and I can't stand that man. By the way, I've learned of a *mela* that's going to be held next month near Allahabad. I'm thinking of going to it."

"What's a *mela*?"

"It's a gathering, a fair. Actually, this *Kumbh Mela* I'm planning to attend is the most sacred festival in the Hindu calendar. It's only held once every twelve years."

"Did this Devi Lal tell you about it?" Cedric asked, his voice tinged with annoyance.

"No, actually it was Nathu Ram. He'd like to attend the festival and asked if he could take a week off."

"He bloody well may not," Cedric blurted out. "Who's going to do his damn work while he's gone? He can have a day off and attend any festival he wants."

"It's two day's train journey from here to Allahabad, Cedric. Millions of devotees travel from all over India to attend this *mela*. I've already told him he can go. He told me the fascinating story about the origin of the *mela*. The Hindus believe that one of the Gods wrestled the *kumbh*, a jar containing immortal nectar from some demons and flew it to paradise. The God carrying the nectar briefly rested at Prayag, the sacred confluence of the rivers Ganges, Yamuna and a mythical river called Saraswati. The entire journey lasted twelve days, and as each divine day is equivalent to twelve years on earth, the *Kumbh mela* is held only once every twelve years. Isn't that fascinating? I'm so looking forward to being there."

"You can't be serious about attending this *Kumbh mela*, or whatever it's called? The place will be crawling with bloody natives. Where the hell would you stay?"

"Nathu Ram said that some of the temples along the confluence of the rivers provide rooms for women pilgrims. I've spoken to Laxmi and she's agreed to go with me."

Cedric had by now learned not to try and dissuade his wife once her mind had been made up. Instead, he started thinking about the arrangements he must make for her safety. He would send a couple of his Indian *sowars* to accompany her without her knowing about it. He would also speak to Nathu Ram and order him to watch out for her all of the time.

"Can I arrange for you to stay with one of the English families in Allahabad?" he asked.

"No, Cedric," Sarah answered firmly, "I don't want you to do that. I'll stay in one of the temples Nathu Ram spoke about."

The day Sarah left, Cedric accompanied her to the train station and instructed the Anglo-Indian station master to see that the train guard kept a close watch on Sarah's first class compartment. Cedric also made the station master send a telegraphic message to each of the stations on the way, asking them to provide any assistance that his wife may need. The two *sowars* who were to guard Sarah were dressed in civilian clothes and seated in a third class compartment. Each carried a revolver hidden under his *kurta*.

Later that day Cedric had gone to the Club in a sour mood and drank heavily all evening. He woke up the next morning with a splitting headache, his body soaked with perspiration and his throat parched. A vein in the side of his head was throbbing painfully. He remembered the strange dreams about his childhood that had plagued his mind all night. His father had come home drunk and his mother hid him in her bedroom closet. Through a crack in the door he could see only the sepia-coloured photograph of his father in the frame with small sea shells glued to it lying on the bedside table. Even though he pressed his hands hard against his ears, he couldn't drown out his father's abusive and vulgar demands of his mother, and her pleas to leave her alone. He had also dreamt of Sarah taunting him, waving fistfuls of money at him.

Cedric stumbled out of bed and took a long drink of water from the jug lying on a corner table. It was Sunday, he remembered, but with Sarah gone, he wasn't going to attend church. Ian Campbell and David Habersham had invited him to go to a local fair with them.

"You'll see some fine horsemanship at the *Ghora mela*, Cedric," Campbell had said. "Some of these natives are bloody good riders."

"This is the last day of the fair," Habersham added. "They'll have a race to crown the best rider and the swiftest horse."

"Do any of us compete?" Cedric asked.

"Hell, no," Habersham answered, "we let the *sowars* race, but none of us will ride with these barbarians."

"Actually, my lad, we know bloody well we'd be beaten by these Pathan riders," Campbell laughed. "That'd be too much for our pride to swallow."

The three men, accompanied by twenty of their *sowars*, rode their horses to the outskirts of Jhelum city later that morning. The *mela* was spread over a large area of open ground. Several ornate tents stood next to scores of make-shift shelters. Along one side were the paddocks where traders offered mules and horses of different breeds for sale. Blacksmiths and saddle makers displayed their crafts in another part of the grounds. Tea and food sellers were everywhere, as were shops selling trinkets and cheap jewelry. Pathan men danced to the loud rhythmic beat of drums. A pall of fine dust hung like a low cloud over the entire *mela*.

Cedric handed the reins of his horse to the *sowar* who, with four of his companions, would keep watch on their horses. "Last year Ian and I left our horses tethered here without posting guards and some bastards stole them," David Habersham related angrily.

"We had to ride a *tonga* back to the cantonment," Ian Campbell added, laughing loudly. "You should've seen the look on David's face. He was ready to shoot every damn native we came across!"

The three of them walked towards the mass of Indians milling around the fair grounds. The fifteen *sowars* followed them closely. The natives stared at the foreigners and slowly moved out of the way. Campbell led them to a saddlemaker's shop and they walked between rows of tables displaying the fine work of the craftsmen. They then proceeded to a roped off area and watched an exhibition by Afridi acrobatic bareback riders. "They're good, aren't they?" Campbell commented.

There was a commotion at the far end of the *mela* and everyone started rushing in that direction. The *sowars* quickly formed a circle and locked their arms together, surrounding their three British officers.

"The winner of the horse race is about to be crowned," Ian Campbell yelled to Cedric over the din of the crowd. They stopped at the edge of a small roped-off clearing where several men were standing on a wooden platform. A silver-studded saddle and a velvet-lined case containing a pistol were displayed on a low table next to the men. One of the men pointed his rifle up in the air and fired. The others raised their hands and yelled, "*Khamosh, khamosh.*" The crowd slowly quieted down.

"Make way for this year's champion horse and rider," the man who had fired the rifle yelled.

People at the far end of the clearing parted. A tall broad shouldered Indian entered the clearing, holding the reins of a magnificent white stallion, and loud applause broke out from the crowd. "Hem Raj, *zinda bad*", they yelled. Garlands of marigolds were placed around his neck, as well as over Kamaan's shoulders. The men on the platform made the presentations of the saddle and the pistol. The crowd roared its approval. Hem Raj raised a hand and turning slowly, bowed to the crowd. When he noticed the three British officers, he stared at them for a moment before turning away.

"What a magnificent animal," Cedric commented.

"That he is, laddie," Campbell responded, nodding his head, "and that chap is one hell of a rider. I saw him win this race last year. No one could even stay close with him."

Sarah had worn one of her saris for the train journey to Allahabad. Just before boarding the train, she spotted Dr. Suri and, to Cedric's annoyance, hailed him.

"I'd like you to meet my husband," she said, shaking his hand. "Cedric, this is Dr. Suri. I met him when I visited the free dispensary in Jhelum."

Cedric ignored the hand the Indian doctor offered and, instead, just nodded at him.

"Are you also travelling by this train?" Sarah asked.

"Yes, madam, I'm headed for Allahabad to attend the *Kumbh mela*."

"Well, what a wonderful coincidence," Sarah said with a smile. "That's where I'm also going. Perhaps you can join me for tea this afternoon."

"I shall be honoured, madam," Dr. Suri answered, bowing.

Laxmi had been very excited about accompanying Sarah to the *mela*. "It is scary to ride train, *mem sahib*?" she asked in English. Sarah had tried to get the *ayah* to speak to her in Hindi but after a few sentences, Laxmi invariably switched back to English.

"Of course not," Sarah answered. "Why, haven't you ever been on a train?"

"No, *mem sahib*, I not. It go so fast. I afraid of falling off."

"You'll be all right," Sarah answered, laughing. "We'll lock the doors securely."

Once the train started, Laxmi could barely contain her excitement. "It wonderful you taking me with you, *mem sahib*, but I not sleep here. At night I must go to ladies third class compartment."

"Nonsense, Laxmi," Sarah laughed, "you'll sleep on that berth right there. Remember, the *sahib* told you not to leave me alone even for a minute."

"If you make me to sleep here, *mem sahib*, I sleep on floor," the *ayah* insisted.

"You'll do no such thing, Laxmi. I've bought you a first class ticket and you'll sleep in your berth." The *ayah* reluctantly sat down on the edge of her berth, but soon felt drawn to the view outside and moved back next to a window. Her hair blowing in the wind, she started singing softly.

"What are you singing, Laxmi?" Sarah asked. "It sounds so sweet."

"It is love song, *mem sahib*," the *ayah* answered, turning around.

"Tell me about it," Sarah persisted.

"It about two young people named Sohni and Mahival," Laxmi explained. "They in love. Sohni was daughter of pot maker. Each night she use one pot her father make to go across river to meet her lover Mahival. One night sister-in-law put unbaked pot outside the door. When Sohni try to cross river, the unbaked clay dissolve and she cry for help. Mahival jump into the swift current but could not save she."

"Oh how sad," Sarah said. "What happened then?"

"Not wanting to live even one moment without beloved, Mahival let fast current take him away and he also drown. They were thus join after death."

"Oh that's such a sweet story, Laxmi," Sarah complimented.

At each stop, Nathu Ram came running to inquire if Sarah needed anything. The two *sowars* sent by Cedric also came and stood discretely on each side of Sarah's compartment.

"Don't worry, Nathu Ram, we're fine," Sarah assured the houseboy. "I would like you, though, to go and ask Dr. Suri to join me for tea at the next stop. Also, instruct the refreshment car to bring extra tea and biscuits."

Dev Suri came and sat in a chair across from Sarah. Laxmi squatted on the floor in the corner.

"Will you be staying long at the *mela*?" Sarah asked, pouring tea into the cups.

"I'll be there for the five main days of the fair, madam, working as a volunteer at one of the medical clinics," Suri answered, accepting the cup of tea Sarah handed him.

"That's very noble of you, Dr. Suri," Sarah said.

"Well, I'm mostly retired now and feel that I should do as much as I can for those less fortunate. My wife was to accompany me but one of our daughters just gave birth so she has gone to look after our grandchild. How long will you be staying there, madam?"

"Please call me Sarah. I'll be there for a couple of nights. I just didn't want to miss being at such a significant event, Dev. Oh, I hope you don't mind my using your first name?"

"No, not at all," Suri answered. "You're right, Sarah, you will see all of India at Prayag. Have you heard the legend behind the origin of the *mela*?"

"Yes, I have. My houseboy narrated the fascinating story to me."

"I hope you don't find our religion with its abundance of Gods to be too confusing."

"When I first came to India I was a little confused," Sarah admitted, "but then my houseboy explained the basic beliefs of Hindus and now I have a much better understanding."

"What I like about my religion is that it is a way of life; it pervades every aspect of each day of our existence," Dev Suri explained. "What bothers me most about Hinduism is its hierarchical caste system. Brahmins, our priests, are at the very top. A Brahmin may refuse to eat food cooked by some one of a lower caste. Below them are the rulers and warriors and then traders and merchants. The lowest of the four are the Shudras: the artisans and cultivators."

"What about the untouchables, Dev. Where do they fit in the caste system?"

"They, unfortunately, are ostracized by the rest of the Hindus and are considered unfit to be included within the caste system. But then we Hindus believe in Karma and reincarnation. We say that what we are when we are born is a direct consequence of our actions of a previous existence. One child is born healthy and in a good family. A second child is born with a crippling disease and is destined to a life of untold suffering. Each child's destiny was determined by its Karma - the fruits of its deeds of a previous existence. We reap only that which we sow - nothing more, nothing less. We are but only clay in the embrace of our Karmas. Now in our present existence we must endeavor to lead a life without sin and perform meritorious deeds so that we may be blessed with good Karmas for the rest of our time on this earth and for our subsequent incarnations."

Their conversation then turned to medical practice in India and in England. Dev Suri asked Sarah about recent advances in drugs and diagnostic procedures. She, in turn, quizzed him about some of the diseases prevalent among Indians. They talked late into the evening and when the train stopped at a station, Dev Suri excused himself and left.

Nightfall came and dinner was brought to their compartment. After they ate, Laxmi insisted on bolting not only the two doors, but the shutters of all of the windows.

"It not safe, *mem sahib*," she cautioned.

"Oh, you're just like my husband," Sarah complained, laughing. "You both worry too much."

Sarah lay down and tried to fall asleep. Her mind kept drifting over recent events of her life and she found it difficult to believe that she had been in India less than four months. So much had happened in such a brief period. Why did she and Cedric drift apart? They had been so happy together before coming to India. She would try harder to work things out.

The train swayed from side to side and its wheels clattered over the rails. Sarah finally dozed off and fell asleep. In the middle of the night, she woke up suddenly to someone urgently shaking her by the shoulders.

"*Mem sahib*, hurry, wake up."

"What's the matter, Laxmi?" Sarah asked, quickly sitting up.

"*Daku, mem sahib*. They outside door," the *ayah* whispered. Over the noise of the train, Sarah heard something pounding on the wooden shutters of the door.

"*Daku, mem sahib*, they come to rob us," Laxmi sobbed softly. "They will kill us," she said in Hindi.

Oh my God, Laxmi's right, Sarah thought. She had read about robbers climbing onto the footboards of trains leaving stations. She pushed the *ayah* away and stood up. What could they do? She went back to her berth and lowered the shutter of the window farthest away from the door. Through the iron rods she saw two shadowy figures hanging on to the handrails and pounding the door shutters with hammers. Her heart racing, she gazed around the compartment, wondering what she could use to defend herself and Laxmi.

The hammering of the shutters stopped. Sarah turned to the door just as a hand appeared through the broken pieces of wood and started groping for the door bolt. Sarah gasped. But at that moment her eyes caught sight of the emptied dinner trays on the corner of the compartment floor. She hurriedly picked up a fork from the tray and, lunging forward, stabbed the hand with it. She heard a man's scream and the hand was hastily withdrawn. Laxmi stood against the far wall, watching wide-eyed, her face frozen in terror. Another hand was thrust through the broken shutters. Sarah was about to lunge at it with the fork when a second hand wielding a long dagger appeared.

Sarah stood helpless watching the door bolt being pushed open. Then she heard a distant pop, followed by a scream from outside the door. One of the hands disappeared. An instant later, there was a second loud noise accompanied by another scream. The dagger fell to the floor and the hand was wrenched from view. Sarah rushed to the door and pushed the bolt shut.

Laxmi slumped down onto the floor and started sobbing.

"It's all right now, Laxmi," Sarah called out, her voice trembling. Her hands were shaking and her knees felt weak. She wiped her palms on her sari and, taking a deep breath, went and knelt down next to the *ayah*.

"Stop crying, Laxmi, we're safe," she said softly.

"The *dakus* will kill us, *mem sahib*. They'll slit our throats."

"No they won't," Sarah answered, putting her arm around the woman's shoulders. "They're gone. They're not there anymore."

That was gunfire she had heard, and wondered who had shot the robbers.

The train was slowing down. Sarah got up quickly and picked up the dagger. She stood staring at the broken shutters of the door, her heart pounding again. But as the train came to a stop, she heard many voices outside. Coolies were rushing to help passengers boarding the train and those getting off.

There was a knock on the door. "Madam, this is the train guard," a man's voice called out in English. "Everything is all right. Please open the door." The *sowars* who had shot the robbers had summoned the train guard as soon as the train had come to a stop. Sarah undid the bolt.

"I'm deeply sorry, Madam. I've been informed what happened. Everything is under control now," the train guard said, taking the dagger from Sarah's hands. "There is another first class compartment to which we will move you right away. Please forgive me for this inconvenience, Madam. I apologize very sincerely."

When the train arrived at Allahabad in the morning, the Station Master there was waiting to receive Sarah. More apologies were tendered for the most unfortunate incident which must have caused Madame to become very upset. Sarah assured the man that she was fine. Would Madame like to rest in the first class waiting room? No, Sarah informed the Station Master, all she needed him to do was hail a *tonga* for her. Then it struck her that no one seemed to have given any thought to the two men who had been shot. They surely must have died and she wondered if there were wives and children left behind.

It was eleven o'clock in the morning. The sun was very bright and it was already getting hot. The path leading from the train station to the confluence of the holy rivers was packed with carriages and carts of all descriptions, surrounded by a mass of people on foot. The *tonga* carrying Sarah, Laxmi and Nathu Ram inched along in pace with those walking. There were a few ornate carriages of the maharajahs among a sea of crude bullock carts, horse-drawn *tongas* and push carts. Pilgrims in the thousands, many who could not afford to pay for a ride, walked. Children were perched on the shoulders of their parents. The lame and the elderly were being carried on the backs of those stronger than them.

Saffron robed *sadhus* by the hundreds walked together, while more important holy men rode atop elephants that lumbered along the path. Groups of men and women devoted to a particular God carried statues and sang hymns in praise of their deity. Various religious groups had set up water stops on the way where the pilgrims could quench their thirst. No one seemed to be particularly bothered by the heat and the dust.

The land on each side of the confluence of the rivers was covered by a tent city extending almost as far as the eye could see. The massive sandbars around which the two rivers flowed before merging also had tents pitched upon them, and were teeming with thousands upon thousands of pilgrims waiting their turn to take a dip in the holy rivers. Sarah looked in awe at the incredible sight before her.

They got off the *tonga* and she paid the driver. "We will go to one of those temples, *mem sahib*," Nathu Ram said, pointing at the shore of one of the rivers. They started walking along a crowded narrow path leading up towards the row of temples high atop the bank of the Ganges river.

A Brahmin priest directed Sarah and Laxmi to a large room on an upper floor of a building adjacent to the temple. There, a woman attendant assigned them two mats, side by side, in one corner of the room. Several other women dressed in saffron-coloured saris were sitting in the room conversing. Sarah placed her small travel case on the mat assigned to her and, followed by Laxmi, came out onto the temple's pavilion overlooking the Ganges.

The pavilion was deserted except for an old woman seated on a small platform under a tree at the far end. She was dressed in saffron-coloured clothes and her long gray hair hung to her waist. Her eyes were closed and she sat cross-legged, with her hands resting in her lap. She appeared frail, but her face was smooth and free of wrinkles. She was very still. Sarah kept looking at her, feeling somehow drawn to her. She slowly walked along the edge of the pavilion towards her.

The women in saffron clothes who Sarah had seen in the room were now coming out onto the pavilion and sat down on the ground in front of the platform. Several elegantly dressed women, bejeweled and wearing richly embroidered silks, appeared out of a side door and sat down on a thick carpet next to the platform.

A few moments passed and then the old woman opened her eyes. Placing the palms of her hands together in front of her, she bowed her head to those sitting around her. Her face was serene: she appeared gentle, and at peace. Seeing Sarah, she called out in a soft voice, "Come, come join us." Sarah moved closer and sat down.

"Let us begin our prayers," the woman said, closing her eyes again. They recited the *Gayatri Mantra* five times, followed by several other Sanskrit mantras. They then sang hymns, their voices blending harmoniously. Sarah could not understand much of the words but found her mind to be soothed.

The prayers over, they all stood up and, by turns, went to pay their respects to the woman on the platform. Sarah hesitatingly followed them. The old woman looked up and smiled at her. "You are not one of us but you wear our clothes," she said softly, in English. "Come, come and sit next to me. Tell me about yourself."

Sarah brought the palms of her hands together and bowed. "My name is Sarah Smythe. I am English," she said, and sat down on the edge of the platform. "Thank you for allowing me to attend the prayers."

"I'm happy to meet you, Sarah. My disciples call me Uma Mata. We are from an order of priestesses living in the Himalayas near Badri Nath. How long have you been in our country?" the old woman asked, resting her hand on Sarah's arm.

"It's been about four months," Sarah answered.

"You seem to have adapted well to our culture."

"I've been fascinated with India since childhood. There's so much that I want to learn."

"Fortunate are those who seek answers and do not allow their minds to stagnate. I hope you find what you are looking for, Sarah. We will now go to bathe in the holy Ganges River. You may accompany us if you wish."

"I would like that very much," Sarah answered, standing up.

They came out of the temple and started walking towards the rivers. The narrow street was crowded but the people parted to allow the saffron-robed women to go through. Uma Mata led the way, resting her hand on the arm of one of her disciples. Sarah walked alongside her with Laxmi behind them. "You have shown great courage by coming to the *Kumbh mela*," Uma Mata said gently, looking at Sarah.

"I wouldn't have forgiven myself if I hadn't."

"I think you'll find what you're looking for, Sarah. I can see it in you. But if you don't, and feel the need, come to our *ashram* in Badri Nath. There is much tranquility in the mountains."

"Thank you, Uma Mata," Sarah answered softly.

They had arrived at the confluence of the rivers. Sarah was again awed by the sight of the *mela* spread in front of her.

"It's incredible, isn't it?" Uma Mata spoke, reading Sarah's mind. "This is my third *Kumbh mela* and I'm still awed. I won't be here the next time, but you will come."

Sarah quickly glanced at the old woman, but couldn't see her face. They had stopped at the edge of the large sandbar. "Tomorrow, at noon, there will be the largest of the daily processions of holy men," the old woman continued, "You must come and witness it. Stand at this point for the best view."

"Won't you come to see it?" Sarah asked.

"No, we'll be leaving early in the morning to return to Badri Nath," the old woman answered, and started walking onto the sandbar.

Conversation was now difficult as the noise of the crowd was deafening. The sounds of drums and bells added to the din, and all but drowned the voices of the devotees singing hymns before the shrines of their particular Gods. The air was heavy with the sweet smells of incense and flowers. The sun shone brilliantly in a cloudless blue sky.

It took them almost an hour to work their way the short distance to the river's edge, and then they had to wait for people in front of them to take a dip in the holy waters and come out. The women went in fully clothed. Sarah held Laxmi's hand and they slowly waded into the water up to their waists. The water was cold and Sarah felt a sharp tingling sensation all over her skin. Like the other pilgrims, she too brought her palms together in front of her face and then immersed her head under the water three times. She stood for a few moments, praying, her eyes closed. Time seemed to have stood still for her and, standing waist deep in the cold water, in the midst of the largest gathering of humans she had ever witnessed, she felt overcome by a deep sense of serenity.

They came out of the river slowly, their clothes clinging to their bodies. Sarah felt strangely cleansed, as if her mind had suddenly been cleared of cobwebs. As they walked back through the crowds, Uma Mata rested her hand lightly on Sarah's arm. They walked to the temple without talking. Sarah changed her clothes and they ate a simple meal served from the temple's community kitchen. Later in the evening, they went into the temple to pray and the priest applied a *tikka* on their foreheads.

The view of the star-studded skies and of the *mela* from the pavilion was breathtaking. Thousands upon thousands of *diyas* and lanterns sparkled along the rivers and on the sandbars. The waters of the rivers shimmered enchantingly in their glow. Sarah stood at the edge of the pavilion, mesmerized. "It is divine, isn't it?" Uma Mata said, walking up to Sarah.

"Yes, I've never seen anything so beautiful."

"You are happy you came, *Saraswati*?"

"Yes, Uma Mata, I am. I've never felt so much at peace with myself."

"*Prayag* does that to those who seek to be illuminated," the old woman said softly. They stood for a few moments without speaking. "Fate has brought you among us for a reason, Sarah," Uma Mata continued. "Your loved one will not accept what you are doing, but it is your destiny. I see greatness in you, and one day you'll heal more than the bodies of those who ail."

Sarah turned sharply to look at Uma Mata. *How did she know about me and what I do?*

"You called me *Saraswati*?" she asked.

"Ah, yes," the old woman answered with a faint smile, "*Saraswati*, the consort of the Creator Brahma, after whom a mythical river is also named. You see, each of us has to have an earthly name, but, as we all have a part of our divine creator within us, we should have a second name as well. Note that the first four alphabets of both of your names are the same," Uma Mata paused for a few moments. Then she spoke again.

"Yes, *Saraswati*; one who gives the essence of one's own self; whose beliefs are rooted in truth; a seeker of self-realization; one who follows a path of righteousness, devotion and service. Yes, Sarah Smythe, *Saraswati* is truly your divine name."

The old woman placed her hands on Sarah's arms. "Well, I must retire now," she said softly. "We'll be leaving the temple before sunrise. Goodbye, Child. You'll remain forever in my prayers. Remember, our *ashram* is there for you. Come to Badri Nath when you feel the need. May Lord Krishna guide your steps through all of your journeys."

Sarah bowed her head. "Goodbye, Uma Mata," she said softly. "Thank you so much for everything."

The long procession of holy men came winding down towards the sandbars of the rivers. Sarah and Laxmi watched from the spot Uma Mata had suggested, and Nathu Ram stood close behind them. Devotees by the thousands crowded on each side to show reverence to the *sadhus* who led ascetic lives in the Himalayas and only came down once every twelve years to attend the *Kumbh mela*. They wore saffron-coloured clothes and had flowing beards and long hair knotted on top of their heads.

The *sadhus* who worshiped Lord Shiva walked with live snakes draped around their necks and iron tridents held in their hands. Followers of Lord Rama had their entire bodies covered with tatoos of the word *Ram*. Other *sadhus* exhibited a variety of penances aimed at purifying their minds and bodies. Some had metal spikes driven through their skin. Others had taken vows of silence and had long iron nails driven through their protruded tongues.

A *sadhu* sitting cross-legged on a cart had his right hand raised high above his head and it was reputed that he had held his hand in that position for years. His fingernails had grown long and had curled around several times. Other *sadhus* had remained in contorted positions for years, resulting in their bodies becoming grotesquely deformed. Each group of holy men was greeted with chants of prayers for the particular God they worshiped. A group of *sadhus* came by who had renounced every comfort of life, even their clothes. They walked together chanting prayers, unmindful of their nakedness and of the curious watching them.

As the procession ended, Sarah and Laxmi were swept along by the crowd which followed the holy men onto the sandbars. Nathu Ram was separated from them. The *sadhus* waded into the waters and chanted *mantras*. They ducked their heads under the water three times and raised their hands in prayer, then proceeded to the tents on the sandbars where they were offered food and gifts. After the holy men had eaten, the devotees and the pilgrims were fed. They all sat on the ground in long rows, and ate the meal served to them on large dried leaves. There was no distinction here by caste or social status. Paupers and beggars ate with the wealthy and the powerful, just as they had bathed side by side in the holy rivers.

Later in the day Sarah and Laxmi had also eaten sitting under the tents with other women pilgrims. They returned to the temple early in the evening. The image of Uma Mata had stayed in Sarah's mind all day. Before nightfall, she went to see the temple priest.

"Thank you for allowing us to stay here," she said, bowing her head. "I am most grateful."

"Everyone is welcome in the temple of Lord Krishna," the priest answered, applying a red *tikka* to Sarah's forehead, "May God grant you health, happiness and tranquility."

"Thank you," Sarah answered, bowing again and turned to leave, but then stopped. "May I ask you something?" she said.

"Yes, of course," the priest answered.

"Could you tell me about Uma Mata? There seems to be something very special about her."

"Oh yes, she is the head of an order of priestesses from Badri Nath," the priest told Sarah. "It is said that she is of royal blood, the daughter of one of the Rajas of Rajputana."

"How did she end up becoming a priestess?" Sarah inquired.

"People say that at a very young age she was married to a maharajah who was considerably older than her. When the maharajah died, the tradition of the Rajput royal families required that his young widow also end her life by the tradition of *suttee*."

"My God, doesn't that mean she would have been burned alive on the pyre of her dead husband?" Sarah asked.

"Yes, that is what the time honoured custom of *suttee* was," the priest explained. "The widow was made to put on her wedding clothes and sat on the piles of wood covering the body of her husband. But in her case, it was said that at the last moment, before the cremation could commence, her brothers rescued her and whisked her away."

"Where did they take her?"

"They took her to the Himalayas and left her at an *ashram* near Badri Nath," the priest answered.

The next morning when Sarah arrived at the train station, the Station Master was waiting to greet her. "Your compartment is ready, Madam," he beamed. "Everything is in order. I've instructed the train guard to keep an extra sharp eye on your compartment throughout the journey."

The train left and sped northwards. Laxmi again sat next to a window and began singing. Sarah lay down on her berth, deep in thought. She was glad that she had come to the *Kumbh mela*. Her mind was at peace and she felt a serenity she had not experienced before. Yet there were questions.

What about Cedric and their marriage? Uma Mata had said, "your loved one will not accept what you are doing." But she was going to do all she could to improve their relationship and make it work.

What about Uma Mata? How did she know so much about me, Sarah wondered. She was so kind and gentle: there was something almost divine about the old woman. Would she ever see Uma Mata again? Would Saraswati ever go to Badri Nath? Sarah wasn't sure, but deep in her heart she hoped and prayed she would.

The Wrath of Kali

The young girl's body was burning with fever and covered with an angry reddish rash. Sarah looked at the thermometer. It read 104.6° Fahrenheit. That was much too high. The girl's glazed eyes stared vacantly, and she was breathing with great difficulty. She kept mumbling, speaking very rapidly. This was the third patient Sarah had examined this afternoon in the Rajpur clinic with somewhat similar symptoms.

One of the other two stricken was the girl's father, a frail man in his forties, who, in addition, complained of a severe headache and violent pains in his back and limbs. His eyes were blood red, tongue inflamed, and his temperature was even higher than that of his daughter. Sarah had given each of the patients pain relievers and instructions to use cold compresses on their foreheads and bodies. She asked that they be brought back to see her the next day.

What could be afflicting them, producing such severe symptoms? She frantically searched her mind for an answer. Suddenly her thoughts went back to the previous week when she had come to Rajpur soon after returning from the *Kumbh mela*. Walking towards the middle of the village, her eyes had caught sight of a dead rat lying in the gutter by the side of the path. Then, closer to the clinic, she had seen a large black rat emerge from a drain hole at the side of a hut. Instead of scurrying away, it had slowly limped along the wall and disappeared into some brush behind the hut.

Now, walking back towards the *tonga*, a dreadful thought kept coming to her mind. No, it couldn't be, she tried to reassure herself: the villagers must be suffering from something else. She must get home and go through her medical books to find out what else could have infected these three patients.

Cedric wanted to go to the club for dinner, but Sarah made an excuse. "I have a terrible headache, darling," she said. "Why don't you go ahead. I'd like to go to bed early, anyway."

After a quick bath and a light supper, she sat down in the drawing room with her medical books and pored through them, trying to match the symptoms exhibited by the patients at the Rajpur clinic. She scanned through the one issue of the British Medical Journal that she had received since arriving in India, and stopped abruptly. There it was, a report of a bubonic plague epidemic that had broken out in Canton and Hong Kong. With a sinking feeling she realized that her patients in Rajpur were suffering from somewhat similar symptoms to those described in this report. My God, what's going to happen if it is bubonic plague.

She had trouble sleeping that night, and early the next morning instructed Nathu Ram to fetch a city *tonga*. "I must go to the Rajpur Clinic," she added.

"But you were there yesterday, *mem sahib*," Nathu Ram answered. "Today is not the day for you to go."

"I need to check on some of the patients I saw yesterday, Nathu Ram," she said, a slight edge to her voice. "Hurry. Get the *tonga* right away."

Riding to Rajpur, she kept mulling in her mind the report she had read last night in the British Medical Journal. Japanese and French doctors working with the victims in Canton and Hong Kong were able to isolate a bacteria they called Pasteurella Pestis which they claimed was responsible for infecting people with plague. They suspected that the bacteria were transmitted by rats' fleas. The doctors were reportedly working on developing a serum.

The medical books Sarah read contained detailed accounts of the plague that had swept through Europe during the fourteenth century. An astounding twenty-five million had died by what had come to be known as the Black Death. There was no cure, and superstitious beliefs of the frightened populations determined their actions. One medical book stated that many believed plague to be a form of divine action, a punishment from God, hence the name *Plaga,* the Latin word meaning a blow administered by divine powers. This belief made the flagellant movement in Germany gain increased popularity during the height of the epidemic. Members of the movement, in hooded white robes with large red crosses sewn to the front and back, reportedly went around beating themselves on their shoulders and backs with metal-spiked leather straps. In 1349 the Pope had banned the practice of self-punishment, and the flagellants started blaming Jews for poisoning their drinking water and causing plague to spread. Thousands of Jews were killed in Strassburg, Basel, Cologne and Meinz.

"Stop here," Sarah instructed the *tonga* driver as they approached Rajpur.

"We'll go further, closer to the village, *mem sahib,*" Nathu Ram said, looking over his shoulder.

"No, no. Stop here, I'll walk the rest of the way."

Laxmi started getting out of the tonga. "No, wait here for me, Laxmi," Sarah spoke firmly, taking her medical bag and heading quickly towards the village.

"Why won't *mem sahib* let me go with her into the clinic today?" Laxmi asked Nathu Ram.

"I don't know," the houseboy answered, shrugging his shoulders. "I don't know why."

Sarah was walking towards the village, deep in thought, when she almost stepped upon a large dead black rat lying in the middle of the path. Then she saw another in the gutter on the side and several more not far from where some village children were playing. Oh dear God, she moaned and hurried into the clinic. Several villagers were waiting, some sitting on the benches along the wall while others squatted on the floor. The man she had examined the day before was lying on a *charpai* which had been carried into the clinic.

"*Mem sahib*, my husband is very ill. Please help him," the woman with him pleaded. Sarah began examining the man. His body was burning with fever, his pulse racing and his breathing very fast, coming in short gasps. "He has been delirious all night and vomited several times," the woman sobbed.

Sarah lifted the man's shirt, pushing it up above his shoulders and lowered his *dhoti*. Her heart sank. There it was, a deep blue, almost black swelling about the size of an egg, bulging from his groin—a definitive sign of bubonic plague. Physicians in the fourteenth century had named these swellings of the glands *buboes,* from the Greek word *boubon*, meaning the groin.

"Have you seen any rats inside your house?" Sarah asked, covering the man's body with his clothing, knowing well that the huts in the village had to be crawling with them.

"Yes, there are some, not too many, though," the woman answered. "Three days ago my husband saw a dead one lying in the middle of our hut."

"What did he do with it?" Sarah quietly asked.

"He picked it up and threw it outside into the fields."

Sarah realized that the entire village could soon be ravaged by bubonic plague, and it may even spread to Jhelum. She had to act swiftly and raise the alarm, but who should she go to? Besides, there were these other sick people waiting to be seen, most suffering from similar symptoms. Their ailments began with fits of shivering and their bodies ached painfully. They felt dizzy, some had vomited and others became delirious. The girl Sarah had seen the previous day had developed a bubo in her axilla. Sarah gently swabbed the swelling with tincture of iodine and the girl screamed with pain. Sarah had no answers for the poor villagers. She gave them pills to relieve the excruciating pain they were suffering and asked that they be returned to their homes. She came out of the clinic and walked in a daze towards the *tonga*. Nathu Ram took the medical bag from her hand.

"We will return home now, *mem sahib*?" he asked.

"What? What did you say? Oh, no, let's see," she said. "Take me to the free dispensary in the city."

As the *tonga* drove away, she looked back at Rajpur. In the glow of the early March sun, the little village, surrounded by lush green wheat fields, looked peaceful. She shuddered, thinking about what must be going on in the rat burrows below the huts.

The *tonga* stopped in front of the dispensary and Sarah went running in.

"Oh my God, it's going to happen here," Dev Suri exclaimed, shaking his head. "I just read about the epidemic in Hong Kong and had wondered if this horror would also strike India."

"Immediate action has to be taken, Dev," Sarah pleaded. "I came to you first. We have to inform the authorities. Who should we go to?"

"We should alert the Civil Surgeon of the General Hospital and also the Jhelum City Administrator in the Commissioner's Office," Suri responded. "There will be other branches of the government that I am sure will become involved."

"Will you accompany me, Dev?" Sarah inquired.

"Yes, of course, I will come with you," he said, getting up.

They went in the *tonga* to the General Hospital. The peon sitting outside the office of the Civil Surgeon informed them that the *Doctor Sahib* had gone to the cantonment to attend an important meeting at the Military Hospital and would not return until the next day.

"Come, Sarah, we must go to the City Administrator's office," Dev Suri said urgently. "It's in the cantonment."

The *tonga* left the General Hospital and started moving slowly along the road towards the cantonment. "Dear God, can't he go faster?" Sarah complained. "*Jaldi challo*," Dev Suri called out, and the driver swung his whip and got the horse moving at a fast pace. Laxmi and Nathu Ram didn't know what was going on, but sensed there was something terribly wrong.

Sarah and Dev Suri were kept waiting outside for a full twenty minutes before being ushered into the office. The City Administrator, Christopher White, sat behind a massive ornate wooden desk. He was a tall lanky Englishman with pale skin and thinning light brown hair. "What can I do for you?" he asked gruffly. "I'm very busy. State your business quickly."

"My name is Doctor Dev Suri, sir, and this is Doctor Sarah Smythe." Suri spoke politely, "I am afraid we have some very bad news. There is a threat of a serious epidemic breaking out in one of the adjacent villages."

"Well then, go and see my Civil Surgeon at the General Hospital," the Administrator answered, waving his hand. "Don't take up *my* time."

"We tried to, sir," Suri answered, "but the Civil Surgeon is at a meeting and will not return until some time tomorrow."

"Can't this blasted problem wait till then?" the Administrator said, raising his voice.

"Mr. White, I believe that several villagers in Rajpur have come down with bubonic plague," Sarah spoke up. "Immediate steps have to be taken to isolate those afflicted and stringent preventive measures have to be implemented at once."

"What are you talking about?" the Administrator said, glaring at Sarah. "Are you a medical doctor?"

"Yes, Mister White, I'm a physician with special training in tropical diseases."

The Administrator calmed down a little. "I thought plague had been exterminated during medieval times," he said.

"Not really," Sarah answered. "Almost half the population of Europe was wiped out by plague in the fourteenth century, and as recently as last year, Hong Kong and Canton were devastated by an epidemic." Leaning forward, she placed her hands on the desk. "It may already be too late, Mr. White. We may be facing a full-blown catastrophe here in Jhelum with thousands upon thousands of lives in danger."

Christopher White stood up. "All right, I'll call an emergency meeting of the City Council for four o'clock this afternoon. I'll send for the Civil Surgeon. I guess the military authorities should also be informed. They like to get their bloody noses into everything that goes on around here." Then, offering his hand to Sarah, he continued, "I want both of you to come back at four and brief the City Council."

The meeting was held in a chamber adjacent to the Administrator's office. A large map of Punjab and another map of Jhelum district hung on one of the walls. Members of the council sat around a long table, with Christopher White occupying a high-backed chair at one end. A framed portrait of Queen Victoria looked down sternly from the wall behind the Administrator. The City Council consisted of representatives from the various branches of the Government, including the police department, civil administration, the health board, the judiciary and the railways. These men were all British. Additionally, there were two Indians on the Council; one, a prominent Punjabi barrister of Jhelum, and the other, a Muslim *Nawab* who owned extensive farmlands and several villages on the outskirts of the city. Seated in chairs along the wall were lesser officials from some of the government branches, as well as Sarah and Dev Suri.

Sarah did not recognize any of the people in the room except Major Alan Duckworth who was there representing the military and sat with the Council members at the table. At exactly four o'clock, the City Administrator cleared his throat.

"Gentlemen, give me your attention," he said, standing up. The hum of conversation around the table quickly died down and everyone turned towards the Administrator. "I was visited by two doctors earlier this afternoon and told that there are several people in the village of Rajpur who seem to be suffering from bubonic plague."

"Did you say the plague?" someone uttered at the table. "Christ, that can't be true." Several men started speaking at the same time.

Christopher White raised his hands. "Yes, you heard me right, gentlemen. The two doctors who came to see me think it's plague, and if they're correct, we may indeed be facing a rather major crisis, especially if the disease reaches the city."

A buzz of conversation spread through the room and a short-statured portly man jumped to his feet. "This is most preposterous," he complained in a loud voice. "Why wasn't I informed first? Why didn't these men come to me?"

"Quiet, every one," Christopher White ordered. "They went to see you, Jeremy, but you weren't at the Hospital."

"Who are these chaps anyway?" Doctor Jeremy Slack, the Civil Surgeon of the General Hospital inquired. "I'd like to know if they are qualified to make a diagnosis of plague."

"Well, the doctors are here with us. Let me ask them to tell you what they found. Doctor Symthe, would you be so kind as to address the Council? Here, come to the head of the table."

Sarah adjusted the end of her *sari* to cover her head and came forward to stand next to the Administrator.

"Goodness me, you're a woman," the Civil Surgeon blurted out. "Are you an Anglo-Indian? Are you a qualified doctor?"

"Yes, I am a woman and a trained physician," Sarah answered back. "My medical degree is from the London School of Medicine for Women."

"Do you know what plague looks like? Have you seen any patients suffering from it before?" the Civil Surgeon persisted.

"No, I haven't Doctor Slack. But I was most concerned yesterday when I examined three patients with rather peculiar symptoms, and remembered seeing a dead rat in the village. Then, today, there were several more dead rats, and I found that two of the patients had de-veloped painful buboes in their axilla and groin. I have no doubt in my mind that it is bubonic plague."

"Do we need to be so alarmed about a few dead rats and a couple of sick natives?" Major Duckworth asked.

"Yes, we need to be very concerned, Major," Sarah answered, turn-ing towards him. "If the disease spreads, it could wipe out half the city in a matter of days, just as it did in Hong Kong and Canton last year."

"How in hell does this disease spread?" one of the Council members inquired. "Isn't there a cure for it?"

"Doctors have theorized that the plague bacteria is carried by rat fleas," Sarah answered. "When an infected rat dies, the fleas attack other rats and any humans nearby. Physicians working with the victims in Hong Kong have, since, been trying to develop a serum, but haven't succeeded as yet. No, there isn't any cure for bubonic plague. All one can do is to try and prevent its spread, and pray."

The Civil Surgeon was about to say something when Christopher White raised his hand. "Gentlemen, there isn't a moment to waste. I'm forming a crisis team. Jeremy, I want you to head it, and report to me daily. You, Doctor Symthe and also Doctor Suri, I am asking you to serve with the team, and I want representatives from the police and the military on it. Gentlemen, get going. Go out to the village immediately and do whatever you have to, but we must prevent this from turning into a full blown epidemic."

A short while later, a small procession of *tongas* and horse-drawn carriages drove through Jhelum City towards Rajpur and came to a stop at the outskirts of the village. Even before getting out of the carriages, they heard sounds of wailing and crying coming from the village.

"The cursed black death has claimed its first victims in India," Dev Suri said softly with a deep sigh. Sarah looked at him with troubled eyes.

Dr. Jeremy Slack led the group towards the village. There were no children playing outside the huts, neither did the village dogs bark to announce the arrival of strangers. "Who is the head man?" Dr. Slack called out loudly in Hindustani. "Come out here. Hurry up."

An old man shuffled out of one of the huts and came running towards the group. He brought the palms of his hands together in front of his face and bowed. "*Hazoor*, I am Bhola Ram, the head man."

"What has happened? Why are your people crying?" the Civil Surgeon asked.

"*Hazoor*, the goddess *Kali* has wrought her anger upon Rajpur. Half the village has fallen prey to a most mysterious illness and seven people have already died."

"Bring one of the sick out here," Doctor Slack ordered. "Do it right away."

The head man turned and hurried back to a group of villagers who had now assembled and stood huddled together. Within moments, a *charpai* was carried out from one of the huts and brought to where the *sahibs* were standing. Lying on the *charpai* was the frail figure of an old man covered with a blanket.

"Remove the man's blanket," the Civil Surgeon ordered.

Before the head man could move, Sarah bent down and gently lifted the blanket. She then slowly peeled the man's shirt away to reveal his body covered with reddish spots and a large deep blue swelling in his groin. The old man's bloodshot eyes were staring at the people around him and he started babbling deliriously.

"Dear Lord, you're right," the Civil Surgeon groaned, taking a step backwards, his face turning pale. "Take him away," he ordered. "Assemble all the able bodied men. I must talk to them."

The men came out of the huts slowly and stood in a tight group in front of the *sahibs*. "I am going to give you some orders which you must all obey implicitly," Jeremy Slack spoke, raising his voice. "Your village has been afflicted with the plague and we must take stringent measures to prevent its spread to other villages and to the city."

The villagers looked at each other, and back to the *sahib*.

"No one is allowed to leave the village without specific permission from the police, who will be posted on all sides. Anyone who is sick will be taken to the hospital and cared for there. Those who die must be cremated immediately. If you see any rats inside your huts or around them, you must kill them at once. Do not, under any circumstances, touch the rats. Use a shovel to lift them and bury them away from the village. Starting tomorrow morning, workers will start putting poison in rat burrows and sealing them. Additionally, the outsides of your huts will be painted with quick lime. Anyone who interferes with the work of the labourers will be severely punished."

"Why must we kill the harmless rats, *hazoor*?" the head man asked softly. "They are God's innocent creatures and do us no harm. We are building a shrine for Kali Mata and will pray for her forgiveness."

"Your goddess has nothing to do with it," the Civil Surgeon scoffed. "The plague is being spread by rats and if they are not eradicated, everyone in your village will die, and the disease will spread to the city. Each one of you will receive a five *paisa* reward for every rat you kill. That is all. You may go now. I will be back tomorrow to see that you've carried out my orders."

Jeremy Slack and his crisis team returned to the City Administrator's office and assembled in the conference chamber. The Civil Surgeon outlined his plan to isolate Rajpur. A decision was made not to move the sick villagers to the city's General Hospital. Instead, the military was asked to pitch tents near the village where a makeshift hospital would be established. Orders were given for a work force of native labourers to arrange for the immediate disposal of the dead, and to paint all of the huts with quick lime. The narrow lanes were to be swept clean and carbolic acid sprinkled along the sides. Employees of the Public Works Department would be directed to drop poison in the rat burrows and to seal them. Adequate numbers of police constables were to be assigned to the village to ensure that all of the orders were carried out faithfully.

It was late in the evening when Sarah returned home. Cedric had already left for the club, leaving word that he would send back the carriage and that she should join him. Sarah was in no mood to socialize but decided to go for her husband's sake. She bathed and changed and rode to the club in the carriage.

Cedric and his friends had just sat down for dinner and were conversing in quiet tones. Cedric saw Sarah enter the dining room and left the table to meet her. "Are you all right?" he asked, putting his arms around her shoulders.

"Yes, I'm fine," she answered. "I could use a sherry, though."

"Come, let me get you one," he said, drawing her close.

"Good evening, Sarah," Ian Campbell said, taking her hands in his. "I understand you were the one who alerted the authorities."

"Well, I was baffled by the symptoms three of the patients in Rajpur were suffering from," Sarah answered. "When I got home last night I read my medical books and realized what they had."

"Dear God, do you think isolating the village and killing rats will prevent the disease from spreading?" Adele Duckworth inquired.

Sarah was about to answer when David Habersham cut her off. "I'd say, spare the damn rats and let the bloody niggers die from their own filthy disease," he blurted out.

"That's a horrible thing to say, Captain," Sarah spoke angrily. "Those poor villagers did not invent plague. The disease was rampant in Europe during the fourteenth century. London suffered through catastrophic epidemics in 1548 and again in 1665 when hundreds of thousands died. In fact, even as far back as 430 B.C., plague was killing millions and brought down the mighty Athenian Empire."

"Well, let's hope it doesn't summon the end of the British Raj here in India," Major Duckworth sighed. "We should be able to contain it and not let it spread. I was most impressed by the swift actions taken by Jeremy Slack."

"How does plague spread?" Ian Campbell asked. "Isn't there a cure for it?"

"It's a very tiny bacteria carried by rat fleas," Sarah answered. "When a rat gets plague and dies, the fleas invade other rats and humans they come in contact with. No, unfortunately there isn't a cure, Ian."

"Oh, how awful," Adele Duckworth moaned. "I do remember reading about the plague that swept through England," she continued. "I thought I also read that people began killing cats and dogs, fearing that they were responsible for spreading the disease."

"Yes, that's true, but that only allowed rats to run about unhindered and spread the disease faster." Sarah added, "Last night I also read an interesting theory on the origin of the nursery rhyme "ring-a-ring o' roses,"

"Tell us about it," Adele Duckworth encouraged.

"Well, some believed that holding fragrant flowers and herbs in front of their face would prevent the foul air from infecting them with plague. The ring 'o roses was supposedly a reference to the rash that appeared on the bodies of the victims, and the pocket full of posies were the flowers and herbs everyone carried with them. A'tishoo is the sneezing which resulted from the disease, and the last line of the rhyme, "we all fall down," is said to mean that everyone afflicted by the disease died."

"Oh how terrible," one of the other women at the dinner table cried. "And I always thought it was such a quaint rhyme. I shan't let my children sing it anymore."

Sarah was relieved when dinner was over and Cedric and she excused themselves. She was exhausted and emotionally drained. She needed to lie down for a few hours. She knew the next few days, if not weeks, were going to be extremely hectic, and she was going to do all she could to help.

Cedric sat in the carriage with his arm around his wife, and they rode in silence. They had slept together in the large bedroom ever since her return from the *Kumbh mela*. She had come back deeply tanned and he had felt strangely drawn to her, seeing her with her dark complexion and the red *tikka* on her forehead.

"Aren't you afraid of catching the disease," he asked. "What if you get plague?"

"There's no danger, Cedric," Sarah answered, turning toward him. "All the books I've read say that doctors and nurses caring for the victims seldom get infected. I would have to come in direct contact with the secretions from the glands of a patient, and then, too, there'd have to be a break in my skin. That's very unlikely."

"I wish you'd leave and go off to Simla for a few days," he spoke after a while.

"What would I do there, Cedric? I'm needed here."

"It's going to get beastly hot here in another month or so. All the British wives and children go up to the mountains for the summer. I can arrange for a bungalow for you there."

"No, Cedric, I'm not going anywhere," Sarah said, sitting up. "I'm staying right here in Jhelum."

"Working among the God damned lepers is bad enough, Sarah, but this plague epidemic is the final straw," Cedric spoke angrily, pulling his arm away. "I want you to go away to the mountains right away."

"Cedric, thousands of lives are at stake and I can't be bothered about my comfort," she answered firmly. "No, I will not leave."

They had reached home and Cedric stormed in ahead of her. "Why the hell do you have to be so blasted stubborn about everything I ask?" he yelled, slamming the door of the smaller bedroom behind him.

Sarah left for Rajpur early the next morning. The servants had been told what was happening in the village, and Laxmi breathed a sigh of relief to learn that she needn't accompany Sarah. Nathu Ram was, however, insistent. "*Mem Sahib* must not ride *tonga* in city alone. I must go with you."

Nearing Rajpur, Sarah was surprised to see that several large tents had already been erected in a clearing next to the village. Jeremy Slack and Dev Suri were there, as were a large number of medical orderlies and nurses. The tents were completely filled with patients. "I'm sorry, Doctor Slack," Sarah apologized, "I should have been here earlier."

"That's all right, Doctor Symthe," the Civil Surgeon answered, wiping his brow. "Another dozen or so villagers died overnight. I've ordered more tents. It's going to be a bloody mess and I'll need every doctor that I can find. Glad to have you here."

The village was abuzz with activity. Scores of labourers were busy: some were applying a watery paste of quick lime to the mud huts, while others went around with buckets of poison, looking for openings to rat burrows. Two young British police officers sat on chairs under a canvas awning that had been strung adjacent to the narrow path leading to Rajpur. Several Indian constables stood behind the officers while others patrolled around the village and made certain that no one left Rajpur. A group of villagers stood together forlornly, watching the activities around them.

Sarah worked all day examining patients and making them comfortable. Tincture of iodine was applied to the buboes as long as they retained their hardness. Once the swellings became soft, they were slit open with sharp scalpels and drained. Laxatives were given to the victims to clean their systems of toxic materials. Hypodermic injections of ether were given to prevent the patients' hearts from failing. They were also forced to drink large quantities of milk to improve their nutrition.

Around one o'clock in the afternoon, food and hot tea was brought and served to the doctors and nurses. Sarah and Dev Suri walked with some of the others to a mango tree close by and sat down under its shade. "Where could the bacteria that infected the rats in Rajpur have come from?" Sarah asked.

"I don't know. It's impossible to tell," Dev Suri answered. "They may have remained dormant in a flea here for a long time, or perhaps the plague was brought by an infected person coming from one of the port cities. Let's hope it doesn't spread to the city," Dev Suri said, looking towards Jhelum. "It'll be a catastrophe if it does."

They, of course, were unaware that throughout the night, hundreds of sick and dying rats had come out of their burrows in and around Rajpur and had crawled through the fields, many towards Jhelum.

Sarah toiled with the rest of the medical personnel in the tents for the next three days. Strangely enough, the village itself had never appeared this clean before. The narrow lanes had been swept and smelt of carbolic acid. The mud huts glistened with the quick lime that had been splashed onto them. Poison had been dropped into all rat burrows and the openings sealed tight. The clothing worn by victims who succumbed to the disease were burned. The medical staff attending the patients were required to wash their hands and arms with soap and water four or five times a day. Each evening, upon returning home, Sarah took a bath, cleansing herself with soap and buckets of water, and then boiled the clothes she had worn during the day.

On Sunday, Sarah did not attend church, nor did she go to Hari Nivas, but instead, spent the day in Rajpur. Then it happened: a dead rat was found in a gutter in Jhelum. By day's end, rats by the scores were crawling out onto the streets and dying. The news spread quickly through the city and the people panicked. Those who could flee packed and left by whatever means they could. The City Council met in an emergency session.

"Why weren't you able to prevent the spread of plague to the city," a Council member demanded angrily of the Civil Surgeon. "Didn't you cordon off Rajpur?"

Jeremy Slack's face turned red. "Everything humanly possible was done. The village still remains isolated, completely sealed off," he answered back. "For all we know, the bacteria may have been transmitted from Jhelum to Rajpur."

"Oh, that sounds absurd," another Council member spoke curtly.

"Gentlemen, please," Christopher White raised his hands, "this isn't the time for pointing fingers. Jeremy," he turned to the Civil Surgeon, "what can you people do now to minimize the spread of the disease in the city?"

"We can implement the same measures we did in Rajpur, Christopher," Jeremy Slack answered, spreading his hands. "and then hope for the best."

"What about the cantonment?" another member of the Council asked. "Can these damn rats swim across the river?"

"Well, the river is a barrier," the Civil Surgeon answered, "but we'll have to control the movement of people between the city and the cantonment."

"Do we need to seek help from Delhi?" Christopher White asked.

"Other than informing them of the potential of an epidemic, we don't need them to come meddling," the Civil Surgeon answered. "Between my hospital here and the Military Hospital, we should be able to provide all the medical personnel we need. If necessary, we can get more from Lahore."

"All right, Jeremy," Christopher White said, standing up, "get going. Now you have a bigger task on your hands."

Sarah had not been to Hari Nivas in two weeks and felt guilt ridden over having neglected the lepers. On Sunday, she decided that she must see how they were faring and went to their village. To her surprise, none of the lepers showed any signs of plague. She had just finished attending to some sores on the leg of one of the women when Devi Lal came running.

"I'm glad you are here, Madame Sarah," he said, catching his breath. "I didn't want to leave without seeing you."

"Oh, it's nice to see you, Devi Lal," Sarah answered, placing an arm around his shoulders. "Are you going back to your village?"

"Yes, Madam Sarah. Our school has been closed and all the students are being sent home," he answered. Then, looking at the lepers, he asked, "Are they all right? The plague has not harmed them?"

"No, they're fine," Sarah answered. "It's as if God decided they have been afflicted enough."

"I'll pray for them and for you, too. Goodbye, Madam Sarah," he said shyly.

"Goodbye, my friend," she answered, hugging him. "God bless you."

An army of labourers was engaged from neighbouring villages and brought into the city. They swept the streets and sprinkled carbolic acid in the gutters. The outside walls of all the homes were bathed with quicklime. Pamphlets were printed and distributed throughout the city instructing residents on the precautions they must take to protect themselves.

But the measures implemented by the Civil Surgeon and his crisis team appeared to be futile, nor did the prayers of the people help. By week's end, the General Hospital was overflowing with victims of the plague and hundreds had perished. The bridge across the river was sealed off by the military and no one other than those on official business allowed to cross.

Most British families had fled the Cantonment and gone to Simla. Cedric had given up trying to persuade Sarah to leave. Their servants were not allowed to come into the Cantonment. Sarah prepared simple meals for herself, while Cedric ate mostly in the officers' mess.

Dev Suri and Sarah were now working all day long and late into the evenings in the General Hospital. Tents had been pitched on the grounds by the military to accommodate the overflow of patients. Large numbers of medical personnel had been brought in from Lahore and Rawalpindi and they all worked day and night under extremely difficult conditions. Jeremy Slack's attitude towards Sarah and Dev Suri was now most cordial and he relied upon them heavily. Weeks turned into a month, and then another, but the plague continued unabated. Over three thousand victims had already died, and those who remained in the city lived in constant fear.

An additional work force of labourers had to be hired from among the untouchable class to deal with the difficult task of disposing the bodies of the dead. Mass cremations were held for Hindus, and common graves were used to bury Muslims. No laughter nor music could be heard anywhere in the city and grim faced people went about their work, wondering if they or a loved one would be the next to be struck.

It was late in the evening and Sarah had just finished lancing a swollen gland in the groin of a young girl in the hospital ward. She came out to the table in the hallway to wash her hands with soap and water. She had been on her feet since early morning and felt exhausted. It was getting dark and she was looking forward to returning home to bathe and change her clothes. Then she noticed Dev Suri sitting on a bench against the wall. Sarah had come to greatly admire the dedication of this Indian doctor who was now not only a professional colleague but her dear friend.

He should be going home and resting, she thought, and walked towards him. Suri sat hunched over, with his head in his hands and Sarah noticed that he was shivering. "What's the matter, Dev?" she asked. "Are you all right?

Dev Suri stood up. "I'm fine, just a little tired," he answered, and would have fallen had it not been for Sarah grabbing him.

"My God, you're burning with fever," she wailed, and lowered him back onto the bench. She hailed a passing medical orderly and they helped Suri to a hospital bed. He was breathing with difficulty and shivering uncontrollably. Sarah covered him with a blanket.

"I've got it, Sarah," he said softly, his teeth chattering. "My head and back ache terribly."

Sarah sent for Jeremy Slack and the two of them examined their colleague. By now Dev Suri was delirious and vomited. Sarah nursed him, applying a cold compress to his forehead. His pulse was racing and his fever very high. An ugly dark blue swelling appeared at the base of his neck and his body was covered with a red rash.

Sarah was near collapse but stayed with him all night, cleaning his vomit, applying tincture of iodine on the bubo in his neck and trying to force some milk down his throat. Jeremy Slack gave him an hypodermic injection of ether.

Towards dawn, Sarah dozed off sitting in a chair next to Dev Suri's hospital bed. She woke up with a start and stood up. The sun was just rising and she went quickly to see what else she could do to make her friend a little more comfortable. But Dev Suri had died sometime early that morning. Sarah didn't know how long she stood weeping by his bed. Jeremy Slack was summoned and gently led her out of the room.

Over the next two weeks the death toll rose sharply. Cedric had to go out of town with his battalion on maneuvers and Sarah felt desperately lonely. She slaved all day at the hospital and even though exhausted, had difficulty sleeping nights.

Then one morning the weather began changing. Ominous churning dark clouds started billowing in and blanketed the skies. The air felt intensely hot and suffocating. The roar of thunder reverberated down to earth and bright bolts of lightning streaked through the clouds and across the horizon.

By the time Sarah reached home that evening, huge drops of water had started noisily splattering the earth. Then suddenly the skies opened up and the rain began falling in torrents. Sarah ran to the lawn in front of her house and sank to her knees. Heavy warm raindrops stung her body and up-turned face like needles. She lingered, arms raised heavenward, letting the rain cleanse her body and mind.

The monsoons had arrived and the parched soil of India was awash, inundated with life-sustaining nourishment. The plague that had claimed over eleven thousand lives began suddenly and inexplicably to subside. Sarah felt numbed. Was it the rain that drowned the rats and stopped more humans from dying? She didn't know but prayed that the epidemic was truly over. The British authorities sighed with relief and returned to ruling India. The Black Death had been dealt with, contained within the city and not allowed to spread. They were pleased: it could have been worse.

The people of Jhelum who had left, started quietly returning to their homes, grim-faced and unsure. They hoped that the Goddess Kali had heeded their prayers and shown mercy. Time passed slowly and there were no more deaths. The people embraced and reassured each other. It was now all right they said. The wrath of *Kali* was over.

Loyalties and Conflicts

$\mathcal{N}$ews about the plague epidemic in Jhelum had spread rapidly through-out Punjab, carried by terrified residents who had fled the city in panic. Accounts of the sufferings of those infected as well as the exaggerated numbers that were said to be dying each day brought terror into the hearts of the people. Temples and mosques were filled with worshipers, all praying to be spared from the dreaded disease.

Kanti, worried sick about her son, was ecstatic when he unexpectedly returned home. She hugged him, laughing and crying at the same time. Her husband was away in Peshawar attending a political meeting and when the other children returned from school, she took all of them to the temple to offer prayers.

"I don't think you should go back to Jhelum, my son," she said later, coming out of the temple. "There are all sorts of problems in big cities. Perhaps you should transfer to the school in Chakwal. I'll speak to your father when he returns."

"No, mother, please don't," the boy pleaded. "My school is very good and I don't want to leave it."

"Well, we'll see what happens with this plague," Kanti persisted. "God only knows how long it will go on."

The other children had run ahead of them. Devi Lal stopped and turned to his mother. "I've become friends with an English doctor lady in Jhelum, Mother," he said softly.

"Oh, is that so?" Kanti answered, turning sharply towards her son. "And where did you meet this lady?" she asked.

"It was in Hari Niwas, the village of the lepers near my school, Mother," he answered, and then added, "her name is Madame Sarah."

"What's an English lady doing in Hari Niwas?" Kanti asked, placing her hands on her son's shoulders.

"She treats the illnesses of the lepers," he answered.

"Well, that's a most charitable act. She must be a very kind person." They started walking again.

"Yes, Mother, she is," Devi Lal said, kicking a pebble on the path in front of him. "She likes Indian people and says that the British should leave and give us our freedom. She wears a sari and, believe it or not, she even attended the *Kumbh Mela*."

"That *is* most astounding, Devi Lal. What else has this Madame Sarah told you?" Kanti asked, sensing her son had something on his mind which he wanted to speak to her about.

The boy hesitated, then looking away from his mother, said, "She thinks that I would make a good medical doctor."

"Oh, and how did the lady arrive at that conclusion?"

"She comes to Hari Niwas every Sunday afternoon and I've been helping her."

"What kind of help do you give her, my son?"

"She's learning to speak Hindi but isn't proficient at it. So I translate for her and I also help her by wrapping bandages after she has treated their wounds."

"Oh dear God. Do you actually touch the lepers, Devi Lal?"

"Yes, Mother, Madame Sarah told me leprosy isn't contagious. A person can only catch it by living among lepers for many many years."

"I hope this Madame Sarah is right, my son," Kanti said with a frown. "How does one become a medical doctor, anyway?"

"Madame Sarah said there must be medical schools in the big cities in India. She suggested I speak to my teachers at school."

Kanti remained silent for a moment and then spoke gently. "But you know what your father expects of you as his eldest son."

"Yes, I know, Mother," the boy answered with a sigh. "But would you please speak to him? Could you ask him if it's all right for me to become a doctor?"

They had reached the front door of their home. "All right, son, I'll do that," Kanti answered, "but I'll wait a few days. Right now your father is very busy. He's been made the head of Azad Hind for our district and has been attending meetings and organizing rallies. But I will mention it to him."

Hem Raj had journeyed to Peshawar and, accompanied by Jagat Singh, had gone to the village of Dera Gulab where a meeting had been called by Nazir Mohammed, Fakir of the Afridis and founder of Azad Hind. The British authorities, alarmed by the increased militant activities of the organization, had recently banned it, labeling it subversive and an enemy of the Crown.

The meeting lasted two days and Nazir Mohammed exhorted his followers to recruit more volunteers and train them in the use of firearms. "Harass the enemy," he urged them. "Raise more money to obtain the latest arms and ammunition. What we can't make or buy, we'll wrest from the enemy. I learnt that the people of a far-away land called America defeated the British and won their independence. If they could do it, so can we."

Hem Raj returned to Karyala excited, determined to make his district unit of Azad Hind the most effective in all of Punjab and the Northwest Frontier. He would organize his freedom fighters into a cohesive force, and they would attack police stations and military convoys. All of India would learn about the brave deeds of the men of Karyala. Upon reaching home, he was surprised to find Devi Lal there, as he had looked with disdain at those who had fled Jhelum. Yet he was pleased to see that his son was safe.

For the next several days, Hem Raj kept busy recruiting trusted volunteers from Karyala and nearby villages of the district. They met secretly and trained in the use of fire arms. They raised money to buy guns and plotted to acquire more.

"I've seen the constables in Chakwal carrying new British made breach loading rifles," Hem Raj told his followers. "The timing is perfect. The foreigners are pre-occupied with the plague in Jhelum and will not worry about a few rifles taken from one of their police stations." His followers agreed and they started planning and training in earnest for the raid.

Kanti finally found a suitable moment to speak to her husband about their eldest son's wishes. "It's so good to have Devi Lal home," she told him. "He's turning into a handsome young man, my husband. He's looking more and more like you."

"Yes, that he certainly is," Hem Raj agreed, smiling, but then continued, "though I can't understand why he spends so much time with his head buried in books." The thought occurred to him that he should take his son with him on the raid of the Chakwal police station, but there might be problems.

He turned to his wife. "Our daughters are also turning into beautiful young girls," he said, reaching out and caressing her face. "In fact it was only today I was thinking that Shanti has started looking so much like you did when we were married. How old is she now?"

"She's twelve," Kanti answered, "but she does look older. Children are maturing so much faster these days. She's going to be taller than me; she's already my height."

Yes, her daughter was certainly maturing fast, Kanti mused. Only last week she had noticed how Shanti's eyes had followed their neighbor's son, Ashok, who had come to play with her brother Mohan Lal.

"Should we start looking for a suitable match for her?" Hem Raj asked.

"No, no," Kanti laughed, "it's much too soon. We can wait." She hesitated for a moment and then continued, "By the way, Devi Lal talked to me a little about what he'd like to do after high school."

"What is it that he wants to do?" Hem Raj inquired. "His future is no secret. Everyone knows that when he grows up, he'll take my place as the head of the family and the chief of our village."

Kanti knew how strongly her husband felt about family traditions and wasn't going to like what she was about to tell him. "He wants to become a medical doctor," she answered softly.

"What?" Hem Raj asked. "Did you say a medical doctor?"

"It seems our son has met an English doctor lady whom he admires greatly," Kanti said, looking away from her husband. "She told him that he would make a very good doctor."

"An English woman?" Hem Raj blurted out. "Our son is getting advice from an English woman?"

"Well, this woman seems to be quite different," Kanti explained, and told him about her conversation with their son.

"That's absolute nonsense," Hem Raj exploded. his face turning red. "No son of mine is going to be a doctor. I'll talk to him tomorrow and put a stop to this rubbish. He's going to be sixteen soon. We should be thinking about getting him married. I'll send for the priest of the Mohyals."

"Why don't you let me talk to our son, my husband," Kanti said gently, placing her hands on his arm. "You already have so much on your mind. Let me do this. Let me speak to him."

"All right, Kanti, you do that. Tell him to stop seeing this English woman and to get these crazy notions out of his head. Tell him that's what I want him to do."

Hem Raj remained in a sullen mood all through the next day. He conducted a brief meeting of the village Council in the morning and later in the afternoon, met with twenty members of Azad Hind that he had selected to carry out the raid on the police station in Chakwal. All the men he had chosen were Hindus and Sikhs, with the exception of Aslam Khan, the chief of the Muslim village of Meerpur. The others, when told about Aslam Khan joining them, had objected. "We can't trust him," they complained. "He'll betray us."

"Nonsense," Hem Raj had scoffed. "He's an honorable man, a patriot just like the rest of us. My wife and his wife have for years been like sisters. We have to unite; Hindus, Muslims and Sikhs, or else we'll remain slaves for ever."

"I still think we shouldn't include a Muslim among us on this raid," Jai Prakash, a Hindu, persisted. Many of the policemen in Chakwal are Muslims and this Aslam Khan may not wish to attack them should there be trouble."

"No," Hem Raj spoke sternly. "My mind is made up. I've invited him and he goes with us. If you have a problem with my decision, Jai Prakash, you can stay back."

"Well, I'll go along," Jai Prakash answered sullenly. "But if things go wrong, remember I warned you."

They assembled on the dry river bed away from the village. Hem Raj squatted on the ground and leveling the sand in front of him, drew a rough sketch of Chakwal.

"We'll carry out the raid in the dark of night," he told the men. Pointing with his finger at the edge of the map he had drawn, he continued. "We'll leave our horses here in a grove of trees next to the entrance to this lane. Surjeet Singh, you and Harish Vaid must stay with the horses. The rest of us will divide into two groups. Aslam Khan, you are to lead one group and approach the town square from the west, past the temple, through this street. I'll lead the other group and we'll circle to the south and come up this street here."

"The entrance to the station is guarded day and night by two constables carrying rifles with bayonets," Aslam Khan spoke in a deep voice.

"Yes, and there'll be other constables along with a British officer or two inside," Hem Raj added. "We'll wait in the shadows until we hear one of the constables in front of the station strike the hour of one o'clock. Make sure that your face is covered with your turban tail, and move swiftly but silently. Aslam, I and my group will proceed first and overpower the two constables outside. You and your men must then rush inside."

"Are we to kill the constables?" one of the villagers asked.

"No, we needn't unless we absolutely have to. Once we overpower them, we'll tie their hands and legs with ropes we'll carry with us. We'll take the rifles and escape before an alarm is raised."

"What about the other constables? Aren't there supposed to be over a hundred of them?" another villager asked.

"They'll be asleep in the barracks behind the station," Hem Raj assured them. "If each of us carries out his responsibility efficiently, we'll be able to get away unnoticed. Do you have any more questions?" he asked.

After a moment, he continued. "We must leave Chakwal quietly and quickly. We'll get our horses and ride back to our villages. Each of us must conceal the rifles that we obtain and lay low in our homes. By the grace of God, we'll assemble here again exactly one week after the raid."

Although pleased with the planning for the raid, Hem Raj left the meeting with a frown on his face. The conversation with Kanti about their son had irritated him more than he thought. How could his son even dream of such strange things, and that, too, on the advice of one of their enemy. On his way home, he stopped at the village school to talk to the teacher and inquired about medical schools and the training of doctors. Later, after dinner, when he and Kanti were alone, he asked her if she had spoken to their son.

"No, my husband, I haven't done so as yet," she answered. "I thought I'd wait a few days."

"Well, don't. Tell him tomorrow morning that I'm forbidding him from seeing this foreign woman. Tell him he's to put all of these ideas about becoming a doctor out of his head. Do you know that as a medical student your son would have to touch and cut open dead bodies with knives and look at what's inside them? Do you know that, as a doctor, he would have to attend to women in labour and deliver their babies?"

"No, I didn't. Where did you hear that?"

"The village teacher told me when I went to see him today. Devi Lal must understand that he is a Mohyal, a Brahmin of the highest order. How can he even think about touching dead bodies and attending to women giving birth? He's Chhibber, a descendant of warriors. If he doesn't wish to take my place as the head of the family, he can join Jagat Singh in Peshawar and fight for the freedom for our country. But I definitely want him to forget this other nonsense."

A week went by and the father and son had not spoken to each other. Hem Raj rode into Chakwal to scout around the police station one last time. He learned that the plague epidemic in Jhelum was over and that schools had reopened. His son will be pleased to hear that, he thought, but decided not to tell him about it right away. This English woman who had been putting such sick ideas in his son's head had to be dealt with first and told to stay away from the boy.

He remembered Kanti telling him that Madame Sarah went to Hari Niwas each Sunday afternoon. The following Sunday, he changed into a fresh set of clothes and rode Kamaan to Jhelum. He found his way to the village of the lepers and waited nearby under the shade of a tree. Time passed, but there was no sign of the English woman. He started wondering if she would come, when, in the distance, he saw a *tonga* approaching. A man in a servant's uniform was seated in the front next to the driver and two women in Indian clothes sat in the back. The *tonga* came to a stop near the tree and one of the women got out. Hem Raj looked at her disinterestedly, but when she spoke, he noticed that her Hindustani was like that of foreigners. Even though the woman's skin had been burnt by the sun, her hair was of a strange light colour.

Hem Raj stepped to the middle of the path. "Are you Madame Sarah?" he asked.

The servant sitting in front of the *tonga* jumped out. "Get away from *mem sahib*," he yelled. "Don't bother her."

"It's all right, Nathu Ram," Sarah waved at him. "I'll be fine." Then turning, she said, "Yes, I'm Sarah Smythe. How do you know my name?"

She had spoken to her servant pleasantly, Hem Raj thought, and she did appear to be quite civil.

"I'm Hem Raj from the village of Karyala," he answered. "My son, Devi Lal, spoke to his mother about you."

"Oh, I'm so very happy to meet you, *Namaste*," Sarah said, smiling broadly and bringing the palms of her hands together in front of her face. "Devi Lal has told me so much about his family. He's very proud of you."

"He has spoken about your work with the lepers and the poor here in Jhelum," Hem Raj responded, surprised at the lack of anger in his own voice.

"Your son is a very special person," Sarah said softly. "I've learned such a lot from him."

"That may be so, but in our culture, he is required to do certain things and to fulfill certain responsibilities which are his as a part of his heritage," Hem Raj explained, wondering why he was being so patient with this woman.

"Yes," Sarah answered, "he told me about your wanting him to take your place as head of the family."

"It's not only what I want, Madame Sarah," Hem Raj answered, his voice turning firm, "but it's his birthright, a sacred duty."

"He's just a boy. How can you expect him to take on such responsibilities?" she persisted. "He has so much compassion in him; you should see him with the lepers. The children simply adore him. He'll make an excellent doctor."

"No," Hem Raj answered angrily. "My son will do what I order him to do. He will finish high school and return to Karyala where he will stay with me and learn to be a man. Keep out of my son's life, Madame Sarah. Leave him alone. I don't want you to see him any more." He turned around and started walking away.

"No, please wait," she called out. "Let me talk to you some more."

Hem Raj did not respond and, mounting Kamaan, galloped away without looking back.

The night was pitch black; even the glow of the stars was masked by the dense clouds that had come rolling in earlier in the day. The freedom fighters rode their horses towards Chakwal without talking. Hem Raj had again reviewed the plans of the raid with his followers and hoped that each would do his part effectively. By raiding a police station, not only would they obtain the latest breach-loading rifles, but it would also help establish his position as a leader in the Azad Hind movement.

When they reached the edge of town, they dismounted and walked their horses the rest of the way to the grove of trees. The men selected to watch the horses stayed back while the others split up and quickly moved away towards the center of town. It was past midnight and the streets were deserted. They stayed away from the area where the rich lived, their homes guarded by watchmen. They reached the town square and Hem Raj signaled his companions to get close to the closed door of a shop.

Across the square, in the faint glow of a fire burning on the ground, they could see the shadowy figure of a police constable. The man held his rifle resting on his shoulder, and was slowly walking back and forth in front of the entrance to the police station. The bayonet attached to his rifle gleamed in the glow of the fire. Hem Raj peered through the darkness but could not see the second constable. He and his men waited, squatting on the ground, resting their backs against the closed door of the shop. The constable guarding the station bent down, and picking a log, threw it onto the fire.

They had been sitting there for some time and Hem Raj could feel his legs cramping. He adjusted the revolver tucked into the top of his *salwar* under his *kameez*, and touched the *kirpan* hanging at his waist. He was now glad that he had resisted the urge to bring Devi Lal along on the raid. His eyes softened thinking about his son, but he was pleased that he had put a stop to the nonsense drummed into his son's head by the foreign woman.

His thoughts were suddenly interrupted by the door of the police station being opened, and he sat up erect. A constable appeared in the doorway, silhouetted against the glow of the lamps inside, and lazily stretched his arms over his head. He then walked over to the wooden post from which a short thick iron bar was suspended. Bending down, he picked up an iron hammer and, swinging his arm, struck the iron bar with it. The loud clanging sound reverberated through the town square, startling Hem Raj and his companions. A dog started barking in a lane on the side of the square. The constable dropped the hammer and shuffled back into the station, closing the door behind him.

A second dog had now started howling. Hem Raj stood up and signalled his companions to follow him. He crouched low and began quickly moving through the town square, hoping that the dogs would continue to bark. He could now clearly see the constable who had turned and was slowly walking away. Hem Raj drew his *kirpan* and racing forward, leapt onto the constable's back, bringing him crashing down to the ground.

He flipped the constable over onto his back and, planting a knee on his chest, placed the point of his *kirpan* at his neck. "One squeak out of you and I'll slit your throat," he whispered. The constable stared at him wide-eyed, gasping for breath. A rag was stuffed into his mouth and his hands and ankles tied with the rope the raiders carried draped around their shoulders.

None of the men had noticed the second constable asleep on a *charpai* against the wall. They had spread out in front of the police station and had taken their positions facing the entrance. Hem Raj waved towards the west end of the square. Aslam Khan and his men came silently sprinting, and assembled in front of the closed door. At a nod from Hem Raj, Aslam pushed the door open and they rushed in. Two Indian constables sitting at a desk were quickly overpowered, as was a British officer who had been sleeping sprawled in a chair with his boots resting on the desk in front of him. The three were gagged, bound and thrown face down on the floor in one corner of the large room. Hem Raj had now entered the station and they quickly located a dozen rifles resting in a rack on one corner. They lifted the guns and were about to run out of the station when someone started yelling outside. "What's happening?" a man was calling out in a sleepy voice. "What's going on?"

Hem Raj looked out the door just as the man in a constable's uniform picked up the hammer and began striking the iron bar. One of the freedom fighters on guard outside ran and knocked the constable down. Several dogs had started barking loudly in the neighborhood and the voices of men were heard coming from the barracks.

"Come on, let's get out of here: hurry," Hem Raj yelled to his companions. They sprinted together in the dark, running away from the police station, carrying the guns they had stolen. More shouts were heard behind them; an officer seemed to be barking orders, yelling at the constables to get their horses. Hem Raj led the way, running through the narrow lanes. Until the alarm was raised everything had gone off smoothly and now he had to make sure that they all got away. A few large rain drops splattered upon the cobblestones of the street, and then it began to pour.

They reached the edge of town and ran into the grove of trees. The earth below was already soggy and sucked at their shoes. They mounted their horses and galloped away towards their villages.

Kanti had stayed up although her husband had warned her that he was going to be late returning. She had asked where he was going but he had been evasive and said that it had something to do with Azad Hind. She admired his patriotism and shared his love for their country but worried about his safety. She hadn't minded when he took part in protests and marches, but now there were rumours that the freedom fighters were becoming more militant. She hoped and prayed that he wouldn't ever be in harms' way.

She came out of her bedroom and stood on the veranda, looking into the courtyard. The night was very still and the sky covered with dark clouds. She felt a warm drop of rain hit her face, and then another and another before the skies opened up with a heavy deluge. She moved back and waited. Then, through the sheets of rain, she saw the large doors leading into the courtyard open, and the shadowy figure of her husband walk in, leading Kamaan by the reins. Sighing, she turned and went back to bed.

It was still raining the next morning when there was a loud knock at the door. Hem Raj was asleep and Kanti had just served the children their morning meal. "Mohan Lal, go and see who it is," Kanti said to her second son.

"Yes, mother," the boy answered, getting up quickly. He picked up a gunny sack lying on the veranda and, covering his head with it, ran to the door. He slid the wooden bolt out and was almost run over by several soldiers who pushed the door open. The soldiers held rifles with bayonets and quickly spread around the courtyard. An English officer entered the courtyard, his uniform covered by a rain cape and a revolver held in his outstretched hand.

"Mother," Mohan Lal called loudly. Kanti came out onto the veranda and stood, surrounded by her children.

"Where is he?" the officer demanded.

Kanti glared back at him. "Who are you looking for?" she asked, her voice defiant.

"We want Hem Raj," the officer yelled angrily. "He is the chief of this village, isn't he?"

"Yes, I am," Hem Raj answered, coming out of his bedroom. "What is it you want?"

Kanti moved next to her husband, grasping his arm, and their children surrounded them.

"You're needed for questioning: come with us at once," the officer ordered, waving his revolver.

"What is it you want to question me about?" Hem Raj asked.

"You'll find out when you get to the police station," the officer answered, with a grin.

These are horse soldiers, probably from Jhelum, Hem Raj was thinking. If it were the police that had come for him, he may have tried to escape, but with so many armed soldiers in the courtyard, he knew it would be foolish, especially with Kanti and the children present.

"All right," he answered, "I'll go put on my turban."

"No, you'll come as you are," the officer ordered, signalling to his soldiers who quickly moved forward.

Hem Raj turned to Devi Lal. "I entrust you with the responsibility of protecting your mother, brothers and sisters," he said, placing his hands on his shoulders. "You, as my eldest son, will now fulfill your duty."

"Yes, father," the boy answered softly.

Shanti and Sheela started crying, clinging to their father. "Where are the soldiers going to take you, *Pita Jee*?" Shanti wept.

"Hush, my children," Hem Raj said, putting his arms around his daughters. "I'll be fine. Help your mother while I'm gone. Your brothers will look after you."

Kanti drew her daughters towards her and held them close. The soldiers gestured with their rifles and Hem Raj walked towards the stable where Kamaan and two other horses were tethered. "No, not the white one," one of the soldiers ordered. Hem Raj glared at him but, picking up a saddle, placed it on one of the other horses.

A crowd of villagers had gathered outside the door and stood silently in the rain. They stared angrily, but stepped aside when the soldiers pointed their rifles at them. The soldiers surrounded Hem Raj and all of them walked their horses down the cobblestone streets. They were led by the British officer still holding his revolver in front of him. Devi Lal and his brothers, along with several men followed them all the way to the edge of the village where the officer gave an order. "Yes, Smythe, *sahib*," one of the soldiers answered and quickly handcuffed Hem Raj. "Get on your horse," the soldier ordered. Mounting their horses, they all rode away at a fast gallop. Hem Raj suddenly remembered, Madame Sarah had used Smythe with her name. Could this man be her husband? he wondered.

They stopped in front of the Chakwal police station and the soldiers pulled Hem Raj off his horse. They took him inside where his handcuffs were removed and he was shoved towards a wooden door. "Get in there," he was ordered. Hem Raj found himself in a tiny cell with the only light coming through a small slit-like opening in the door. He turned to the door and peered out of the slit. Two British officers were standing in the middle of the room, talking to each other. He recognized one as the officer they had gagged and tied in this very room that night. The other was the young officer who had arrested and brought him from Karyala. The two seemed to be arguing, speaking in English.

The officers then walked out of the station and Hem Raj moved away from the door. Although it had stopped raining by the time they had reached Chakwal, his clothes were soaking wet. He took off his shirt and squeezed the water out of it. He put his shirt back on and sat down on the floor in the corner of the cell. He hadn't eaten since early the previous evening and his wrists felt sore where the handcuffs had rubbed against the skin. He wondered what they were going to do to him. They couldn't have recognized him, as all but his eyes had been completely covered by the tail of his turban. Could Aslam Khan have betrayed him? No, the Muslim was an honorable man. They had arrested him since they must suspect that he was somehow involved with Azad Hind. His anger turned towards the Indian soldiers, the traitors who for a uniform and a few rupees were selling their souls to the enemy. He would remember their faces.

His thoughts were suddenly interrupted by the door being swung open. The same soldier who had locked him in the cell earlier, now ordered him out and handcuffed him. He was pushed out of the police station and made to get onto his horse. Led by the British officer, they rode through the town. The streets were crowded with people who quickly got out of the way to allow the horses through. Chants of "Hem Raj *Kee Jai*" rang out when the people recognized who the soldiers were taking away.

They came out of the town and kept riding east. They must be taking him to Jhelum and these soldiers must be from the cavalry regiment. Hem Raj had heard about the torture of prisoners in Jhelum jail and wondered if that's what they would do to him.

It was past noon when they approached the outskirts of the city, but instead of riding towards the jail, the soldiers turned into an area where Hem Raj had never been before. The streets were wide and tree-lined, and soldiers on horseback were everywhere. His clothes were now dry but his wrists were raw, chafed by the handcuffs.

A tonga was coming from the opposite direction. The officer raised his hand and the soldiers stopped their horses. The officer dismounted and walked towards the tonga which had also stopped. He spoke to one of the women sitting in the back. They seemed to be arguing and then the officer returned and, mounting his horse, gave a command to the soldiers to start riding. Hem Raj glanced at the woman in the tonga and recognized her. So it's your husband who has humiliated me, he thought, angrily turning away, not seeing the sadness in Sarah's eyes.

They rode past what appeared to be a parade ground and then went between rows of barracks. They came to a stop in front of a squat brick building with its narrow wooden gate guarded by armed sentries. The soldiers dismounted and led him through the door into a courtyard. They removed his handcuffs and once again prodded him with their rifles towards a row of cells along one wall. He was pushed into one of them and the door slammed and bolted behind him.

Hem Raj sat down in one corner of the cell, resting his back against the wall. He rubbed his forehead with his hands and ran his fingers through his long hair. His throat felt parched and his body ached. He dozed off until a short while later when the door to the cell opened and he was hauled out. This time his hands were handcuffed behind his back and he was taken into a room at the far end of the courtyard. A British officer was standing next to a desk. He was slim and tall and his small eyes appeared to be sunken in his skull. Hem Raj was made to sit on a chair in the middle of the room. The officer adjusted his tunic and came and stood in front of the prisoner. "What's your name?" he asked gruffly in Hindustani.

Hem Raj glared back at him. The officer repeated his question, and then slapped Hem Raj across the face. Stunned by the blow, Hem Raj leapt to his feet and lunged forward. He struck the officer with his shoulder, knocking him to the ground. The two Indian soldiers grabbed him by the arms and dragged him back to the chair.

"Tie him up," the officer yelled, getting up. One of the soldiers took a rope hanging from a nail on the wall and did as ordered. "Should I beat him up, Habersham, *sahib*?" one of the soldiers asked.

"No," the officer answered, "leave that pleasure to me." Swinging his arm, he slapped Hem Raj across the face. "Now, tell me your name and where you're from," he asked.

"You know who I am and the name of my village," Hem Raj answered with a sneer.

The officer clenched his fist and struck Hem Raj's face. "Answer my questions, you swine, or I'll have you shot. Who else helped you with the raid on the Chakwal police station last night?" he yelled.

Hem Raj felt his mouth filling with blood but remained silent, a stubborn grin frozen on his face.

"All right, he's all yours," the officer said, turning to the soldiers and walked out of the room.

The soldiers took turns beating him and Hem Raj lost all sense of time. First they used their fists and then one of them picked up a cane and repeatedly struck him on his shoulders and back. Then the door to the room opened.

"All right, that's enough," he heard someone say. "Put him back in his cell and give him some food." Through eyelids that were almost swollen shut, he recognized the British officer who had come to arrest him in Karyala; Madame Sarah's husband.

His torture and questioning by the same British officer and the pair of Indian soldiers continued for the next two days but his tormentors got nowhere. Each day Madam Sarah's husband had come in and had him sent back to his cell. Then the beatings stopped but he was kept locked up for three more days.

On the sixth day since being brought to Jhelum, he was again taken into the room where he had been tortured. The officer whom the soldiers had called Habersham *Sahib*, was sitting behind the desk.

"The British government is releasing you," he spoke sternly, "but you'll be under constant surveillance. Should even a shred of evidence show up of your involvement in this or any other raid on government property, you'll be arrested immediately and I'll shoot you personally."

Hem Raj did not answer. He knew he had stood up to them. He had beaten them. A grin appeared on his face.

"Take him away," the officer ordered with a wave of his hand.

As he was being led out of the room, he saw Madame Sarah's husband coming towards them. The two looked at each other for a moment before the soldiers hustled Hem Raj away.

He rode back towards his village, planning in his mind the revenge he swore he would extract. Each of them, the foreigner and the two Indian soldiers, would pay with their damn lives. He would first make them suffer.

He arrived home unshaven and haggard. Kanti opened the front door and gasped. "I'm all right, dearest," he said, taking her into his arms. "Don't worry. They tortured me but I didn't break. I won. It's good to see you, Kanti. It's good to be home."

"Oh, I'm so happy you've returned, my husband," she answered, wiping her tears. "Let's forget what happened. It's over."

Hem Raj led his horse into the courtyard. "No, it isn't over, Kanti," he said, his eyes cold and angry. "I can't forget what they did to me. It most definitely is not over. This, I promise you, is only the beginning."

Revenge and Compassion

Hem Raj was now obsessed with his yearning for revenge. He rode into Chakwal each day and pestered the leaders of Azad Hind to let him lead an attack on the British in Jhelum. "That will be nothing short of suicide," he was told. "We can't take on an entire regiment of lancers, especially in their own backyard. Wait," they counseled. "Let our national leaders decide when and where we should strike."

He returned to his village, cursing his tormentors in Jhelum; the British officer and Indian soldiers, and now the cowards in Chakwal who seemed to be afraid of a good fight.

The day he had almost decided to give up on them and plan something on his own, a messenger rode in from Chakwal with an urgent call from Nazir Mohammed asking all freedom fighters to proceed to Peshawar. The messenger did not have details about why they were being summoned, but could only add that it was a matter of utmost importance. They were to travel to Peshawar by train and were to contact Jagat Singh. Hem Raj was instructed to muster as many fighters as possible from his district. "You need not bring your guns, but expect to be gone about two weeks," he was told.

He went around eagerly contacting several of the men who had participated in the raid on the Chakwal Police Station. "It's something big," he told them. "I think we'll finally be able to deliver a major blow to the enemy."

"We'll go with you," they all responded eagerly.

"You won't invite Aslam Khan this time, will you?" Jai Prakash asked. "Look what happened to you after the Chakwal raid."

"He had nothing to do with it, damn you," Hem Raj answered angrily. "Had he informed on me, the authorities would not have released me."

"Why are you so obsessed with trying to unite Hindus and Muslims? We are different. It won't work," Jai Prakash retorted stubbornly. "I saw your elder daughter on the riverbed the other day, smiling at something a Muslim boy told her from atop the cliff. I suppose that doesn't bother you."

"Hem Raj's face turned red. "Don't you ever dare say anything about my children, Jai Prakash," he yelled. "If you do, I'll break every bone in your body. In fact, I do not want you to accompany me to Peshawar. You're not fit to ride with us."

"That's fine with me," Jai Prakash answered, walking away.

Hem Raj then rode into Meerpur and invited Aslam Khan to journey with him.

Yet Jai Prakash's words kept bothering him. "I don't want our daughters to play down on the riverbed any more," he told his wife that evening.

"Why, my husband?" Kanti inquired. "The river is dry this time of the year. There's no danger."

"Just do as I say, Kanti," Hem Raj spoke curtly. "Tell the girls they are not to go down to the riverbed any more."

Early the next morning, accompanied by ten men, he left for Peshawar. He hadn't spoken much to his eldest son except to tell him that his school had reopened and to remind him that he was not to see the English woman. Before leaving he told Mohan Lal that, as now the eldest son in the house, he was responsible for the protection of the family.

The men were traveling light. Hem Raj carried a cloth bag hung from his shoulder in which he had a change of clothing, soap and razor, and the revolver he had won in the horse race at the recent

Ghora Mela. He was pleased to once again have Aslam Khan by his side. He had come to admire the young Muslim. Whenever they meet, Aslam would inquire after the children and "sister Kanti." That's how Hindus and Muslims should treat each other. He would not allow any religious conflict in his district.

They arrived by train in Peshawar late in the afternoon and spent the night in the homes of members of Azad Hind. Early the next morning, accompanied by Jagat Singh, they rode in *tongas* to Dera Gulab. The village now resembled a military camp with heavily armed men on horseback guarding all approaches. Several tents had been pitched in a clearing within the walls of the village. Freedom fighters summoned from as far as Amritsar and Lahore had come to Dera Gulab. Men in the hundreds were being served hot, sweet tea and *naans* baked fresh in clay *tandoors*. Their religious differences forgotten, at least for the time being, Hindus and Sikhs drank the tea and ate the *naans* provided by the Muslims of Dera Gulab.

Around mid-morning, the tall giant-like figure of Nazir Mohammed appeared, accompanied by several of his deputies. The head of Azad Hind moved through the crowd of men, stopping now and then to shake hands.

"*Salaam*, my brother," he said, embracing Hem Raj. "I'm delighted that you've joined me. I heard about your grand raid on the Chakwal police station. Come, stay by my side. We'll fight the enemy together."

They walked to the middle of the clearing. All the men stood up and moved closer. Nazir Mohammed raised his hands and started speaking. "I'm pleased to see all of you, my brothers. The moment has come when we have to attack our enemy in force. For the last month we have received terrible news of the brutal actions of the British authorities in the Swat valley. They've killed thousands of our brethren, burnt their villages, and slaughtered their cattle. *Insha-allah,* we shall extract revenge. Those of you without horses will be provided mounts. Those who don't have arms will be given guns. We'll leave at noon and ride north to Mardan and then proceed northwest from there. The foreigners control Malakand Pass during daylight hours. Their foot soldiers are garrisoned in a fort at Chakdara a short distance beyond the pass. The soldiers patrol the pass on horseback from sunrise to sunset and also guard the wire bridge across the Swat river north of the fort. We'll attack the fort and capture it. We'll trap and annihilate the British soldiers who massacred our people in the valley." Raising his rifle into the air, he bellowed, "*Inkalab.*" A thousand voices around him answered, "*Zindabad.*"

Horses, guns and swords were provided to those who did not have them. Late that afternoon, close to twelve hundred armed freedom fighters rode out of Dera Gulab. Young boys left behind to guard the village cheered them. Women stayed inside their homes with their children and prayed for the safe return of their husbands and sons. Nazir Mohammed, with Hem Raj next to him and Jagat Singh and Aslam Khan following them, rode at the head of the column. Their mood was jovial: they hailed each other. Hindu, Muslim and Sikhs each called out their religious slogans.

"*Shri Ramchander Jee Kee Jai,*" sang the Hindus.

"*Allah-o-Akbar,*" yelled the Muslims and "*Jo Bole Sonehal, Sat Sri Akal,*" intoned the Sikhs.

Dusk had fallen by the time the long column of riders reached the tribal village near Mardan and set up camp for the night.

The next morning, accompanied by several men from the village to serve as guides, the freedom fighters started riding towards Malakand, climbing further into the hills. Close to five hundred tribal men from adjacent villages joined them along the way. By late afternoon, they were approaching the Malakand Pass. Plans for attacking Chakdara Fort had been worked out in detail by Nazir Mohammed. They would leave their horses at a base camp at the southern end of the pass and towards sunset, enter the pass on foot. Traversing the pass, they would stop short of the fort. The attack on the fort would occur early the next morning.

The mood of the men was now somber and they rode silently. Hem Raj adjusted the bandolier around his chest and touched the revolver at his waist. The humiliation of his arrest in front of his family, and the beatings he endured flashed through his mind. He hoped his tormenters from Jhelum would be among the enemy they were to engage.

They set up their camp and entered the pass on foot just as the sun was setting. Marching rapidly between its high granite walls, they stopped a short distance from the fort to rest and eat the food they had brought with them. Four men were sent ahead to scout the fort and its surroundings. Upon their return the freedom fighters spread out and began climbing over the rocks in the faint light of the stars. They surrounded the small fort and crept towards its front gate. They rested in the cold, taking turns sleeping curled amongst the rocks, and were all awakened before dawn.

As the sun rose over the mountains, the fort gate was swung open and four Indian soldiers came out to stand guard in front of the gate. The freedom fighters readied their guns. Moments later, two dozen British foot soldiers came marching out. As soon as they had cleared the gate, Nazir Mohammed's voice bellowed "Fire," and the British soldiers went down in a hail of bullets. The four soldiers guarding the entrance frantically attempted to close the gates, but now the freedom fighters, with swords and revolvers drawn, had already begun rushing in.

Horses tethered in the courtyard of the fort were struck by gunfire and their loud neighing mingled with the screams of the soldiers struck by bullets. Soldiers from the back rampart of the fort were now firing at the intruders and several of the freedom fighters were hit.

Fierce hand to hand fighting began but in a little more than an hour the fort had been overrun by the freedom fighters. All but a few of the three hundred Indian and British soldiers had been killed. The jubilant victors ransacked the barracks and the officers' quarters. Nazir Mohammed, waving a bloodied sword, barked out orders. The freedom fighters who had died were to be buried outside the fort and several others who were injured were to be helped back to their camp.

Hem Raj moved from one downed freedom fighter to the next and gave instructions to the men around him. He bent over a figure on the ground and, stunned, went down on his knees. It was Aslam Khan. His face was ashen, his eyes glazed and a deep red stain was spreading slowly on his *kurta*. His hand reached out and Hem Raj grasped it. "Take the *tabeez* from around my neck and give it to Ali, my eldest son." Aslam spoke, his voice barely audible, "Tell him to look after his mother and brothers."

Hem Raj was about to answer when the hand he held went limp. He reached out and closed Aslam's eyes, his own beginning to cloud. He lifted the Muslim in his arms and slowly walked out of the fort.

Three injured British soldiers were dragged out of the fort and tied spread-eagled to stakes driven in the ground. They were stripped of their clothes and jabbed with swords. The freedom fighters were able to extract from them the information they were seeking.

Two regiments of lancers had ridden into the valley beyond the fort a month ago to quell the resistance of the local tribesmen and open up free passage to the town of Chitral. One of the cavalry regiments was then to stay on in Chitral and the other was to return.

Nazir Mohammed turned to Hem Raj. "I want you to lead a scouting expedition down into the valley," he said. "Take twenty men with you. Ride these cavalry horses and proceed speedily. Find out how far into the valley the enemy has gone and when they might be returning."

Hem Raj felt dejected and rode deep in his thoughts, leading the men down into the valley. Why had he asked Aslam Khan to join him? There were enough men from Karyala who had already agreed to accompany him. He had carried Aslam's body up onto a small hill near the fort and had buried him. He did not know any Muslim prayers but bowed his head and stood in silence next to the grave, holding the *tabeez* in his hands. He would carry it back with him and personally give it to Ali. First he would send Kanti to break the news to Noor and to be with her.

Soon the riders reached the first tribal village. Nothing remained of it but a few charred pieces of wood. Fruit trees in a small grove adjacent to the village had been chopped down and a narrow field along the valley had been burnt. The branches of the only two large trees in the village had been cut down to deny the tribesmen any shade during the boiling heat of summer.

The freedom fighters watched in stunned silence and then rode on deeper into the valley. They went past one village after another, all showing the same savagery and destruction. In the last village, they came across an old man and several women shuffling through the ruins of what had been their homes. They sobbed and told of the brutality of the horse soldiers. All of their men and even young boys were killed. Women and children who could get away had run into the mountains. There was nothing left of their homes and their farms.

"We'll get revenge," the freedom fighters consoled the survivors. "The foreigners will pay for this. We promise you."

They were not quite a third of the way to Chitral and it was getting late in the afternoon. They swung their horses around and rode back towards Chakdara Fort.

The fort had been stripped of everything of value and set on fire. The freedom fighters then returned to their base camp at the southern end of Malakand Pass.

Each day, scouts rode through the pass and down into the valley but returned with nothing new to report. On the fifth day, late in the evening, they came back and excitedly informed their leaders of having seen cavalry scouts.

"The enemy is returning," Nazir Mohammed said, his eyes ablaze. "We'll be ready for them. Tomorrow morning we'll take our positions on each side of the pass, both at its northern and southern ends. Hide yourselves well behind boulders and maintain complete silence," he instructed his followers. "The foreigners would have seen what we did to their fort and will be alert. We'll attack only after the bulk of the cavalry has entered the pass. Wait for me to fire the first shot."

That night they held a feast in their camp and sang and danced around campfires. Early the next morning, they walked back into the pass and climbed up the rocks to take positions on each side. The sun had started rising and the night's cool was being replaced by a warmth that would soon become intense. They waited quietly and patiently, talking to each other in whispers. The excitement Hem Raj had felt earlier while climbing with Nazir Mohammed to the front of the pass had now been replaced by boredom. It was past noon and there was no sign of the British cavalry. His thoughts drifted back to his village and home. He tried to imagine what Kanti must be doing and his eyes softened. How dearly he loved her and his children. He hoped that he hadn't been too harsh towards his eldest son. His fingers touched the *tabeez* he was carrying back for Aslam Khan's eldest son. Ali was now to serve as the head of the family, but he was just a young boy. He would need guidance from an elder and Hem Raj resolved to be there for him. He would help Ali and treat him like one of his own sons.

His thoughts were suddenly interrupted by the sound of horses snorting in the distance and then he heard the clatter of their hooves on the rocky path of the pass. He tensed and peered over the top of the boulder in front of him. Nine riders appeared, entering the pass from the north; a British officer and eight Indian *sowars*. They were riding at a slow trot, scanning the granite walls on each side. Nazir Mohammed had raised his hand to caution the freedom fighters. The scouting party was to be allowed to go through and only when the bulk of the cavalry was within the pass would they attack. How easy it would be to pick them off, Hem Raj thought, keeping the red tunic of the foreigner in the sight of his gun.

It was now intensely hot and the rays of the sun reflected off the rock-strewn path below. Hem Raj used the tail of his turban to wipe the perspiration from his face. He smiled at the good *kismat* of these soldiers whose lives were being spared today because they had been given the otherwise hazardous duty of acting as scouts.

The soldiers had disappeared towards the south and the pass was once again empty. Then they heard the sounds of the approaching cavalry. They entered the pass four abreast, led by three British officers; their brass buttons and metal-tipped lances glistened in the sun. The British in their white pith helmets and the Indians in their khaki turbans rode with the jauntiness of seasoned cavalrymen. They, of the 11th Bengal Lancers, had completed their campaign successfully, destroying all resistance through the entire length of the Swat valley. Even though they had found the Chakdara Fort in ruins, they were headed back to Jhelum for what would certainly be a rousing welcome and many decorations.

The British officers leading the formation were directly below them and Hem Raj recognized the tall slim officer with sunken eyes who had beaten him in Jhelum. He jerked his rifle and sighted it on the head of the man who had so humiliated him. His finger on the trigger itched, but gritting his teeth, he slowly turned away to look at the rest of the lancers riding past him.

They kept coming, and soon the entire pass was a sea of riders; horses and lancers slowly moving towards the south. Suddenly the deep voice of Nazir Mohammed resonated throughout the pass. "*Inkalab Zindabad*," and a single shot rang out. In an instant, hundreds of other guns began firing. Their thunderous explosions echoed through the pass and mingled with the screams of men and horses struck by bullets. Two of the three British officers who had led the regiment had already died, shot out of their saddles by the first barrage of bullets. The third drew his revolver and yelled "Draw your rifles." The soldiers obeyed and, firing at the cliffs on each side, followed their officer into a trot and then a full gallop. The freedom fighters at the southern end of the pass were now shooting down at them. Only a handful of lancers made it through the pass, the path behind them littered with their fallen comrades.

Unable to break through, another officer barked an order and the *sowars* leapt off their horses, bringing their rifles with them. They quickly took positions behind some of the larger rocks along the side of the pass and tried to shoot back. But the lancers were trapped, pinned down by the gunfire coming at them from every direction.

A British officer, revolver in one hand and a drawn sabre in the other, yelled orders at the *sowars* near him and they started climbing up the steep slope of the pass. Many were shot and fell, but others reached the freedom fighters and fought them fiercely.

But the soldiers were outnumbered. "Rush to the south end," Nazir Mohammed yelled at Hem Raj. "None of them must escape." Hem Raj ran scrambling over the rocks on his way along the cliffs. Gasping for breath, he climbed down towards the path leading away from the pass. He raced around a large rock and suddenly came across a British officer about to mount a horse. In an instant he raised his rifle and was about to press the trigger when the officer turned and Hem Raj saw his face. The two men stared at each other and then Hem Raj slowly lowered his rifle.

"Get out of here, ride away," he said, gesturing with his hand.

The look of fear on Cedric's face started turning to surprise. "Why are you sparing my life?" he asked suspiciously.

Hem Raj glared at him for a moment, then answered in a cold voice, "I don't want my son's friend to be made a widow."

"What if I get back and tell the authorities about you? They'll hang you."

Hem Raj quickly raised his rifles, pointing it at Cedric. "Give me your word that you won't," he said.

"Can you trust the word of an Englishman?" Cedric asked, "Enough to bet your life on it?"

"Yes," Hem Raj answered, lowering the rifle to his side. "Only because he's wedded to Madame Sarah."

A grin appeared on Cedric's face. "Alright then, you have my word as an Englishman," he answered and climbed onto his horse. "Perhaps I shan't cause Madame Sarah's friend to be made an orphan either. At least I don't think I shall," he said, looking down at Hem Raj before spurring his horse and galloping away.

Doubts and Decisions

*E*ven though the plague epidemic was over, the loss of thousands of lives and the death of her dear friend Dev Suri, had left Sarah feeling deeply saddened and depressed. She had thrown herself into her work at the Rajpur Clinic and at Hari Niwas, and also started volunteering at the free dispensary in the city.

Cedric had been gone over two weeks and she was feeling desperately lonely. "I don't know when we'll return," he had said. "It might be awhile. All I know is that it's something big. The entire bloody regiment is being sent and we're taking provisions for an extended campaign. Look after yourself while I'm gone, darling."

A letter from her father had also arrived a few days earlier, telling her that her mother was ill. "You needn't worry, darling," he wrote. "She's receiving excellent care."

Sarah had returned to Hari Niwas, hoping that she would see Devi Lal. He wasn't there, but one of the leper women gave her an envelope.

"*Chotta sahib* came this morning and asked that I give this to you," she said.

Sarah tore the envelope open and started reading the short note it contained.

Respected Madame Sarah,

I hope you are well and that God protected you while you took care of the victims of the plague. I have been very much wanting to see you, but my father has forbidden me from doing so, and I must obey him. He believes very strongly in our Indian traditions and in my responsibility as his eldest son. I hope you will understand. My science teacher has given me an application for admission to the Medical College in Lahore, but my father has forbidden me from trying to become a medical doctor. The matric examinations will be held in December and I don't know what I will do after that.

I pray for you daily, and also hope that your respected husband is well.

Yours faithfully,

Devi Lal

Sarah wrote and told him that she was pleased he had returned to school and that she understood his father's feelings. She mentioned Doctor Suri's passing away and the sadness she felt. She wished him well in his matric examinations and hoped that he would keep in touch with her through letters. She mailed the letter addressed to him at his school.

The days passed but Sarah remained melancholy. The servants, especially Nathu Ram and Laxmi, fussed over her. They accompanied her for long walks along the river each evening and Laxmi chatted incessantly about her life growing up in her village, and asked questions about England.

Almost a month went by and yet there was no news from Cedric. At the church one Sunday morning, Adele Duckworth whispered to Sarah that she had heard from her husband. "They are up north, punishing some of the tribes for causing trouble." Sarah prayed for Cedric and the other men.

Then one day when she returned from the Rajpur clinic, she found Cedric home. "Oh, it's great to see you, darling," she cried, rushing into his arms. "I've missed you so terribly."

"It's good to be home, Sarah," he said softly, his voice faltering. "It's good to be home."

Sarah raised her head and looked at her husband's face. He appeared gaunt and tired. "Are you alright, darling? Did something go wrong?"

Cedric freed himself from his wife's arms and sat down on the sofa. "Everything went wrong, Sarah," he whispered. "Every bloody thing that could have went wrong."

Sarah sat down next to him and held his face with her hands. "What happened, my love," she asked gently.

"They're all gone, Sarah," Cedric started sobbing. "David Habersham, Ian Campbell, Alan Duckworth, the VCOs and hundreds of *sowars*—they were all killed. More than two-thirds of the regiment was wiped out."

"Oh, darling, I'm so terribly sorry," she said, taking him into her arms and gently rocking him. "Poor Ian, Alan and David, it must have been horrible."

"Yes, it was," he moaned. "We were ambushed. We didn't have a bloody chance."

"Oh dear God," she gasped. "What about poor Adele Duckworth? Has she been told?"

"Yes, she knows by now," he answered, turning away.

"Perhaps I should see her. She must feel devastated. I'll go this evening," she said, standing up and taking Cedric's hand. "Come, let's go out. Let's walk by the river," she urged.

She led him through the garden and the back gate. They walked in silence for a few moments and then Cedric started talking. He told her about their campaign in the Swat Valley. He spoke about their return and the shock of finding Chakdara Fort in ruins. He told her about their being ambushed in the pass.

"There were thousands of natives sniping down at us from each side of the narrow pass. A couple of our officers and a handful of sowars made it through, but the rest of us were trapped. I ordered my squadron to draw their sabres. We dismounted and fought but didn't have a chance. There were too many of them. One of them even had me in his gun sight but let me escape."

"Oh thank God for that," Sarah said. "Thank God you were spared."

"You aren't going to believe this, Sarah, but it was your friend Devi Lal's father who spared my life."

"Are you telling me it was Hem Raj?"

"Yes, Sarah, none other than him," Cedric answered with a dry laugh. "Most of them were *Afridis* from tribal villages around Peshawar with a few Hindus and Sikhs helping them," he added.

"Did he say why he was letting you go?" she asked.

"He said he didn't want you, his son's friend, to become a widow."

Sarah turned her head and looked away. "What happened after he let you go?" she asked.

"I just rode away towards Mardan and came across old Bidley-Halden slumped over his horse, half dead," he answered.

"You rescued Colonel Bidley-Halden?"

"Well, I grabbed the reins of his horse and we got to Mardan by nightfall. The next morning, with reinforcements from a cavalry regiment stationed there, we rode back to Malakand Pass. The *Afridis* had disappeared and we buried the dead *sowars* just south of the pass."

"What about Ian, Alan and David?"

"We brought their bodies back to Mardan for burial in the British Cemetery."

"Oh, I'm so sorry darling," Sarah said, holding his hand. "But I'm so grateful to God that you're home safe."

"It's your Indian friend's father who spared my life, Sarah. I should really say that it's because of you that I'm still alive."

"Did he say anything else?" she asked.

"Yes. All he wanted as a guarantee that I wouldn't tell on him, was my word as an Englishman. Figure that one out."

"You haven't told the authorities about him, have you?" she asked, glancing up at him.

"No, not as yet. Not quite as yet," he answered, turning away.

"You gave him your word, Cedric. He spared your life. You mustn't betray him," she pleaded.

"Sarah, he's a murderer. God only knows which of my fellow officers he gunned down and how many of the *sowars* he killed. Besides, I also swore allegiance to my country and the crown."

"Cedric, I abhor violence; you know that. But this was a battle not of their making. You and your soldiers went in and massacred their people. How can you blame them for fighting back? You mustn't betray him, darling. Please. We owe him your life."

Cedric turned to his wife. "I don't know what I'm going to do, Sarah," he said softly. "I really don't know."

"What will happen now?" she asked.

"Well, our troops will go into their territory and burn a few more of their villages and kill more of them."

"Will that stop them?"

"Not really," he answered. "They'll wait a month or so and then attack us, and we'll go and destroy more villages. It's a never-ending bloody cycle."

"What about now?" she asked.

"I don't know. I guess I'll be needed to help rebuild the regiment. We'll have a job to do," he answered. She held his arm and led him back towards their bungalow.

Sarah continued receiving letters from Devi Lal each Sunday and answered, telling him what she was doing. He had written that his matric examinations would soon be over and he was going to be returning to his village. He was sad at not being able to see her and wished her well. His teachers had helped fill out the application for admission to the Lahore Medical College. He was going to ask his mother to again plead with his father to allow him to become a doctor.

Cedric came home one day and told Sarah that he had been given a week's leave. "Let's go to Lahore for Christmas, darling. We'll have a marvelous time," he said with a smile which Sarah hadn't seen in weeks.

She wanted to say no, but didn't have the heart to deny him the change that she felt he so desperately needed. She went to see Doctor Jeremy Slack and arranged for two of his young Indian house surgeons to look after her patients while she was away.

They stayed in the elegant Empress Hotel on the Mall and went to polo matches and attended a string of parties. The weather was delightfully cool and the gardens were exploding with bright colours. The Christmas Eve and the New Year's Eve balls at the Gymkhana Club were particularly gala affairs and Sarah met a number of the social elite of Lahore. Doctor Reginald Jones, the principal of the Medical College, shook her hand.

"So, you are Doctor Sarah Smythe," he beamed. "I've heard such splendid accounts of your work in Jhelum during the epidemic. Although I must say, I imagined you to be a fussy old matron and certainly not such a beautiful young woman."

Sarah blushed and changing the subject, told him about her friend, Devi Lal, and his having applied for admission to the Medical College.

"Why don't you come and visit the College, my dear," Doctor Jones beamed, taking her hands. "You can find out if your friend has been accepted."

Sarah went to the Medical College the next day and was delighted to learn that Devi Lal had indeed been granted admission and based upon his grades and the recommendations of his teachers, was offered a full scholarship. Her young friend was going to be ecstatic. But then she remembered her conversation with Hem Raj and his stubbornness. If only she could convince him what an excellent physician his son would make. Perhaps she should plead with him once more.

At a cavalry regiment dinner that night, Sarah heard several officers congratulating Cedric. One of them mentioned the Military Cross.

"Why that's splendid, darling," Sarah said, the moment they were alone. "Why didn't you tell me? I'm so proud of you."

"There's nothing to be proud about, Sarah," he answered. "I don't deserve a medal. They wouldn't have given me one if they knew how I got out alive."

"But you led your men with such courage, darling, and besides, you did save Colonel Bidley-Halden's life."

"I stumbled upon him, Sarah. Anyway, I don't think I'm going to accept the award."

"You must, darling. You've earned it," Sarah insisted.

The week flew by and they returned to Jhelum. There was a note from Doctor Jeremy Slack marked urgent waiting for Sarah, asking that she contact him immediately upon her return concerning a matter of utmost urgency. Although it was late in the evening, Sarah went to the General Hospital. Jeremy Slack was still in his office working through a pile of papers on his desk. "Oh, I'm delighted to see you, Sarah. I sent the note over only this afternoon. Thank you for coming so promptly."

"We just returned from Lahore, Jeremy. Your note said it was a matter of utmost urgency."

"Sarah, I've received a telegraphic message from the City Administrator of Bombay," Jeremy Slack said, picking up a piece of paper from his desk and handing it to her. "They've had several cases of bubonic plague reported in different parts of the city and are fearing a full-blown epidemic."

"Oh dear God," Sarah gasped. "The plague will cause havoc in a congested city like Bombay."

"They've asked us for help, Sarah. They are counting upon our experiences here. I'm planning to leave for Bombay in two days." Taking Sarah's hands into his, Jeremy Slack continued, "I can't think of anyone more qualified than you to help them in Bombay, Sarah. Will you go with me? I'll make arrangements for your travel and stay there."

"I don't know, Jeremy," Sarah answered. I have my work here. I'll need to talk to Cedric. He won't like it. How long would I be gone?"

"You can return whenever you please, Sarah. You have to convince your husband that it's important for you to go. As far as your work is concerned, I'll see to it that your patients are looked after."

"I'll talk to Cedric, Jeremy, but I won't leave until Monday. I want to go to Hari Niwas once more. There are a few loose ends I need to try and tend to."

"That's great, Sarah. I'll make train reservations for you leaving Monday," Jeremy Slack said, shaking her hand.

Sarah returned home and told Cedric what Jeremy Slack had wanted to see her about.

"You aren't going, are you?" he asked, sighing deeply.

"I must, Cedric. I must help them," she answered softly.

"Well, here you go again abandoning me and running away for some bloody noble cause," he retorted angrily. "Your place is here with me. Don't you realize that? You should worry about what happens to me and take care of me. But no, all you're interested in is helping these damn natives."

"I probably won't be gone too long, Cedric," she pleaded. "They need me. They can use the experience I gained here in Jhelum."

"I don't think you're going to be away for a short while, Sarah," Cedric blurted out. "I think it's going to be for a bloody awful long time. This might be the damn last time we're together."

"How can you say such a horrible thing, Cedric," she cried.

"You're the one who's running away. You don't give a damn about us. Go, go ahead, but don't count on my being here when you return," he yelled.

"I'm tired, Cedric, very tired, and I've got a busy day tomorrow. I don't want to argue anymore. I need some sleep," she said, walking into their bedroom.

She could not fall asleep and tossed around in her bed almost the entire night. She felt confused and angry and wished Cedric would be a little more understanding. By going to Bombay she could conceivably help save thousands of lives. What was more important than that?

The next morning she wrote a letter to Devi Lal telling him about her meeting the principal of the Medical College in Lahore and her visit to the college. She congratulated him for receiving admission, and a full scholarship. "I enjoyed being given a tour of the classrooms, laboratories, and the hospital wards," she wrote. "Now when you write and tell me about what you are doing, I'll be able to visualize it clearly." She told him about the plague epidemic in Bombay and that she was going there for an indefinite period. She wrote that the superintendent of the General Hospital had assured her that he would have a physician go to Hari Niwas once a week. She closed by wishing him well and telling him that she would write to him from Bombay.

She instructed Nathu Ram to engage a *tonga* and deliver the letter to Devi Lal in Karyala.

"Am I to take a *tonga* all the way to Karyala and back, *mem sahib?*" the houseboy asked.

"Yes, Nathu Ram. I want you to do that. I also want you to give a message to Devi Lal's father, Hem Raj. Ask him if he could please come to Hari Niwas this Sunday at noon as there's a matter of great importance that I would like to discuss with him."

Nathu Ram did as instructed and, traveling to Karyala, knocked on the door of Hem Raj's house. Kanti opened it and the houseboy brought the palms of his hands together in front of his face.

"*Namaste Jee,*" he said, "I have a letter here for Devi Lal from my *mem sahib*, and also a message for *Shree* Hem Raj."

"Devi Lal is away from home but will return shortly," Kanti said, taking the letter from the man. "And what is the message for my husband?" she asked.

"*Mem sahib* has requested if he could please come and see her this Sunday noon at Hari Niwas,"

"Why does your *mem sahib* want to see my husband?" Kanti asked, a frown appearing on her face.

"I don't know, but *mem sahib* said it was a matter of great importance."

"All right, I'll give him the message," Kanti answered, remaining at the door for a few moments after Nathu Ram had left.

When Devi Lal returned, Kanti gave him the letter but did not tell him about the message for his father. Hem Raj came home in the evening and Kanti spoke to him after dinner, when they were alone in their room. "A man servant from Jhelum came to see you today, my husband," she said.

"Oh, whose servant was he? What did he want?" Hem Raj asked, taking his turban off.

"He had a message from Madame Sarah," Kanti said, looking at her husband's face. "She asked that you come and see her in Hari Niwas on Sunday."

Hem Raj turned sharply to look at his wife, and then turned away. "Why would she want to see me?" he asked.

"The servant didn't tell me why, except to say it was a matter of utmost importance," she answered. "Will you go?"

"I don't know," he answered. "I'll see."

Sunday morning Kanti watched her husband shave and change into a new set of clothes.

"I think I'll ride into Jhelum today and see what Madame Sarah wants. I have to talk to the Azad Hind leaders there, anyway," he said, not meeting his wife's eyes.

"Will you be back in time for dinner?" she inquired.

"Of course I'll be back," he answered, tying his turban carefully.

Sarah had attended church with Cedric and then went to Hari Niwas, wondering whether Hem Raj would show up. As they neared the village she turned in her seat and saw him standing next to his white horse. Her hand rose to her throat and her heart seemed to have missed a beat.

"*Namaste*," she said softly, walking towards him. "I'm so glad you came."

Hem Raj bowed his head. "I'm pleased to see you," he said.

"I wanted to thank you for sparing my husband's life."

"He gave me his word not to disclose my identity," he said, looking into her eyes.

"It might be wise, perhaps, for you to go away some place where you are safe, at least for some time," she said.

"Why? Isn't his word good?"

"I think it is, but there might have been others who recognized you."

"No, I won't run and hide. The cause is greater than my life." They started walking towards Hari Niwas.

"I'm going away to Bombay tomorrow and I wanted to see you before I left," she said, looking up at his face.

"Why do you have to go?" he asked gently.

"There is a major plague epidemic there and I've been called to help."

They were nearing the village, and stopped. "How is Devi Lal?" she asked. "How is he doing?"

"He's fine," he answered.

"I was in Lahore earlier this week," she continued. "The people at the medical college there are very impressed with how well your son has done in school. They have offered him not only admission, but also a full scholarship."

So that's what it was, Hem Raj thought, angrily. All she's interested in is my son. His eyes slowly hardened. "Had I known this was the reason you wanted to see me, I wouldn't have come," he said coldly. "My mind is made up. My son will do what he's told. He must fulfill his obligations to me and to his family." He climbed onto his horse and looked down at her. His eyes softened for an instant. "May God be with you always," he said, and wheeling his horse, galloped away.

Kanti had anxiously waited for her husband to return from Jhelum. Although she wasn't expecting him back until late evening, she kept looking at the front door each time it opened. She had not met

Madame Sarah, but her son had told her how beautiful she was. She is English and married. Why did she want to see my husband? Devi Lal had told her what Madame Sarah had written to him. Kanti had seen the excitement in her son's eyes and was happy for him. But she also knew her husband well.

"Will you plead with him, Mother?" Devi Lal begged. "I really wish to join the Medical College. Mother, there's so much suffering. As a physician, I can serve so many. You can't imagine how much help the lepers have received from Madame Sarah. She gives them such comfort. I'd like to be like her. Before I left school to come home, I went to Hari Niwas to bid farewell to the lepers and made them a promise. I told them that I would return one day and God willing, it would be with the skills of a doctor so that I may repay their friendship and the many lessons they taught me."

"I want you to do what's in your heart, my son," Kanti answered gently. "I'll bring it up before your father again. I'll talk to him."

Kanti wanted her children to be able to achieve their dreams and not let traditions of their culture hold them back. She would plead with her husband to give their son the freedom to fulfill his heart's yearning.

It was late in the evening by the time Hem Raj returned. Kanti served him a meal and he ate in silence.

"How was your trip to Jhelum?" she asked him later.

"Oh, it was all right," he answered. "I saw Madame Sarah for a couple of minutes."

"Is that so?" Kanti said softly. "What did she want?"

"She told me that Devi Lal has been granted admission to the Medical College in Lahore and had received a scholarship. She appealed to me to let him go."

"Yes, our son also received the news. He has asked me to talk to you. He wants to become a medical doctor and serve the sick and the poor. Perhaps you should give him permission and your blessings, my husband."

"No, never," Hem Raj exploded. "Let me talk to him right now," he said, walking out onto the veranda.

"Devi Lal," he hailed. "Come down here." He sat down on a chair on the veranda and Kanti came and stood in the doorway behind him. Devi Lal came down from his room and brought the palms of his hands together in front of his face.

"Sit down, I wish to talk to you." Hem Raj said, controlling his anger.

"Yes, father," the boy answered, taking the chair across the table from his father.

"Your mother told me that you wish to enroll in the Medical College in Lahore."

"Yes, father, I would very much like to do that, and would like to receive your blessing."

"No, I am against it. I forbid it," Hem Raj said, his voice beginning to tremble. "You are my eldest son, Devi Lal. You will take my place of honour as the head of the family and chief of our village. This is your birthright, your privilege, and a sacred duty."

"I'm very grateful for all I've received, father," the boy answered softly. "But there is so much suffering. As a doctor, I can be of help to many. Mohan Lal is only a year younger and is more capable of following in your footsteps than I."

Hem Raj's face was turning red. "You are a Mohyal, a Brahmin, Devi Lal," he spoke slowly, "a descendant of brave warriors. It's inconceivable that you would agree to touch defiled bodies and sick people." He then stood up and pointed around him. "Look, as the eldest son, you will inherit all of my land and wealth. If you don't want that, then go join the freedom fighters and help rid our country of these foreigners. But forget this nonsense about wanting to become a doctor. I'm ordering you to obey me."

Sarah left for Bombay feeling sad and confused. Cedric came to the station and awkwardly stood on the platform. She had hoped that they would have slept together her last night in Jhelum, but he had gone into the second bedroom and closed the door behind him. They hadn't spoken much on the way to the station, and briefly embraced before she got onto the train. She sat down at the window, looking at him as the train pulled away. Why did she feel there was something final about this parting? The train gathered speed, and she began sobbing.

A week went by, and Devi Lal had not been able to decide what he was to do. Defying his father was going to be very painful, yet he yearned to follow a path by which he felt he could be of so much help to so many. He went to the temple often and prayed. Kanti sensed the turmoil in her son's mind and asked God to help him make the right choice.

In the end, Devi Lal decided that, as painful as it was going to be, he had to defy his father. Hem Raj had gone to Peshawar to collect rent from their tenants and would not be back for a week. Devi Lal told his mother of his desire to leave for Lahore right away. Kanti tearfully agreed that it was best for him to go while his father was away.

Leaving Karyala where he was born and raised, and traveling to the far-away city of Lahore was frightening. He was going to miss his family terribly, but his mother promised to write often.

His brothers carried his small tin trunk down the winding lanes to the edge of the village. Kanti had given him all the money she had at home and accompanied him, holding his hand in hers. Devi Lal was to take a *tonga* to Jhelum, where he was to board a train for Lahore. He hugged his brothers and sisters, and then, bending down, touched his mother's feet. Kanti took him in her arms. "May Krishan Bhagwan bless you and protect you at each and every moment, my son," she whispered, tears streaming down her face.

Devi Lal, choking back his tears, climbed into the *tonga*. His heart ached as it had never done before. Had he made a mistake, he now wondered. Could he stay away from his family? He felt panicked.

Maybe he should tell the *tonga* driver to turn around and take him back. But the man was wielding his whip and the horse was moving at a fast pace. Perhaps he could go as far as the railway station. Maybe the train to Lahore today was going to be canceled.

But as they entered Jhelum city, he knew that he couldn't go back. The train wasn't going to be canceled and now that he had made a choice, he had to go through with it. He bought a ticket to Lahore and was told that the train wasn't due for another three and one-half hours. He looked around the empty platform, wondering how he should pass the time. Then it occurred to him; he could go to Hari Niwas and see the leper children one more time.

He picked up his trunk and engaged a *tonga*. Yes, it would be nice to see his friends and take them a gift. He bought some fruit and, climbing into the *tonga*, gave directions to the driver.

But as the *tonga* approached Hari Niwas, he noticed there was something terribly wrong. Nothing appeared to have remained of the village except a few charred pieces of wood and piles of rubble. He got off the *tonga* and ran to the middle of the ruins. He looked around, stunned. Even their shrine under the big peepul tree had been destroyed. What could have happened? Who could have done this? A farmer was going by herding a few head of cattle.

"What happened to the village of the lepers?" Devi Lal asked.

"Oh, the huts were set on fire in the middle of one night last week," the farmer answered. "It was the work of some thugs from the city."

"Why did they do that?" Devi Lal asked angrily.

"Who knows what makes criminals perform such evil deeds," the farmer answered, raising his hands.

"What happened to the people who lived here?" Devi Lal asked.

"Most of them perished in the fire. Some of the children who survived were carted away by the police to another city," the farmer answered, running after a calf that had strayed away.

Devi Lal sat down on the stone platform of the ruined shrine and looked at the pathetic remains of the huts. What terrible men could have done such an awful thing to these poor people. He imagined the leper children at play and the women performing *aarti* during their Sunday prayers. He could see Madame Sarah caring for the lepers and smiled a little thinking about her speaking to them in her broken Hindustani. He prayed for them all.

When Hem Raj returned from Peshawar and entered the court-yard of his house, he found Kanti and the children seated on a *charpai* on the veranda. He waited, but Shanti and Sheila did not come running to hug him as they always did when he returned home from a trip. "What's the matter, children?" he called out. "Isn't anyone happy to see me back?"

Kanti stood up and came towards him. "Welcome home, my husband," she said quietly. "It's good to have you back."

Hem Raj walked onto the veranda and, removing his turban, wiped his face with it. He hugged his daughters and placed his hands over the heads of his two younger sons. "Where's Devi Lal?" he asked.

The children looked at each other and then at their mother. Kanti came and placed her hand on her husband's arm. "Devi Lal left three days ago, my husband," she said softly.

"Where did he go? Is he in Jhelum?"

"No," Kanti answered, looking into his eyes, "he's gone to Lahore."

Hem Raj's mouth fell open. "Has he gone to join the Medical College?"

"Yes, I'm afraid he has," Kanti answered, looking away.

Hem Raj staggered and sat down in a chair. He tried, but was unable to speak. Then his eyes narrowed and the muscles of his jaw tightened. He stood up and without uttering a word, stormed into his room. Later that evening, he wrote a short letter to his son.

You have disobeyed me and I'm disinheriting you. From now on you have no right or claim whatsoever on any of my lands and property. Further, I am forbidding you from setting foot in this house ever again.

Devi Lal felt devastated. Although he had expected to be cut off from the family, the finality of his father's words was something he wasn't prepared for. He prayed a great deal and threw himself into his studies. His mother wrote to him twice each month and periodically enclosed a rupee note in her letters.

He also received a letter from Sarah saying that the plague epidemic in Bombay was not going well and she felt terrible that thousands were dying. She said she missed Jhelum and their walks along the river, and hoped the inhabitants of Hari Niwas were being looked after.

Devi Lal answered at once to inform her about the tragedy that had befallen Hari Niwas and the lepers. Three weeks later he received a letter from her.

> I was shocked by the news that you gave me about what had happened to Hari Niwas and the lepers there. I sent a telegraphic message to Doctor Jeremy Slack and have since received full details about the tragedy. It appears that a gang of thugs from the city began extorting money from the lepers. Unable to get the amount they demanded, the thugs set fire to the lepers' huts during the middle of the night. As you know, leprosy deadens the senses, the person does not feel pain. Most of the adults, therefore, perished in the fire. The children who survived were taken away by the city authorities and moved to a leper asylum near Rawalpindi, north of Jhelum. I know how this must sadden you as it has done me. Doctor Slack has informed me that all of the miscreants were apprehended and are being tried. He has assured me that the full measure of the law will be applied in dealing with the thugs.
>
> With my prayers for you,
>
> Your friend,
>
> *Sarah*

Time passed and Devi Lal gradually became accustomed to his life in the college hostel and to the demands of his medical studies. He was learning a great deal and spent most of his free time in the library.

Kanti wrote and told him that his father had again gone to Peshawar. She was fearful that he was becoming much too deeply involved in the freedom movement. She also informed him that they had gotten his brother, Mohan Lal, engaged to a girl from a good Mohyal family from the nearby village of Bhaun, but that the wedding date had not as yet been set.

Sarah wrote that almost a year had passed since her coming to Bombay, and yet the epidemic had not abated. She said that they had recently received a small amount of a new serum which was showing promise, but that the demands were outstripping the supply of the serum.

Devi Lal had now begun the clinical phase of his medical training. The pain and suffering he witnessed in the free wards of the Medical College Hospital only made him more convinced that he had made the right choice. He immersed himself into his work and gave every free moment of his time to the care of those afflicted.

Sarah wrote that after devastating the city's population for two years, the plague epidemic seemed to be dying out. She confided that she was feeling physically and mentally drained and had been advised by her colleagues to take a prolonged period of rest. As much as she hated leaving India, she had decided to return to England and stay in the home of her parents. She gave him her address in Willoughby on the Wolds and asked that he reply to her there. She did not mention anything about her husband accompanying her.

Devi Lal felt saddened by the thought of her going away so far from him. Other than the work at the hospital, his only source of comfort was the letters from his mother and from Madame Sarah. He hadn't seen either in over two years, but each had provided him with infinite support. His mother he loved so very dearly and, although he had known Madame Sarah for a brief period, she had come to mean something very special to him. Now he was concerned about her well-being. She had written that she was physically and emotionally drained. What about her husband: why wasn't he taking care of her?

That evening Devi Lal went to the temple on the hospital grounds and knelt down before the altar. He prayed for the well-being of his family in Karyala, for his brothers and sisters and for his father and mother. Then he prayed for Madame Sarah. "Lord God, protect my friend through her journey back home. Grant her peace of mind and good health, and let her healing hands continue to provide solace and comfort to those who ail."

Relationships and Fears

Cedric had first met Natalie several months after his return from the battle of Malakand Pass when he was asked to interview applicants for the position of regimental clerk. She was young, skinny and short in stature. Her skin was light brown and her black wavy hair was long, almost reaching her waist. The most noticeable feature about her face were her large eyes that looked at him with childlike candor.

She had introduced herself as Natalie D'Souza, and then had quickly added, "I'm really an Anglo-Indian and a Roman Catholic," implying by the tone of her voice that she was almost British and certainly superior to native Indians. The thick coat of rouge on her cheeks reminded Cedric of the street walkers on White Chapel Road. He had hired her, but then hadn't seen her for some time, getting busy traveling to surrounding villages to help recruit *sowars,* and buy horses. Then, back at the Regimental office it seemed that he was running into her almost daily. Although he smiled and greeted her warmly, he didn't make any attempts to start a conversation.

With Sarah gone, the bungalow felt empty and Cedric was spending most his free time at the club. At night he lay in bed thinking about how deeply in love he had been with her when they had first met. After their marriage he had found the physical side of their relationship somewhat difficult to deal with. Throughout his life he had been burdened by a sense of guilt that there might be something wrong with him. Yet he loved his wife dearly and had made the best he could of their relationship.

Cedric believed that India had changed Sarah. Her obsession with everything Indian and her compulsion to help the natives had driven him, at times, to almost hating her. By making him promise not to betray her friend's father, she had forced him to withhold vital information from his superiors about what really happened in the Malakand Pass. A pang of jealousy coursed through his mind by the thought that Sarah may have been attracted to the Indian. Now her leaving him and running off on another of her bloody missions of mercy was the last straw.

After arriving in Bombay, Sarah had written fairly regularly, telling him about her work and life in the big city. But as time passed, her letters became less frequent. Then, a little over two years after she had left, he received a short note from her saying that she was returning to England and wasn't sure how long she'd be gone. She hoped that he was well and promised to write again after reaching her parents' home in Willoughby on the Wolds.

Cedric didn't feel sad nor angry, but instead, was somewhat relieved. Perhaps it was best they hadn't seen each other before she left. He could go on with his life without any emotional encumbrances and she could do whatever she bloody well pleased.

Over two years had gone by since the ambush in the Malakand Pass. The 11th Bengal Lancers, once again restored to full strength, were ordered to enter the territory of the *Afridis*, north of Peshawar. They left eagerly as the humiliating and costly defeat in the Malakand Pass had not been forgotten.

But their task wasn't easy and the campaign lasted several months. Autumn went by and winter brought its woes. They did destroy several *Afridi* villages, including Dera Gulab, but much to their dismay, Nazir Mohammed and his followers escaped deeper into the Frontier. After being gone six months, the 11th Bengal Lancers returned to Jhelum.

Tired from this tedious and dangerous campaign, Cedric now yearned to return home to England. He applied for six months leave and within a month, sailed for London. The seas were calm and this time he found the voyage to be not too bothersome. He stayed at the Cavalry Officers Club at Aldershot and went to see his mother in her flat near Bow Road in the East End of London. She was not in good health but still worked at the hospital where now she was a waitress in the canteen.

Cedric wanted her to quit working and offered to get her a flat in a better area of the city but she refused to move. "This is where I've lived all of me life," she insisted. "I'm an East-ender. I wouldn't be 'appy any place else." Cedric went to see her once each week and took her out to dinner. He gave her some money, although she tried not to accept it.

After a couple of months in London, he became bored, and traveled north by train to Scotland. He stayed in Edinburgh at an inn outside the city, and went for long walks. His mind seemed to be at peace here and he was able to reflect over the past few years. He had not made any attempts to contact Sarah and wasn't even sure if she was still in England. He didn't think there was any future for them together. He certainly wasn't in love with her anymore and he didn't see why they should remain married. Upon his return to London, he went to the offices of a barrister and filed for divorce, on the grounds of her deserting him, and their incompatibility. The moment he stepped out of the barrister's office after having signed the papers, he felt strangely relieved.

Although he still had more than two months left of his leave, he went to the War Office and asked to be sent back to his regiment. He couldn't believe it, but he was actually eager to return to Jhelum. In a short while, therefore, he once again boarded a steamer headed for India.

Devi Lal was nearing the end of his medical training and, at age twenty, had turned into a handsome young man. He had taken to wearing western clothes in the hospital but continued to wrap the traditional turban around his head. He had grown a moustache and, although not as broad shouldered, he resembled his father quite a bit.

Madame Sarah had written and told him that because of her feeling of constant fatigue and a persistent cough, tests were carried out and she was diagnosed to be suffering from tuberculosis. She was now staying in a sanitorium near Welling in Kent. She wrote:

> This is a beautiful area of England. It's summer and the flowers are in full bloom. It reminds me so much of my home in Jhelum. I don't know how long I'm to stay here at this sanitorium. I guess it will be until I'm declared cured. I'll then return to my parents home and decide what to do with the rest of my life. If you wish to write to me, and I do hope you will, as I enjoy reading your letters, you may address them to my home in Willoughby on the Wolds. My parents will then forward them to me. You must be nearing the end of your medical studies and will soon become a doctor. What a glorious achievement. I'm so very proud of you. Do write and give me all of your news.
>
> With affection,
>
> Your friend,
>
> *Sarah*

Devi Lal read the letter a second time. He knew that Madame Sarah must be receiving the latest treatment. He sat and wrote her a long letter. He conveyed his deep sorrow at her having contracted tuberculosis.

> You have a strong will, Madame Sarah, and are a most decent human being. I know that God will heal you and you

will continue to serve mankind. Yes, I am very excited about completing my studies. I know there is so much more that I have to learn and am pleased to inform you that the Medical College has offered me a position as house surgeon in its hospital. After completing this assignment, the Ministry of Health in Delhi will then give me a four year posting as a physician somewhere in India. This will enable me to fulfill the requirements of the scholarship I received.

I hope that your honorable husband is in good health. I pray for you daily and ask God to remove all obstacles before you.

Yours faithfully,

Devi Lal

The letters he received from his mother continued to contain news of the family and of the village. She wrote that his father had earlier returned after a two week's absence, with the very sad news that her dear friend Noor's husband had been killed in a battle against the British.

Since then I have tried to tell your father to curtail his involvement in the freedom movement, but he tells me that the momentum is on our side and Azad Hind must continue its activities more vigorously. Your brother, Mohan Lal's, wedding will take place next spring. I pray for you each night, my son, and I'm certain your father also does. Perhaps time will soften him, for I know that in his heart he cares for all of you, his children.

She closed with her love, blessings and prayers.

Devi Lal received his medical degree and started working as a house surgeon. He had stood first in his medical college final examinations and was awarded a gold medal. His superiors at the hospital were greatly impressed with his diligence and began giving him increased responsibilities.

Towards the end of his year as a house surgeon, he was summoned to the office of the Principal of the Medical College.

"'Well, well, come on in Devi Lal!" Doctor Reginald Jones beamed, shaking the young Indian's hand. "I've received splendid reports about your work as house surgeon. That's jolly good, but I dare say it didn't surprise me. I fully expected that of you. Would you like a spot of tea? It's beastly hot, but then I've found drinking hot tea actually makes the heat more bearable."

"Thank you, Doctor Jones," Devi Lal answered politely. "I don't wish to bother you."

"It's no bother at all, old chap," Reginald Jones answered, ringing the little bell on top of his desk. An Indian servant quickly materialized through a side door. "*Chai lao*," he was told.

"*Accha, sahib*," the servant answered, bowing.

"Where were we?" Doctor Jones said, turning towards Devi Lal. "Oh yes, I was about to give you some good news." He picked up a piece of paper on his desk before him. "Guess what, Devi Lal, your orders have come through from the Ministry of Health. You're being assigned as a District Medical officer to the town of Myitkyina."

"Oh, is that so?" Devi Lal answered, taken aback. "I don't think I even know where this place is."

"I'm sorry, didn't I tell you?" Dr. Jones responded. "It's the northernmost town in Burma, quite remote, in the foothills of the Himalayas."

The servant had slipped back into the room carrying a large tray which he set down on a table against the wall. Devi Lal accepted a cup of tea from him.

"This will indeed be a splendid opportunity for you to practice the medicine you've learned here with us, Devi Lal," Doctor Jones said, taking a sip of his tea. "I think you're very well suited for this position."

"Will I be working with other physicians in this town, Doctor Jones?" Devi Lal asked.

"Oh no, old chap. You'll be it. You'll probably have a nurse or two helping you. There isn't another town within a hundred miles of Myitkyina. By golly, you'll have the run of the district. Believe me, even the chief of police and the district commissioner have to stay on the good side of the medical officer."

Devi Lal knew little about Burma other than what he had learned in his high school geography class.

"You'll find the Burmese a delightful people," Reginald Jones continued. "A very friendly and hospitable lot. I should warn you, though, watch out for their beautiful women. I've heard they're most charming. I won't at all be surprised if within a year or two one of them gets you to say 'I do'!"

Devi Lal laughed. "No sir, I'll be in no hurry to get married. I want to fulfill my service obligations as quickly as possible and return to Punjab."

"Well, we'll just have to wait and see, won't we?" Doctor Jones laughed.

"When will I be leaving, Sir?" Devi Lal asked.

"You've got two months. The ministry will be sending you a train ticket to Calcutta, and also book your steamer passage to Rangoon."

Devi Lal stood up to leave. "Thank you very much, Doctor Jones," he said, bowing.

"Good luck, Devi Lal," Doctor Jones said, standing up and shaking the young Indian's hand. "I envy you," he added. "You're going to find the next few years to be most exciting. Do write and let me know how things turn out. God bless."

Burma, that sounded so far away, and they'd given him only two months before he had to leave. He would have to miss his brother's wedding. But then it occurred to him that his mother hadn't said anything about his attending it. He had to prepare for the journey and he had to see his family before he left. Oh dear God, he had to. He hadn't seen them for almost five years. He would write to his mother and ask if he could come to Karyala, even just for a day. "I do not wish to disobey my father," he wrote. "But perhaps you and my brothers and sisters could meet me just for a little while at the outskirts of the village. Please, mother, please write and tell me that I can come to see you.

"I have been assigned as a District Medical Officer to a town in a very remote part of Burma. I will have to serve there for four years and only God knows what may happen during all of that time."

Tears filled Kanti's eyes when she read her son's letter. She would plead with her husband to allow their son to come home. She had to see her son before he would be gone for another 4 years.

"No, absolutely not!" Hem Raj answered angrily. "I have disinherited him. If you and the children wish to see him, you can meet him elsewhere in the village. You could meet him at the temple. But he's not to set foot in this house."

Kanti wrote and told her son that she would also be heartbroken if he were to leave for this faraway land without letting her eyes rest upon his face at least once more. "You must come, my child. I, your brothers and sisters will be waiting for you eagerly at the temple on the day you tell us you'll come." She wrote nothing about her conversation with his father.

The day before he left for Karyala, Devi Lal received a letter from Madame Sarah.

I'm still in the sanitorium, but I've been declared cured. It's a relief, although I'm a little sad about the thought of leaving this place. It's so peaceful and I've had a lot of time to think and sort things out in my mind. I know that I'd like to return to India, but it can't be to Jhelum. There are too many bittersweet memories of my life there and I'm not quite ready, at least for now, to face them. I don't know where my husband is. I should say my ex-husband. He had filed for a divorce which went through recently. I should have written to you about this earlier, but didn't wish to burden you with my problems. In many ways, I'm relieved to place that phase of my life behind me.

Some time back I had written to Uma Mata in Badri Nath. Remember, I had told you about meeting her at the Kumbh Mela. From the very moment I first saw her, I had felt inexplicably drawn towards her. She's asked me to come and stay in their Ashram. She wrote that there is an orphanage as well as a leper asylum, both in dire need of medical care. I've decided to go to Badri Nath as soon as I've attended to some personal matters here in England. I don't know how long I shall stay there. I'll have to wait and see. Perhaps the tranquility of the mountains will help me find piece of mind. I will come to see you when I arrive in Lahore. May God bless you.

Fondly,

Sarah

Devi Lal journeyed to Karyala and ran all the way up to the temple. Kanti looked at her son through tearful eyes. Devi Lal bent down to touch his mother's feet. "Oh my son," she sobbed, taking him in her arms. Shanti and Sheila started crying. Mohan Lal and Sohan Lal stood by, fighting back their tears. Devi Lal embraced each of them. "You've all grown so big," he said to them. Kanti led them to one corner of the temple.

At first they didn't know what to talk about. After all, they hadn't seen each other for almost five years. Then each started speaking, as if making up for all of those years in the few hours they had together. He told them about Medical College and his work and about Burma. They asked a thousand questions. All too soon it was time for him to leave. Kanti wanted so much not to cry. Her son must take away happy memories of his family. "Let's go to the shrine and pray together," she said with a forced smile. "We'll pray together again the very first day that you return, my son."

They came out of the temple and started walking silently. "Mother," Devi Lal said softly.

"Yes, son," Kanti answered.

"Mother, I'd like to see our house once before I leave."

Kanti nodded and looked away, unable to hold back her tears anymore. She took her son's hand and led him towards their home. The door to the courtyard was ajar. Devi Lal looked in, slowly, caressingly running his eyes from one end of the house to the other. His eyes had begun to mist and he didn't notice his father lying on a *charpai* under the large banyan tree. Hem Raj had seen who was at the doorway and, quickly closing his eyes, feigned sleep.

Devi Lal brushed his eyes and, seeing his father asleep under the tree, gasped. He quickly turned to his mother, his eyes imploring. Kanti nodded and gently nudged him through the door. The palms of Devi Lal's hands came together in front of his face. He entered the courtyard, his heart exploding with emotions he had kept bottled up for the past five years. He walked quietly towards the *charpai* under the banyan tree and, so as not to waken his father, very gently touched his feet. He looked at his father's face one last time, and prayed silently. Then, as a final act of reverence, he lifted his turban from his head and placed it next to his father's feet. "I vow not to wear a turban until I've received your forgiveness, my father," he prayed, his lips moving soundlessly. He turned and slowly walked towards the door, thus not noticing the tear that rolled down from the corner of his father's eye, nor the hand gently rise to bless him.

He returned to Lahore and, within a month, left for Burma. He felt forlorn and dejected. He had brought such pain to his father and mother. Would he even recognize his brothers and sisters the next time he saw them? The train on which he was riding roared south from Lahore, taking him away that much further from his family. Madame Sarah had written that she would soon be travelling to Badri Nath and would stop in Lahore to see him. But she had not come. When darkness came, he fell asleep, unaware that in the middle of the night he and Sarah had come within a few feet of each other, as their trains, traveling in opposite directions, roared away, carrying each to fulfill a destiny drawn for them by the embrace of their Karma.

A Cloud Over the Moon

" *T*hat was not a very sensible thing to have done," Hem Raj said, looking at Ali and his five companions. "You shouldn't have attacked the foreigners without first clearing it with me or with one of the other leaders of the movement. And then, the least you could have done was to divide up and ride off in different directions. No, you had to flee all together straight to Meerpur. You might as well have stopped by at the police station in Chakwal and given them directions to your village."

He looked at their faces: Ali and the rest, young men, who had acted rashly, without thinking about the consequences. He probably would have done the same at their age. They had ridden out past Chakwal and onto the road towards Jhelum, looking for some excitement. From a distance they had seen two carts drawn by pairs of mules and laden with what appeared to be supplies coming towards them. What interested them more were the dozen or so British horse soldiers escorting the carts. The young men quickly turned their horses around and, riding a short distance back towards Chakwal, hid in a wheat field by the side of the road. When the carts came near, one of them became nervous and fired his rifle at the horse soldiers. The others also quickly fired their guns and then, getting onto their horses, fled through the fields. They rode through Chakwal and on to Meerpur. One of them had confessed to his father what they had done and Hem Raj had been summoned.

"Stay inside your homes at all times," he commanded. "Don't even stick your heads out of windows. The British must have started hunting for you already. If they come for you, let me know right away. I'll try and have you smuggled to the Northwest Frontier."

"The jackasses," he muttered, riding back to his village. He would see to it that no harm came to them. He must protect especially Ali. Hem Raj felt distraught and frustrated. Although the Azad Hind now consisted of hundreds of thousands of freedom fighters spread throughout the country, they seemed to be ineffective in freeing the country. "It's not as if our men aren't brave," he had said to Kanti. "Thousands have already given their lives. But the odds are so heavily against us. Look at what these foreigners have done. They've gone to the poorest villages throughout the land and recruited men to join their armies. They have soldiers from every province of India willing to serve them more faithfully than dogs. How can we defeat the British when we are so divided?"

"I feel suffocated," he told his wife. "I can't breathe this air of oppression while being witness to the treachery of my own people. We are worse than slaves. Do you know they have signs outside their eating places which read 'Indians and dogs not allowed'? Yet there are Indian servants who cook and serve meals to them. Do you know there are loose women in the cities who, I'm told, willingly sell their bodies to the foreigners for a few coins?"

"You mustn't lose faith," Kanti tried to console her husband. "You will succeed, I know you will."

But Hem Raj was inconsolable. His eldest son had gone to this faraway country and he wasn't sure if Mohan Lal was capable of bearing the burden that one day would be placed upon his shoulders. How fate had caused his family to be affected by the actions of these foreigners. If only Madame Sarah hadn't interfered with the affairs of his family. Thinking about her, his anger abated a little.

She was different, and now Devi Lal had written and told his mother that she had returned to her country. He wondered if he would ever see her again.

The three young girls swayed their hips enticingly, twirling in front of the British officers lounging on sofas in the drawing room of their bungalow. Four men sat in one corner playing Indian musical instruments. The girls stomped their feet on the floor, making the tiny bells around their ankles jingle in harmony with the music. Cedric had been back in Jhelum just a few months but was already tired of this weekly ritual of his bungalow mates. After drinking heavily all evening and ogling the dancers, they would each grab a girl and stagger to their bedrooms.

The first few times, Cedric had allowed one of the girls to accompany him into his bedroom, but kicked her out after a short while. Soon he dropped all pretense and although he drank with his companions and watched the girls dance, he kept them out of his bedroom. His friends chided him. "Come on Cedric, don't be such a bloody bore," they yelled. "Let these cute things teach you a trick or two."

But they soon gave up and stopped pestering him. Although he had looked forward to returning to Jhelum and to his old regiment, he had already started feeling unsettled and lonely. When he went to the club in the evenings a few unattached young women who had traveled from England to be with relatives and to meet eligible bachelors, gushed over him but he felt ill at ease and avoided them. The only person he now seemed to be able to converse comfortably with was Natalie D'Souza. They chatted whenever she brought some papers into his office or occasionally at her desk when he happened to walk by.

One day she came into his office and asked to speak to him. "Yes, certainly," Cedric answered with a smile, "What can I do for you?"

"Oh, it's nothing, sir," she said, fidgeting with her hands. Then quickly looking at him, she blurted out, "Will you do me the honour of having dinner with me on Saturday night, sir? I would very much like to cook for you."

Cedric chuckled. "Why, of course, I'll be delighted to," he was surprised to hear himself say.

Oh, you will?" she looked at him with her large imploring eyes.

"Yes, Natalie, I'll be pleased to," he answered.

"That's wonderful, sir," she gushed. "I'll write out directions to my place. Will seven o'clock be all right?"

"Yes, that'll be just fine," he answered with a smile.

Her house was on a narrow lane on the fringe of the city. Cedric was pleasantly surprised at the neat little garden in front of the small bungalow into which Natalie led him. "My grandfather built this house when he moved to Jhelum from Goa," she explained. "My mother lived here with me until three years ago."

"It's a lovely home. Where's your mother now?" Cedric asked.

"She died during the plague epidemic," Natalie answered softly.

"I'm sorry to hear that, Natalie, truly sorry," he said, taking her hands into his.

"I have some Scotch whisky for you, Lieutenant," she said, pointing at a bottle on a table in the middle of the room.

"Thank you, Natalie. I will have a drink," Cedric said, and then added, "only if you stop calling me Lieutenant. My name is Cedric."

"Oh, all right, Lieutenant, I mean Cedric," she answered, laughing.

Dinner was enjoyable and Cedric relished the food she served him. They ate sitting at a small table in the kitchen and chatted freely. She told him about her childhood and her father. "He was English and worked as a foreman for the city municipal department. He left for South Africa when I was three years old, telling my mother that he would send for us. But we never heard from him. My father had named me Natalie, but I have no memory of him. After he left, my mother started using her maiden name of D'Souza."

Cedric told her about growing up in London and his training at Sandhurst. They talked about the Lancers and he spoke about their campaigns in the Frontier.

It was getting late and Cedric got up to leave. He had drunk more of the Scotch whiskey than he should have. "Won't you stay awhile longer?" she asked, her eyes imploring.

"I should be leaving, Natalie," he answered. "It's past midnight."

She came and stood in front of him. "Please stay," she pleaded, placing her arms on his shoulders. He felt a little unsteady on his feet. She came into his arms and he began kissing her, holding her in a tight embrace. She took his hand and led him towards her bedroom. He stopped at the door and freed himself. He felt panicked and didn't think he could go through with it.

"Come, Cedric, please come with me," Natalie whispered, nestling her face against his chest and locking her arms around his neck. Her perfume permeated his head and her body pressed hard against his. She held his hands and he followed her into her bedroom. They made love and afterwards he fell asleep in her arms.

He woke up in the morning to the sounds of her humming softly in the bathroom. The sun was shining through an open window and he could hear a peacock's call from a distance. He thought about the night. It was strange, but for the first time ever he had been able to make love without any sense of guilt. Maybe there was nothing wrong with him after all. Or was it Natalie who was able to help him be himself.

He placed his hands behind his head and began looking around the neat little bedroom. He saw himself in the mirror of the dressing table and looked down at the array of small vials and bottles in front of the mirror. There were two framed photographs on the dressing table and he glanced at them. One was of an Indian woman wearing European clothes. He turned to the other, and sat up with a jerk. The frame had little sea shells glued onto it and the faded sepia-coloured photograph showed a man in a suit, with the tips of his mustache waxed to a fine point, standing in the middle of an ocean-front amusement park. The lower right hand corner bore a signature—Jonathan Smythe.

"Oh, my God," Cedric moaned, leaping out of the bed. He felt faint and almost fell. "Oh, dear God," he mumbled again, staring at the closed bathroom door. He got dressed quickly and ran, stumbling out of the room and away from the little bungalow.

He got home, overwhelmed with guilt. What a failure he had been all of his life at everything he had attempted. He was a loser, a fake, and now this. He brooded all day and refused to accompany his bungalow mates to the club for lunch. Instead, he took a bottle of Scotch and locked himself in his bedroom.

Later in the evening the dancing girls arrived and his companions dragged him out to the drawing room. He stayed with them, drinking heavily, but after awhile stumbled back into his bedroom. He had a splitting headache and gazed around the room through half-closed eyes. He saw his service revolver on the bedside table. He staggered over and picked it up. He stared at it for a few moments; then, placing its barrel against his temple, pulled the trigger.

Early in the morning, an Azad Hind messenger from Chakwal rode into Karyala and raced up to Hem Raj's home. "The British horse soldiers are coming to Meerpur today," he said urgently. "Our police informant got the message to us late last night. The horse soldiers are coming from Jhelum with orders to round up the men who ambushed and killed three of their men."

"I knew this was going to happen," Hem Raj blurted out, cursing in his mind the young hot heads. "All right, thanks for the warning," he said, placing his turban on his head. I'll have to get the men out of the village at once, he was thinking. They'll have to somehow get to Peshawar. He tucked his revolver into his *salwar* and picked up his rifle. He saddled Kamaan and rode out to Meerpur.

The village had been on edge ever since the ambush by the young men, and the lookout tower had been manned day and night. When Hem Raj rode into the village square, the elders were there to meet him. "Hurry, we don't have time," he called out, jumping off his horse. "Get the men together. Where's Ali? We've got to get them to safety."

The young men were brought out, all looking pale and scared. "Ride west," Hem Raj instructed them. "Then turn south and go to Khushab. Proceed to the house of one Saleem Khan. Tell him that I have sent you. Tell him that I am the one onto whose wrist his wife had tied a *raakhi* twenty years ago. Tell him everything and ask him to get you to Peshawar."

A village elder was about to say something when a man from the watchtower called out urgently, "I see riders approaching from the east." A moment later he yelled again, "There's another group of riders coming from the north."

Hem Raj was thinking furiously. The British were making sure that no one would escape towards the Northwest Frontier. He turned to Ali. "Ride out of here. Take your friends with you. Come on, get out," he yelled. "Head west and don't stop until you get to Khushab. May God bless and protect you." Yet he feared that the horse soldiers coming from the north would see the riders escaping towards the west. The soldiers must be diverted: their attention had to be drawn away. Hem Raj leapt onto Kamaan and, spurring the horse, raced out of Meerpur, heading towards the north.

The soldiers saw him approaching and spread out. Hem Raj nudged Kamaan and turned east. The soldiers coming from the north also changed direction and began chasing him. Hem Raj quickly fired his rifle at them and dug his heels into Kamaan's sides. "*Inkalab Zindabad,*" he muttered under his breath as the horse broke into a full gallop. He placed Kamaan's reins between his teeth and drew his revolver. A soldier racing towards him fired. Weaving Kamaan from side to side, Hem Raj fired both his revolver and the rifle. One of the soldiers was hit and fell off his horse.

Hem Raj fired again, hitting a second soldier moments before a bullet ripped through his own left shoulder. The reins fell out of his mouth and a trickle of blood ran down his arm. "*Inkalab Zindabad!*" he yelled at the top of his voice, firing both his revolver and the gun towards the soldiers. Then two bullets tore into his chest and his body jerked violently. He felt a sharp, searing, stabbing pain in his lungs. His rifle and revolver fell out of his hands and he slowly slumped forward onto his horse's neck. Kamaan did not break stride, but instead, turned and started galloping towards Karyala.

The horse soldiers slowed down and stopped to go to the aid of their fallen comrades.

Kamaan reached Karyala and started slowly climbing up the cobblestone street. The horse was foaming at his mouth and its white coat was stained crimson with the blood of his master slumped over his neck. Men, women and children of the village came out of their homes and started silently walking behind the horse. Kamaan reached the door of his master's house and came to a stop. Kanti came running and screamed. Mohan Lal and Sohan Lal came running and, gently sliding their father off his horse, carried him to the *charpai* under the banyan tree. Kanti cradled her husband's head in her arms, tears streaming down her face.

Hem Raj opened his eyes slowly and reached up with a trembling hand. "No Kanti, no clouds must ever mar the face of the moon," he moaned, and Kanti wiped her tears away. His eyes closed for a few moments and then he looked up at his wife again. "I'm sorry, Kanti, but I couldn't let them take Ali and the others away. They would have been shot."

"Hush, my husband, save your strength," she whispered. "Mohan Lal has gone to fetch the *hakeem*. He'll help stop your bleeding."

Hem Raj closed his eyes. "If my doctor son were here," he whispered, with a faint smile on his face, "he would have been able to save me. Kanti, we've had a good life together. You've raised our children well."

Shanti and Sheila knelt at the foot of the *charpai*, crying and gently massaging their father's feet. Hem Raj gazed at their faces and they came closer. He placed his trembling hands on each of their heads. Mohan Lal came running in with the *hakeem* behind him. Hem Raj shook his head. "No, my son, my time has come. I want you to be strong. Look after your mother, your brother and sisters."

Mohan Lal's eyes filled with tears. "We'll seek revenge, *Pita Jee,* it will be blood for blood. I give you my pledge."

Hem Raj nodded slowly and, turning towards Kanti, he tried to smile. He gasped and his eyes slowly closed. Kanti clasped him in a tight embrace and began sobbing.

The next morning, every lane of Karyala was thronged with thousands who had come from neighbouring villages and towns. Hem Raj's body, lying on a wooden pall, was covered with a silk sheet and draped with the tri-coloured Indian National flag. A red tikka had been applied to his forehead. The pink shawl to which Kanti's *dupatta* had been tied when they were married was wrapped around his shoulders. Garlands of marigolds adorned his neck and the turban of his eldest son, Devi Lal, lay on his chest, clasped between his hands.

Village elders of Karyala and Meerpur; Hindus, Sikhs and Muslims, in trembling voices, pledged to unify their people. Their hero's sacrifice of his own life to save six young Muslims would not be in vain. They then vied with each other to serve as pall bearers. The funeral procession began, led by Mohan Lal walking Kamaan, saddleless, his white coat still stained with his master's blood. The crowd chanted, "*Shaheed Hem Raj kee jai!*" Kanti and her children, accompanied by Noor and the women of the two villages, followed, weeping silently. Villagers showered their hero's body with rose petals.

The procession slowly wound its way down the cobblestoned streets to the cremation grounds toward the east of the village. The body was gently lowered onto a pyre of sandalwood logs. A Brahmin priest performed the religious ceremonies and the last rites. Mohan Lal, as the elder of the two sons present, lit the pyre which gradually consumed Hem Raj's mortal remains.

Later that night, Kanti stood alone on the terrace of their home. In the faint glow of the moon she could make out the cremation grounds in the distance. Scenes of her past flashed through her mind; their marriage and their life together. How caring and gentle he had been towards her. She remembered his loving caresses, his not letting her ever cry. He would brush her tears away. "No, my dearest," he would smile and say, "no cloud must ever mar the face of the moon."

She remembered his courage, his burning desire to set their country free and his fervent wish for men from all faiths to live like brothers.

A bright shooting star streaked across the night sky, startling Kanti. "Goodbye my dearest husband," she whispered, choking back her sobs. "May God bless and guide your soul. I know you'll live again to fight for our freedom. I know you'll bring joy to the hearts of those you'll love."

A small dark cloud slowly moved across the face of the moon. A teardrop rolled down Kanti's cheek. A gust of wind blowing from the cremation grounds brushed the teardrop away. The little cloud sailed aside and no longer marred the face of the moon.

Glossary

Aarti—A ceremony to pay homage to God

Accha—Yes

Ahimsa—Hindu and Buddhist belief in the sacredness of all living creatures, a doctrine of non-violence

Allah-O-Akbar—Muslim saying meaning God is great

Ayah—Maid servant

Azad Hind—Free India

Baksheesh—Gratuity or gift of alms

Baraat—Bridegrooms entourage

Bindi—A red dot applied to the middle of the forehead by Hindu women indicating that they are married

Chai—Tea

Chapaati—A round thin flat wheat flour bread baked on a griddle

Charpai—A cot made of a wooden frame with intertwining strands of thin rope stretched across the frame

Chotta—Small, little, young

Cowrie—Brightly marked hard, small shell of a tropical marine mollusk

Daku—Bandit

Dholkee—A small two-sided drum

Dia—Small round clay vessel with oil and a wick

Diwali—Hindu festival of lights depicting victory of good over evil

Dolee—A palanquin in which a bride is carried to accompany her husband after their wedding

Duppata—A long, light veil worn by women draped around the shoulders and head

Fakir—A Muslim or Hindu ascetic or religious mendicant

Ghee—Clarified butter

Ghora Mela—Horse fair

Hakeem—A local medicine man, a native physician

Hari Niwas—God's Abode

Hazoor—Master

Hey Bhagwan—Oh God

Hey Prabhu—Oh God

Inkalab Zindabad—Long live freedom

Insha Allah—God willing

Jaimala—Flower garlands exchanged by the bride and groom at the time of a Hindu wedding

Jai Ram Jee Kee—Salutations to Lord Rama

Kajal—A cosmetic black powder used as an eye liner and beauty mark

Kamaan—Bow for shooting arrows

Kameez—Shirt

Khamosh—Silence, silent, quiet

Khansama—Cook

Kikar—Acacia tree

Kirpan—Small dagger

Kismet—Fate

Kurta—Shirt

Lakshmi—Hindu Goddess of wealth

Lao—Bring

Lathi—A stout long stick

Lohri—A Hindu festival

Maata—Mother

Madhuparkha—A part of the Hindu wedding where the bride and groom share a drink of honey and yogurt

Mandap—A wooden structure decorated with flowers under which

Hindu wedding ceremonies are held

Mehandi—A cosmetic paste made from Henna leaves, applied to the hands and feet producing orange-red patterns

Mem—A lady. Used to refer to British women in colonial India

Milni—A ceremony of greeting and welcome at the beginning of a Hindu wedding

Mohyal—A subcaste of Brahmins

Mullah—A Muslim cleric

Naan—Flat round wheat bread baked in a clay oven

Namaste—Greetings to you, respectful salutation

Namaskar— Same as *Namaste*

Nawab—A ruler or governor or a prince

Paisa—A copper coin in the Indian monetary system equivalent to 1/100th of a rupee

Parmatma—God

Pathan—A Northwestern Muslim tribe of the Indian sub-continent

Peepul—A tree held to be sacred by Hindus

Prabhu—God

Pundit—A Brahmin scholar, a learned person

Punkha—Fan

Raakhi—Colourful strands of thread, tied by sisters around the wrist of their brothers during a yearly festival

Rani—Queen

Rivaz—Cultural tradition, custom

Rupee—The basic monetary unit of India

Sadhu—A Hindu ascetic, a holy man

Sahib—A title of respect equivalent to master or sir, first used for the British in colonial India

Salam—A Muslim greeting meaning peace

Salwar—Baggy pants narrowing around ankles worn by North Indian men and women

Sari—A colourful garment worn by women in India, consisting of six yards of a light fabric with one end wrapped around the waist like an ankle length skirt, and the other end draped over the shoulder

Sehra—A silver ornament with a veil of flowers hanging from it, placed in front of the turban of a groom at the time of a wedding

Shaheed—Martyr

Shehnai—A flute-like reed Indian musical instrument

Shree—Formal way to address men, like Mister

Sowar—An Indian cavalry soldier, a rider

Tabeez—A talisman worn around the neck or the arm

Tandoor—Clay oven

Thaali—Platter usually made of brass

Tikka—A gold ornament worn by women which is suspended over the forehead, attached with a clip to their hair

Tonga—A two-wheeled horse drawn carriage with back to back seats

Prem Sharma was born in Mandalay, Burma and at the age of ten faced the ravages of World War II when the Japanese invaded the country. After experiencing devastating bombing raids during which their home and much of the city was destroyed, the Sharma family fled Mandalay. They undertook a month long perilous journey through dense jungle and over treacherous mountains—much of it on foot—to reach India and safety.

As an angry and rebellious young boy Prem Sharma became involved in India's struggle for freedom from the British. Then he met and was greatly influenced by Mahatma Gandhi and his teachings of compassion and nonviolence. In 1947 India received its freedom and the nation of Pakistan was created. Prem Sharma witnessed bloody ethnic rioting as 680,000 Hindus and Muslims butchered each other to death.

The profound influences of these defining moments of his youth were further ingrained in his mind by visits to the House of Ann Frank in Amsterdam and to a Nazi Concentration Camp in Austria.

Prem Sharma studied dentistry in Edinburgh, Scotland and came to the United States in 1961. After an illustrious career in professional education, he recently retired as Associate Dean and Professor at Marquette University, School of Dentistry. A recipient of numerous national and international professional and civic awards, Dr. Sharma has provided leadership in a variety of scientific and civic organizations. He currently serves on the boards of six state and national community organizations and is a frequent speaker on race relations and religious harmony.

Karma's Embrace is the first part of Prem Sharma's trilogy. Part two, *Mandalay's Child* was published in 1999 and has received wide acclaim.

The saga continues...

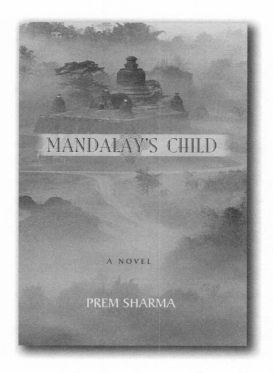

MANDALAY'S CHILD

A NOVEL

PREM SHARMA

In the next book of this trilogy, *Mandalay's Child,* Devi Lal's idyllic existence as a prominent physician is shattered when the Japanese invade Burma in 1942. With his daughter's husband missing in action, Lal and his family flee toward India. Traversing dense jungle and mountains, traveling often on foot, they finally reach safety and settle in a poor neighborhood of a large north Indian city.

Devi Lal's grandson joins a group of patriots fighting for India's freedom from the British. His granddaughter Sophia becomes a youthful follower of Mahatma Gandhi.

Tragedy strikes again when in 1947 India is granted independence and communal rioting erupts, resulting in the brutal slaughter of over 680,000 people.

The setting of the novel then moves to Ireland, Austria and England where the story ends.

From the annals of Man's tragic inhumanity toward man, Sharma weaves a remarkable story of courage and generosity, of hope and faith, that ultimately reminds us of the indomitability of the human spirit.

"...extremely moving, and the reader cannot help but think of the current Kosovo refugee situation. Prem Sharma is a skilled storyteller combining suspense, coming-of-age themes and spirituality. ...the narrative is compelling."
—*ForeWord Magazine*

"His prose is fluid and his tale compelling. Prem Sharma's novel is as much allegory as history and more the quest for meaning than memoir. He has embroidered tragedy with the articles of hope and valor. For the poetic soul it is a pilgrimage worth making..."
—Rabbi Francis Barry Silberg, Ph.D., D.D.
Author of *The Philosophy of Moral Values*

"I am in awe at the historical breadth and poetic quality of *Mandalay's Child*. From the opening hymn to the closing line, this novel is a moving and unforgettable experience. At this time in the world's history where violence and inhumanity are almost taken for granted, this novel speaks of the courage and compassion, the hope and faith we need to make this a better world."
—Rev. Robert A. Wild, S.J., President Marquette University

"*Mandalay's Child* is an extraordinary addition to the grand old tradition of epic literature. Covering historical themes as vast as World War II in the Far East and the traumatic birth of modern India, Prem Sharma brings history to life in the struggles of a family attempting to survive adversity and, even more, to defiantly pass on a legacy. Prem Sharma has produced a literary experience that will touch your soul."

—Arthur Flowers, Professor, Fiction, Syracuse University Creative Writing MFA Program; Author of novels, *De Mojo Blues* and *Another Good Loving Blues*